Praise for Joe Meno's previous books

Hairstyles of the Damned

"Meno is a romantic at heart. Not the greeting card kind, or the Harlequin paperback version, but the type who thinks, deep down, that things matter, that art can change lives." —*Elgin Courier News*

"It's a funny, sweet and, at times, hard-hitting story."
—*Chicago Sun-Times*

"[Meno] writes in the most authentic young voice since J.D. Salinger's Holden Caulfield." —*Daily Southtown*

"Meno's language is rhythmic and honest, expressing things proper English never could." —*SF Weekly*

Bluebirds Used to Croon in the Choir

"In only a few pages per story, Meno crams in loss, healing, familial bonds, unrequited love and understatement to spare."
—*San Diego Union-Tribune*

"An odd, romantic, and compelling group of tales." —Bookslut.com

"A jazzy collection of short stories and little moments . . . musical tales of love and loss with hardly a word wasted." —*Kirkus Reviews*

How the Hula Girl Sings

"Mr. Meno is a superb craftsman whose language is simple and direct and never loses sight of its origins." —Hubert Selby, Jr.

Tender as Hellfire

"We're hooked." —*NewCity Chicago*

The Boy Detective Fails

joe meno

Punk Planet Books
Chicago

Published by Punk Planet Books/Akashic Books
©2006 Joe Meno

Punk Planet Books is a project of Independents' Day Media.

Illustrations by Koren Zelek
Author photo by Joe Wigdahl
Cover design by Dan Sinker and Jon Resh
Book design by Pirate Signal International

The angel food cake recipe on page 332 is courtesy of the Angel Food Bakery, 1636 W. Montrose Ave. Chicago, Illinois.

***To the astute reader:* It may be of interest to you to note, for purposes of decoding the hidden story placed within these pages, that A=N.**

ISBN 10: 1-933354-10-0
ISBN 13: 978-1-933354-10-1
Library of Congress Control Number: 2004106233
First printing

Punk Planet Books
4229 N. Honore
Chicago, IL 60613
books@punkplanet.com
www.punkplanetbooks.com

Akashic Books
PO Box 1456
New York, NY 10009
Akashic7@aol.com
www.akashicbooks.com

For:
K.Z.
D.S.
J.T.
J.R.
M.Z.
J.V.

"Genius: the ability to prolong one's childhood."
—H.L. Mencken

CHAPTER THIRTY-ONE
THE MYSTERIOUS IDENTITY
OF THE BOY DETECTIVE

It is no parlor trick: There is a skull and, in the dark, it is glowing. Somehow it is now floating above us all. Listen: The skull is speaking. It is saying your name. It knows about you and your favorite flower and all about your tenth birthday. But it does not matter. You are not convinced. For some reason, you are still full of doubt. You stare into the dark, looking for wires. Grasping for strings, you hold your hands out.

ONE

Dear Reader,

The story thus far, as you may have forgotten: Even as a young boy, Billy Argo showed an uncanny talent for solving puzzles of almost every configuration, arrangement, and design.

That is all.

No—it was more than a talent. It was a kind of very sad genius, so that in the end, the very sad genius appeared on the boy detective the way a child born with a deformity—a missing hand or one leg shorter than the other—might make the same adolescent distant and dreamy; like a birthmark in the shape of an elephant smack dab on the forehead, it led Billy to be somewhat shy, somewhat withdrawn, though not at first. No, at first the boy was at play: happy, daring, secretly cunning.

In the stark world of Gotham, New Jersey—small white houses and green, murky woods surrounding a modern factory town, home to both the Mold-O-Form Plastic and Harris Heating Duct plants, a burg bustling with both Prosperity and its companion Crime—Billy would run hand in hand with his younger sister, Caroline, and behind them, their childhood friend, a husky neighborhood boy by the name of Fenton Mills, would often come calling.

Through the nearby grassy field, with the chimneys of the plastics factory churning black clouds in the distance, the children would hurry, shouting, trampling the fuzzy white puffs of dandelions and sprawling knotty underbrush. Their hideout was an abandoned lot which was wide and silver and green with enormous, expressive daisies. The lot had remained unsold—being too filthy with lead after an explosion during the days when the land had been home to the old

Drip-Less Paint Factory. Above the dirt of an unmarked grave and beneath the shadow of the abandoned refinery, the children would play their own made-up games: Wild West Accountants! in which they would calculate the loss of a shipment of gold stolen from an imaginary stage coach, or Recently Divorced Scientists! in which they would build a super-collider out of garbage to try and win back their recently lost loves. Together, forever, they would explore the near-dark world of wonder and mystery.

The boy detective in his youth was pale with dark wispy hair and was generally a nervous child, both quite short and strange-looking for his age. There was an incident in the boy's elementary school cafeteria involving a bully named Wayne Meany III concerning Billy's unusually large eyes. One day, Billy, sitting unsuspecting beside his younger sister, felt a pronounced thump at the back of his head. When Billy turned, the back of his cranium sore, his face red, he discovered a knotty green apple lying there on the floor. Wayne Meany III laughed and pointed, then remarked, "How do you like them apples, owl-eyes?" Billy pondered the question for a moment but did not have a proper answer. His eyes were indeed large and wise, and yes, somewhat unbecoming, but with his sister and their one true friend, those same eyes would be central in examining a collapsed ant hill or measuring the size of a wrecked nest of speckled robin eggs, carefully held amongst all three pairs of their small dirty hands.

His sister, Caroline, both blond and petite, was the charming one: always taking notes in her white-and-gold diary, a perfect record of all their discoveries; always curtseying; always learning French, or so it seemed. Her favorite word? *Jejune*, as in: "What they force us to wear as school uniforms is very *jejune*."

Their neighbor friend, Fenton, short and chubby, sweaty, and always out of breath, followed last in his small red beanie, his mother's solution for the boy's persistent psoriasis. The portly boy always reminded the others when it was getting too dark, admonishing them when he thought that what they were doing might somehow make their parents worry.

It was a summer that never ended for the three of them: a summer of games and puzzles and surprises.

It was a summer that, lying in bed, we wish we had once had.

TWO

When Billy Argo turned ten, he received a True-Life Junior Detective Kit from his aunt Eunice for his birthday. The family was all there in the small yellow kitchen: Mr. and Mrs. Arg o, Billy, Caroline, their older brother Derek, in visiting from the Navy, and the neighbor boy, Fenton. Billy, on that day, wore a small blue party hat, along with his favorite blue suit and clip-on tie, which featured an orange owl along its wide center. The family stood around him at the white linoleum table, cheering, handing him gift after gift. *Hooray,* they said, *the boy is one year older. Hooray, we are all one year closer to our deaths.*

The gifts that year had been quite lackluster: From Mr. Argo, Billy received a woodworking set, which was not recommended for anyone under the age of eighteen and had to be taken back. From Mrs. Argo, a new blue cardigan which was exactly the same size as the previous year's and thusly too small. From Caroline, a set of colored markers which produced fruit smells and which all looked suspiciously used. From his older brother Derek, a record entitled *Mood Music for the En- terprising Bachelor*, a gift which his mother called "perhaps somewhat inappropriate, but thoughtful nonetheless."

Finally, Billy stared down at his last gift, wrapped in blue paper, which proclaimed, *Happy Birthday to a Fairly Nice Boy!* Standing beside Billy, Caroline and Fenton clapped obnoxiously, pulling on each oth- er's paper party hats, wildly blowing their noisemakers in each other's ears. Ignoring them, Billy opened the box from his aunt. When all three children saw what was inside the package, the noisemakers went deadly quiet in their mouths and there was a profound and immediate silence. Within the box, there was more than their small eyes, hearts, and minds could grasp in a single glance: a magnifying glass, a pencil, a pad of paper, a fingerprint set, a number of real lock picks, a pair of binoculars, an eye patch, a working flashlight, and a fake black beard with a matching mustache.

What happened then was this: The lost part—the silver, misplaced key to his heart, the part of him that seemed to be missing—had been suddenly found. Words were not necessary. The room was still as the boy detective took the magnifying glass in his hand and began to do what he had always been meant to. At once, the mysterious, the unknown, and the unidentified moved from the shadows into sharp contrast before his eyes. It was at that moment that the boy detective first began to detect.

It went exactly like this: Billy held up the magnifying glass, the lens bringing the wondering faces of his family into perfect sharpness, their soft expressions suddenly becoming serious, each a portrait of some hidden secret. Billy spied his older brother with the magnifying glass, as he was the relative standing the closest, and Derek immediately confessed that he was gay. Also, that he hated life in the Navy.

After the drama that followed, in which Mrs. Argo dropped the birthday cake out of nervousness and Derek hugged Billy and apologized for ruining his younger brother's birthday, the boy detective laid in his bed and wondered what other strange discoveries might now be awaiting.

Within two weeks, the answer came. Staring at the front page of the *Gotham Daily*, the children found a picture of themselves staring back, beneath a headline that read:

BOY DETECTIVE SOLVES STRANGE MURDER CASE

Kid Sister and Neighbor Boy Help Out

From that front-page photograph, this interesting description: Billy, Caroline, and Fenton accepting congratulations from hefty Mayor Pierce, a shady union-supported candidate with an enormous bald head, all four of them in front of the Gotham Town Hall with a galley of news reporters before them shouting question after question and flashing their flashes. In the accompanying pictures, the children look wonderfully composed and serious. Billy, in his blue suit and clip-on tie, holds the detective kit's magnifying glass to his right eye and wears the eye patch over his left. Together, Caroline in her white dress wearing the beard, and Fenton with the mustache and his beanie, hold a simple drawing depicting a stick figure disguised as Abraham Lincoln running with a long-barreled pistol; Lincoln's one long stick leg is stuck in a large gray crayon-colored mansion where the victim, a Sir Tobias Earl, was shot to death, while the other leg stretches into the entrance of the local wax museum (where, with the boy detective's insight, the perpetrator was found hiding). In the front-page photograph, the Mayor stands unconvinced beside the children, the round man in a wrinkled black suit, his own mustache both weak and droopy; at first it seems he is offering to shake their hands but then, fearing he may look foolish, he simply presents the children with the reward offered by the grieving millionaire's family. The Mayor holds up the gigantic white check, the amount of $1,000.00 almost as indecipherable as the embarrassed *Congratulations*, he seems to be muttering.

Within a week or two, then, another clue, and another headline:

BOY DETECTIVE SOLVES FATAL ORPHANAGE ARSON

Kid Sister and Neighborhood Boy Lend a Hand in Murder Investigation

Another photo from the front page once again: Outside a dilapidated, still-smoking orphanage, the charred embers of a swing set and dormitory rising like skeletal ribs in the distance, young Billy points at a crooked-looking fireman being led away in handcuffs by two bearded policemen, all of whom are frowning sadly. Caroline and Fenton look on with disapproval. Caroline is holding up a smudgy fingerprint belonging to the guilty fireman. Fenton again stands with a drawing that illustrates the suspect's motive: a scribbling of the burning orphanage, doodled children burning in their sleep, while buried beneath, an immense cache of pirate's treasure lies quietly, clearly illustrated with the familiar shapes of gold doubloons and a smiling skull adorning the chest. In a subsequent photograph, Billy and the other two children are given a second award by the Mayor, again on the steps of City Hall. The Mayor, chagrined by both the scandalous rogue fireman and the children's crime solving abilities, which some critics believe call his entire administration into question, this time deigns to shake their hands, while spotty, faceless townspeople stand by applauding.

BOY DETECTIVE DISCOVERS URANIUM DEPOSIT

Children Save Town from Bankruptcy

In this photo: Billy and Caroline and Fenton wear large miners' helmets, their single cyclopic lights aimed in the dark at a great green glowing rock. Caroline points to a long silver radiation detector, which Billy holds, smiling widely, the long handle of the device leading to a wide arching head which is lit up madly. Once again, the kids shake hands with the Mayor, who, hunched into the opening of the mine and overcome with sweat, looks altogether foolish. He has begun to show the sure signs of his imminent mayoral defeat: His face is completely smeared with dirt, as are the newspaper stories concerning his lazy police force. The Mayor, being the Mayor, looks downright humiliated, but does his best to smile the politician's winning smile, not fooling anybody.

BOY DETECTIVE SOLVES FLYING SAUCER HOAX
Three Dead at the Scene

With the advent of these triumphant newspaper clippings, Billy Argo's parents, Jack and June Argo, couldn't have been more proud or happy. Mr. Argo was a judge advocate general, an officer in the Navy, and a world-class bantam-weight karate champion. Oftentimes, he would be found in the backyard breaking bricks with his bare fists, or would not be found at all, flying off in the middle of the night to help prosecute a wayward sailor. His wife, Mrs. Argo, was a world-renowned Nobel Prize-winning chemist and amateur artiste. When she was not busy in her lab, inventive with her rows and rows of Bunsen burners and powdery silver chemicals, she would paint portraits of famous world leaders. When they were not occupied with their own work, both parents gladly encouraged their son's determined sense of justice and unyielding curiosity.

Through all of Billy Argo's trials and tribulations stood his charming sister Caroline, who was always darling and a real ace with the fingerprint set, and their loyal sidekick and friend Fenton, whose belief in the decency of man and certainty concerning the triumph of good over evil was unshakable. The three of them had all pledged to the three cardinal rules of detection, which young Billy had, of course, invented, and were later recorded in Caroline's diary with perfect penmanship:

Cardinal rule #1: the boy detective must solve any inexplicable mystery
Cardinal rule #2: the boy detective must foil any criminal caper he can
Cardinal rule #3: the boy detective must always be true to his friends

Between them, soon enough, all foul riddles, all wild hoaxes, all staged problems were solved quickly, with joy, fondness, and surrender.

THREE

The boy detective's most memorable case: The Haunted Candy Factory (but we may be getting ahead of ourselves already).

FOUR

Trouble began the following year when Caroline, bored with always being the boy detective's assistant, requested a magic set for Christmas. That wonderful morning, the silver Christmas tree blooming with false white light, Caroline tore through the boxes and boxes of other gifts to find the crinkly silver gift-wrapping that held a True-Life Junior Magician Set. In her small, starchy white nightgown, Caroline pulled apart the box, her fingers working ferociously against the paper. Billy looked on with dismay and fear. From within the box, Caroline yanked out a black top hat, and immediately a white dove took flight, fluttering and flitting above the family members' heads. Gleeful, the girl clapped, chasing the bird wherever it landed, ignoring the gift Billy had bought for her: a brand new magnifying glass, decorated with a gold ribbon around its handle.

"What will you name your bird?" Mrs. Argo asked.

"Margaret Thatcher," Caroline replied, without giving it a second thought. Billy turned, pouting, opening a gift from his father: a taxidermy kit and set of torque wrenches. For him, it was the worst Christmas ever.

For several months, then, Caroline was completely disinterested in her older brother's adventures.

BOY DETECTIVE EASILY BUSTS SILVER SMUGGLERS ON HIS OWN

WONDER BOY DETECTIVE UNMASKS TAROT CARD FAKE WITHOUT ANY KIND OF ASSISTANCE AT ALL

The boy detective took his sister's absence very badly. The two children were often found in the small white hallway between their bedrooms shouting, cursing each other with ferocity: "You simple-minded dwarf!" or "You hopeless barbarian!"—enigmatic insults neither understood fully. In their disagreements, Caroline simply stated that magic was more fun because it worked on the notion of wonder and mystery. Upon hearing this, Billy threw her magic set on the floor, arguing magic was fun only for irrational, childish babies.

Most of these contests ended the same way: Caroline, alone in bed, crying.

A strange, important, event occurred one day: Caroline's magic-set dove, Margaret Thatcher, born with a silent and inoperable heart defect, quite naturally passed away, falling on its side, dead in its shiny silver cage. It was a true shock, seeing the puffy white bird lying there dead, staring strangely back at her from beyond the world of the living. Caroline, at once, lost all interest in magic of any kind. Quite sure the ghost of the bird would return to haunt her unless it was given a proper interment, Caroline begged her brother Billy for his help. Together, the two children made amends and gave the beloved pet an appropriate burial, hiding the remains within a strongbox beneath the Argos' front porch.

And like that, Caroline was happy to accompany Billy on his adventures once again.

BOY DETECTIVE CRACKS CASE OF THE UNBREAKABLE SAFE

BOY DETECTIVE QUIETS THE MYSTERY OF THE SINGING DIAMOND

BOY DETECTIVE PULLS THE PLUG ON THE PHANTOM LIGHTHOUSE

An excerpt from Caroline's diary at that time reveals the joy of their continuing escapades:

> *all the other girls are wearing skirts and makeup.*
> *some worry about their hair and nails,*
> *but i'm not interested in that. i'd*
> *much rather climb into a dark mine. i'd much*
> *rather follow Billy into the dirt. sometimes*
> *he can be quite hard to tolerate. sometimes he can*
> *act rather bossy, but he can also be very sweet.*
> *i often wonder, stepping quietly behind him,*
> *could it be that he also enjoys my company? i am*
> *not very talented with codes and puzzles but i am*
> *actually very professional with the fingerprint set and am*
> *very diligent in taking notes, even in the dark,*
> *doing quite well documenting all our adventures.*
> *it is good to be needed for something.*
> *additionally, i have a notion that Billy has a fear of*
> *heights, while i do not, and also, he is afraid of*
> *bats: their sounds are enough to start him*
> *panicking. there is something in their delicate wings that*
> *really makes him shiver, though he acts quite brave*
> *whenever our good friend fenton mills is*
> *around. what i truly love the most are our secrets together.*

Many months after the dove's unexpected death, Billy and Caroline were to be found hiding under their slanted, white wood porch, having dug up Margaret Thatcher, studying the remains of the stiffened dead dove with Caroline's new magnifying glass. In that moment, a sacred vow of trust was made, both brother and sister now mesmerized by the inexplicable nature of dying: If on one of their dangerous adventures, one should first pass into the greatest and most profound mystery— that of unyielding mortal expiration—then he or she would send back word, as evidence of a post-corporeal world, of which Caroline argued for and Billy against.

The word they chose, as solemn proof of some kind of afterlife, was shared with no one other than themselves, not Fenton Mills nor their parents. It was with a matter of a most serious pride in which the Argo children took their word, their oath, and their silence. The single word, *abracadabra*, was written twice on a single piece of Caroline's pulpy notebook paper, then folded into edible size. Each child swallowed the word and then they shook hands to keep it as a blood pact, to be revealed under no circumstance, ordinary or otherwise.

FIVE

Their perfect childhood having perfectly ended, the boy detective left his sister Caroline and friend Fenton for the prestigious, mahogany halls of the Greater New Jersey University and Pharmaceutical College to study criminal law, in hopes of becoming a leading international criminologist. He finished his final case on the day of his high school graduation:

BOY DETECTIVE GRADUATES HIGH SCHOOL EARLY
Solves Celebrity Double Murder Same Day

COLLEGE NOW FOR BOY DETECTIVE
New Mayor Fears Crime Already Back on the Rise

The boy detective soon found himself shaking hands with his father, kissing his mother, hugging Caroline and Fenton, and waving goodbye to the world he knew so very well. It was the first time any of them could remember that they would not be together. And each took to facing their loneliness in their own way:

• At the college library, Billy, surrounded by disintegrating brown books and looking homely in a narrow blue cardigan sweater, studied harder than ever, hoping to finish his criminal law degree two years early.

• Caroline, recently sixteen, took ill and remained in bed for weeks at a time, mysteriously heartsick with the onset of late pubescence, as her doctor diagnosed it. For months, Caroline lay under her gold-colored sheets, listening to records by Joan Baez and the Carpenters, staring at her detective diary and then, all at once, and quite uncontrollably, she would begin crying.

• Young Fenton Mills became dangerously overweight, ballooning up to well over three hundred pounds, his body impossibly expanding in all directions, like an overinflated blimp. He was featured on several talk shows of the afternoon variety and developed a nearly religious following among housewives and cleaning ladies. His photo at the time frequently appeared on *Fenton FOREVER* T-shirts and bumper stickers.

Instead of passively enduring her continued depression, Caroline, once again exhibiting her ambiton and courage, decided to follow in her older brother's footsteps. Her first case was investigating strange rumors of ghoulish moans and wails at an abandoned cave, which had at one time harbored the city's ancient stockpile of mustard gas and had been promptly closed for public health reasons. Caroline, alone, crept past the opening of the barricaded cavern, with signs which read, Danger! and No Trespassing! treading lightly through the poorly fitted boards into the strange mischief of the dark night.

She was, sadly enough, unable to ever solve the strange case on her own. Shortly thereafter (*and here we are just speculating*), perhaps out of humiliation, pride, or defeat—or so badly missing the wonderful life of adventure and companionship her older brother had always made real—poor Caroline did a terrible thing.

As she stood naked in the family's grimy white tub, black candles burning, her tape player warbling "Yesterday" by the Beatles, the shower issuing a woozy, constant stream of steam, Caroline slowly slit her bared and tender wrists with a razor blade snapped from a pink disposable Petite Lady Shaver, the plastic formed in the factory not more than a mile down the street. In a moment, then, the girl collapsed with a terrible thud, her head hitting the faucet, her body falling limp against the tile flooring.

The sound of their daughter's fall interrupted Mr. and Mrs. Argo's studied reading of their respective newspapers that evening. Lowering their pulpy pages and looking at each other confused, they knew at once there was some significant trouble. Within a few moments, there was a panicked phone call, then their firm hands were under the girl's willowy neck, and Caroline was being wheeled out on a wobbly silver stretcher, Mr. and Mrs. Argo walking beside her, trying their best at comfort but only actually talking to each other nervously.

—It will be all right.

—It will be better than all right. Everything's going to happy once again, you'll see.

—Let's just hope for all right.

—Yes, yes, I'm sorry.

Caroline survived the tragedy, but was never the same fine, carefree girl ever again. No more running in fields or investigating caves; no longer was she ever barefoot. Instead she grew into someone else, asking her parents to now call her "Patient 101174," and refusing to remove the plastic bracelet the hospital had forced her to wear. Caroline began draping herself in black clothes and black makeup, becoming something much more miserable, much more distraught, much more blank-eyed than she had ever been.

If only after this first incident the boy detective had been called, if only Caroline's secret had then been told, the end may have come out differently, but no. Perhaps Mr. and Mrs. Argo decided it would be better to keep mum Caroline's mistake, not wanting to unduly worry Billy, who was at the time carefully composing "Secret Criminal Plots in Abandoned Amusement Parks," the subject of his first semester's final paper, the grade of which we all now know was merely a C-, the lowest the boy detective ever received in his academic life.

No, it was all kept hush-hush from the boy detective for his own good.

Within a few months of that first incident, Caroline found herself lying beside a bevy of strange, pimply faced boys, French-kissing them in the nearby field—the one she had traipsed through as a younger girl—whispering dirty words to them in the vacant woods, following them into the privacy of her own empty bed and empty room. Caroline, taking off her see-through black top and short vinyl skirt, would wink at the boy once, and then, at the end of their tryst, would smoke a cigarette and laugh to show how little she cared about any of it. But secretly, she hated each and every boy, and they simply stared at her terrified and then awkwardly left.

The day Caroline let a boy named Butch, a dopey fellow with a peach-fuzz mustache, have his way with her, pinning her against the door of her closet, the metal hook on which she hung her schoolbag jabbing into the back of her head again and again, she closed her bedroom door and cried one last time, and her detective diary remained shut once and for all.

Some time later that same week, the boy detective's sister was expelled from Villa Victoria Private Academy for pulling the fire alarm and calling the principal a "turd." The very night Billy Argo was finishing up his second quarter exams—specifically, a test on "White American Serial Killers"—Caroline found herself very alone. Standing naked in the tub, she slowly slits her wrists once again.

There were no records or candles this time.

Within her left hand, there was only a piece of torn paper inscribed with the message *abracadabra*. And then a fall: a final, startling collapse.

Mr. and Mrs. Argo were not on the premises that evening, having been invited to accept Gotham's award for Truly Above-Average Parenting.

The moment he found out, the boy detective began to reconstruct the crime scene in miniature, determined to prove that sister Caroline was the murder victim of some masterly plotted and nefarious revenge scheme. *It could have been the work of the Thinker, no doubt, had the Thinker still been alive,* he told himself. *Perhaps Dr. Menace.* Using a darling diorama and several small paper dolls, he was still unable to dissuade the police coroner, a Mr. Thorn, to rule that the tragedy was anything but a suicide.

—But look here, Mr. Thorn, the window was left open. And these strange red markings along her neck.

—Billy, I wish there was something I could do.

—And the message. Certainly she knew she was in danger from someone.

—Yes, I'm terribly sorry, Billy.

At the funeral, Billy, unsure of what to wear and so deciding on his owl tie and a blue cardigan, stood at the coffin crying beside his boyhood friend, Fenton, who was more enormously overweight than ever and had to walk with the assistance of two sturdy steel canes. Neither one said anything to each other. Mr. and Mrs. Argo themselves would not come near the pale white casket. They hovered around the expensive hors d'oeuvres and bickered about why their eldest son, Derek, had decided not to show. In the measured silence of that room, the boy detective could not refrain from mumbling the same, repeated, *Why? Why? Why did this happen? Who is responsible? What kind of strange plot was the cause? What villain was behind such a terrible act?* It was a mystery that would not lift its veil for a single moment, something so murky and unclear that Billy felt himself beginning to disappear into the profound darkness of it simply standing there.

The boy detective turned finally in his grief and, in whispers, began to blame his lifelong friend Fenton for not having looked after Caroline while he was away.

—You. You are to blame. You let this happen.

—No.

—You ought to have told me she was in danger.

—How was I to know?

—How were you to know? Look, look at her now. How can you look at her and ask that?

—But how was I to know? How was I to know?

The boy detective, thin and frail in his blue cardigan sweater, his owl-eyes wide as saucers, his small white hands open and shaking, continued yelling at Fenton, who in return could only continue sobbing, the pasty white funereal flowers getting drenched under the large boy's interminable tears. In the end, Billy simply but angrily pointed his finger at Fenton, who accepted the blame and cried helplessly into his own hands as an apology. It was the last time the two ever spoke in person.

So distraught was the boy detective that he was unable to finish his schooling at the university. He moved back in with his prize-winning but guilt-ridden parents, who, as best as they could, offered guidance, advice, and book after book about learning how to grieve.

Many months passed like this—crying in bed, lying on his stomach, listening to his sister's Carpenters records, caressing the fingerprint set—until, soon enough, Billy Argo, heartbroken boy detective, decided he would follow his sister into the most profound, irreversible, and unperceivable mystery: death. Billy stood in the tub, his skinny chest shaking, naked, holding a razor blade from his father's traveling kit against his wrist. He then made the incision and collapsed with a similarly terrible thud, which reverberated throughout the house once again.

The sound of their son's sudden mistake interrupted Mr. and Mrs. Argo's somnambulant evening. Both now on Quaaludes and familiar with the aching noise of that particular kind of crash, they lowered their newspapers and looked at each other grimly. Within a few moments, an ambulance siren was wailing, Billy was being wheeled out on a wobbly silver stretcher, his parents walking beside him, trying their best at comfort but only blaming one another nervously.

—You let this happen.

—No, you let this happen.

—No, you did.

—No, you did.

Unwilling to make the same mistake again, and truly worried for Billy's happiness, the Argo parents decided it would be best if the boy detective was temporarily hospitalized upstate at the St. Vitus Institute for the Infirmed and Mentally Ill. Soon enough, Billy found himself sitting in St. Vitus' placid green dayroom on a plastic-covered couch, feeling his own bandaged wrists and listening to the steady hum of foreign soap operas on TV and the strangely calm voices of the interminably lost beside him.

All around the dayroom, at small brown card tables, various mental patients in various states of mental illness spent hours putting together a variety of jigsaw puzzles— pictures of kittens, national monuments, historical figures, all in various states of disarray—their faces very serious, their hands very busy. Without a thought, Billy would often look up from his damaged wrists and turn, offering his help. Soon enough, Lincoln's beard would be restored, a Great Dane would find its legs, the Pyramids their third side; all the available puzzles in the room quickly solved.

In the end, the boy detective's stay at St. Vitus lasted more than ten years. The truth was this: At first, Billy did not want to go back home and purposefully failed any kind of examination meant to evaluate his readiness for readmission into the outside world. But then, it should be known, after being administered enough Thorazine, Billy became as unresponsive as the next overly medicated patient and simply disappeared into the slumbering universe of his own grief.

A decade later, with state-wide budget cuts and the appointment of a new hospital director, Dr. Kolberg, St. Vitus' unnecessary psychoactive medication therapy soon dwindled, and patients once thought to be profoundly comatose began to again register all the symptoms of life. Billy rose from his drug-induced stupor, gripped the silver-framed sides of his bed, scratched at his strange, bearded face, and began howling Caroline's name. It was a single thought the boy detective carried then, in his blood and head and heart: Discover who had brought about Caroline's death and punish them with equal parts terror and despair.

Within a few days and after a welcome shave, Billy passed all the required tests and a hasty, if not entirely accurate, prognosis was made, at which time the state board saw no need for the boy detective to remain at St. Vitus, and so Billy was released. The hospital staff—a matronly nurse with red hair named Mrs. Hemmings, in particular— were helpful in finding him a room at Shady Glens, a state-sponsored assisted-living facility, and a productive job in the city so that he could find a way to negotiate the rest of his life within a world that he continued to see as dangerous to strangers and heartless to the friendly.

The boy detective once again waved goodbye to his parents, who came to see their son off as he climbed aboard a bus bound for downtown Gotham. Billy was thin, his face gaunt, and he wore his faded blue sweater. His head was nearly shaved, two circles of baldness glowing above each ear, the skin made clean for a final bout of electro-convulsive therapy. The boy detective climbed through the door, found a seat beside a window, and watched as his parents slowly and momentously disappeared. Looking down into his lap, Billy touched the thick white scars on his wrist, then felt the two bare spots on his head. He looked up again and waved, though his parents were no longer anywhere in sight. Instead, off in the distance, across the great river, and growing more faint each moment, were the silver and green searchlights of the mysterious and unwelcoming metropolis of New York City.

It was like that.

In the end, it was not so very strange.

And yet still Billy Argo could not have known how unexpectedly this boy detective's life was about to change.

CHAPTER THIRTY-TWO
THE CASE OF THE
BROWN BUNNY

What do people think of the boy detective?
The bus driver: always punctual.
The mailman: very polite.
The police chief: an uncanny eye for clues.
The schoolteacher: has a very large vocabulary.
The banker: found my daughter's missing leg.
The rocket scientist: quite bright.

ONE

In our town—our town of shadows, our town of mystery—it seems our buildings have, without reason, begun to disappear completely. Still full of their loyal inhabitants, the buildings and the people all disintegrate soundlessly. The air has been hard to breathe, full of regret and the glassy voices of the unsurprised dead. Our commuters have begun carrying photographs of their loved ones with them to work. On the bus, we look at each other, pictures of our sad wives and doubtful children huddled close to our chests, quietly imagining the silent elaborations of our own deaths. We are disappointed coming home that evening because the many photos betray our cowardice: We live in a town that is disappearing, and worse, like the buildings, our hope is gone and we are no longer surprised by anything.

Only look now: past the remaining silver skyscrapers, glinting high along the horizon; past the shadowy green river; look over the small city park dedicated to some founding father whose name has long been lost; past the statue of an armless man astride a bronze horse; beyond the small white houses and narrow gray streets to the end of a gruesome cul-de-sac, the lane hidden among the smokestacks of the town's remaining factories, and there we see the Shady Glens Facility for Mental Competence.

Look closer still and we will discover a small figure standing there on the sidewalk staring up sadly at the square-shaped building. It is the boy detective, now aged thirty, who has finally been released: *hooray*. For many reasons, he is still unhappy. He stands before the strangely modern building, Shady Glens Facility for Mental Competence, yellow suitcase in hand, and is very disappointed. The boy detective thinks:

Oh, dear. The boy detective thinks: *I do not quite like the looks of this place.* He feels a sob coming on but fights it with his teeth. He looks up, pushing his black bifocals against his face, and blinks.

As noted, the facility is modern, very rectangular, white with dull brick and thick black bars that give the windows—certainly the eyes of the place—a feeling that it is also clinically unhappy. But there is no mistake: The weak, gray numbers beside the glass security doors exactly match the sloppy handwritten numbers on the slip of white paper in Billy's trembling palm, reminding him of a conversation with Dr. Kolberg that went exactly like this:

—Are you ready to return to the outside world, Billy?

—No, definitely not, sir.

—Well, you can't stay here forever now, can you?

—Why not? I'm not bothering anybody, sir.

—Because it's not healthy. You're a very special young man, Billy. It's time you found that out on your own, out there. The world may not be as terrible as you think.

—I would like to stay here one more month, if I may, sir.

—One more month? Why?

—Summer will be over, sir. I can't go out there if it's going to be summertime.

—And why not?

—I wouldn't want to see any young girls playing. I would not want to see any flowers outside.

—Why?

—Because everything happy right now is going to die.

—But Billy . . .

—I would not like to be reminded of anything pretty.

—But Billy, of course, anything might . . .

—I would not like to be reminded.

—OK, OK. We will see what we can do, Billy.

Doctor Kolberg did all he could so that Billy was finally re-leased after the school year had begun and the flowers had already started wilting.

The boy detective looks up suddenly. A pale blond girl is shouting at him from her front lawn across the street. Beside her, a small young boy is silently frowning.

"Do you see my bunny's head over there?" the girl shouts.

It is none other than Effie Mumford, age eleven, an adolescent, female, and very awkward-looking. What you must know about Effie is that she has won the local, state, and national science fair for the past three years. Also, she is hopelessly in love with amateur rock-etry. Additionally, she is an interminable social pariah, a long-suffering possessor of many, many unstoppable runny noses, a silent victim of reoccurring eye infections, and a future prize-winning neurobiologist. One last important fact about Effie Mumford: She does not like to be touched. Not by anyone, not ever.

As per her usual routine, Effie is dressed wildly inappropriately, in her white and purple winter jacket, which she wears year round, well into the hottest months of summer, white scarf around her neck, fur-lined hood pulled up, entirely covering her small head.

Beside her is her younger brother, Gus Mumford, age nine, a square-headed dark boy who is smarter than all of his teachers in the third grade, and yet who is known for being a bully. Only that morn-ing, Gus raised his hand to answer a puzzling question about the assas-sination of Abraham Lincoln and noticed that his teacher, Miss Gale, rolled her eyes at him and called upon Missy Blackworth instead. Is it the boy's fault that his hands are so large and square-shaped? Is it his fault that he was born loving the sound of muted flesh against muted flesh? He does not want to be the third grade bully, and yet he is. He does not want to hit Lucy Willis in the ankle with a stone at recess, but for some reason, he does. The boy, Gus, stands silently gazing downward, as he does not ever speak to anyone, horrified by the bloody shambles so near his feet.

Billy looks at them both, squinting, pointing at himself questioningly.

"Are you shouting at me?" Billy asks.

"Yes."

The boy detective pushes his black bifocals up his face.

The girl may be blond. There are a few strands of her hair waving over her forehead and she is wearing thick purple-framed glasses. Billy can see one of her eyes has a white patch over it.

"Do you see my bunny's head over there?" the girl asks again.

The boy detective turns and looks around, then shakes his head.

No is what his head is saying, but it takes a few moments for his mouth to say it.

"No."

"Oh, OK. It's definitely missing then."

The boy detective thinks this: *?*

Like a quiet explosion—with the introduction of this, a new puzzle, the nearly knowable answer to the strange question lying somewhere before him—Billy finds his feet are moving. His tiny black-and-white notebook is out of his pocket and already he is writing. He hurries across the street and stands beside the girl, staring down at where she is looking. There, exactly as the girl has claimed, is a small, fawn-colored rabbit—but headless—the animal's neck a disastrous flood of blood and tendons, its great wound decorated with silver specks of small buzzing flies, two pairs of small ballerina slippers still on its feet.

"What is the meaning of this?" Billy asks.

"Its head isn't on its body."

"Yes. Or so it would seem."

The boy detective is already investigating: measuring, tabulating, a black-and-white blueprint, a detailed diagram of the missing bunny head is already magically appearing at the end of his pencil. He introduces himself like this: "My name is Billy Argo. I am a detective."

"A detective?"

"Yes. What is your name?"

"Effie Mumford." With that, she wipes her runny nose. Beside her, Gus, her brother, only squints suspiciously.

"And what is his name?" Billy asks.

"Gus Mumford. But he doesn't speak."

"I see. And why not?"

"His teacher won't call on him in class. He writes notes, though."

The boy detective stares at the strange little dark-eyed boy, who passes him a small piece of white paper. It says: *Hello stranger*

The boy detective nods at the note then asks: "When did you see this bunny last?"

"I don't know. Last night. Before I went to sleep," Effie replies.

"Is this a random occurrence or has anything like this ever happened to you before?"

"Nope. No way. It's a total surprise. It's very surprising to me."

"As it should be."

"It's pretty gross."

"Yes. Very gross, indeed." The boy detective makes a note of this in his notepad: *Very gross.*

The girl says: "I don't think its head is up here. We've looked around the front of the house pretty good."

Gus Mumford hands the detective another note: *Will you help us look?*

Billy nods, staring at the strange boy again.

The three of them walk around the side of the brick building, searching in the dark green bushes, beneath the sturdy white porch, in the small gray alley. "Mr. Buttons!" the girl calls, slapping her leg. "Mr. Buttons!"

"It is very unlikely that it will come when called now."

The boy detective and the girl stare at each other for a moment. They look behind two silver garbage cans, but to no avail. All they uncover is a sprung mousetrap and a withered corsage.

In a moment, Mrs. Mumford comes to the door. She has short dark hair, blue eyes, and looks quite lovely in a navy dress with ruffles. She stares at the strange man on her front lawn. "May I help you?" she asks.

"I'm a detective. I'm here to find out what happened to the bunny."

"Effie, I told you to please put Mr. Buttons in the trash."

"We are figuring out what happened to him, Mom," Effie argues.

"Well, don't make a mess. We're eating in a half hour."

"OK."

"That goes for you, too, Gus, dear."

Gus Mumford nods, hating to be reminded of anything he already knows. He holds up a note: *Fine!*

"And no playing with chemicals, you two. I don't want you playing around with chemicals again."

With that, Mrs. Mumford disappears, going back to her cleaning. The boy detective and the Mumford children stare down at the bunny's headless body once more.

"Now then, I will ask you this important question, Effie and Gus Mumford: Do you know anyone who would want to do this?"

"Yes. Everybody, practically, of course."

"Why?"

"Because they're hateful. I get first place in everything at school and people hate me for it."

"Who hates you for it?"

"Hateful people. The girls especially."

"They hate you for winning at school?"

"Yes."

"I see." The boy detective makes another note. "What grade are you in?"

"I was double-promoted. I am in the eighth grade."

"The eighth grade? How old are you?"

"Eleven."

"Oh, I see."

The boy detective and the two Mumford children stand staring down at the small brown body.

"So," the girl says.

"Yes?"

"So, are you going to find its head or not?" the girl asks.

"No. It does not look like it."

"No?" the girl asks.

"No. I don't think it's very likely."

"You're not a very good detective, are you?"

"No. I am afraid I am not."

They stare down at the rabbit's body then, in awkward silence, no one quite sure what should be said next.

TWO

It is a scientific fact: There is more crime in Gotham, New Jersey, than you may think. It may truly surprise you. It is like a terrible wax museum, haunted by the eerie faces of the recently deceased. The crime world of Gotham, New Jersey, each year, can be best viewed like this:

19 murders
67 rapes
706 robberies
739 assaults
1,173 burglaries
2,400 larceny counts
1,095 auto thefts
Crime index = 785.8 (higher means more crime; U.S. average = 330.6)

It is a town that truly needs a boy detective. The boy detective has forgotten just how badly.

The boy detective hoists his yellow suitcase to his side and does not move. He does not want to go inside Shady Glens Facility for Mental Competence. He does not want to live there, no, no, no, not at all. Inside, it will smell like a strange brand of instant mashed potatoes. Inside, someone will be screaming a song Billy does not know. The stillness of the angular building and the pasty pallor of his fellow patients—steady and sad-eyed in their medicated gaze, shuffling back and forth in white robes along the front lawn of the facility—give the boy detective cause to think, and what he ponders is this: that the cause of this imbalance, of theirs and his, in this day and age, remains only a cloudy vapor at the far end of some scientist's muddled microscope. Whether it is a chemical disturbance, a psychologically traumatic event, or some inhuman environmental strain that has unhinged them and him so badly, it is the mystery of his infirmity that the boy detective finds most terrifying.

What is also somewhat frightening is how his own treatment continues as only a highly scientific guessing game. Billy is, at the moment, being treated for several illnesses: as a major depressive and an obsessive compulsive. His own therapy combines cognitive behavioral techniques (meant to lessen his compulsion to finish crossword puzzles, close cabinet doors, complete songs other people are whistling) with a daily dose of two hundred milligrams of a serotonin reuptake inhibitor—popularly, Anafranil, or medically, Clomipramine (meant to slow serotonin absorption rates in his brain). Also, two kinds of antianxiety medication which he has been instructed to take at his own discretion: Ativan, which acts quite quickly during the onset of panic, and Seroquel, which remains in the system longer though does not work quite as fast. Why do these drugs work? We do not know. What is the cause of the illness to begin with? Who knows? No one. Strangely, it is also this mystery—the perplexity of the sickness, the cause of his unresolved unhappiness, this unanswered crime perpetrated within the shady, secret underworld of Billy's mind—that makes the boy detective so very depressed and causes the quite obvious hand twitch which has just begun to make its appearance.

At that moment, as he walks across the street and opens the double glass doors, the boy detective knows he is in the exact place he has feared to be: looking back over his shoulder at the inevitable world of mystery.

It follows, then, that the boy detective thinks this: *I am going to find out why Caroline committed suicide, punish whoever is responsible, and stab myself as soon as I have the chance.*

THREE

At soccer practice, Effie Mumford is the worst thing ever, of all time.
We mean it: With her purple winter jacket on and hood pulled up,
she has absolutely no peripheral vision; her persistent runny nose
forces her to stop and blow her mucus on her sleeve frequently;
her glasses usually fall off and get trampled by less awkward, more
athletic kids; if the ball is ever kicked in her direction, she will run
toward it overexcited and she will trip before she can make contact,
skinning her knees; she will try and steal the ball from her own
teammates. As per the regulations of the American Preteen Soccer
League, she must play each game for at least four minutes. It is
during these four minutes that many contests involving her own
Gotham Cougars are often lost. Accordingly, her team has made up
a song about her:

> E-F-F-I-E
> *We don't want her*
> *You can have her*
> *Just send her back to gaylord camp*

At soccer practice, earlier that very day, the ball was accidentally
kicked in her direction. Effie charged toward it, shouting, "I got it! I
got it!" and tripped, falling directly on her face.

"You are the biggest gaylord I have ever seen," one of her teammates said, a pink-cheeked girl with a brown ponytail, standing over
her. The girl's name was Parker Lane. She had small shorts and blue
eye shadow and came down hard with the heel of her spiked shoe

right upon Effie's eyewear, smashing the glasses, already bandaged with several gobs of transparent tape. "We hope you go blind."

Holding her hands over her ears, Effie said, "I'm not even here right now, I'm at the North Pole." She picked up the shards of her glasses and ran away quick.

It should be noted that Mr. Buttons, the bunny whose head has gone missing, had been part of Effie Mumford's science experiment for the upcoming school science fair. Like nearly all of Effie Mumford's recent experiments, it concerned the nature of evil. For nearly three months, Effie Mumford had placed a record player beside Mr. Button's cage and would then note the general effects different kinds of music, speeches, and songs had on his nervous system, reflexes, and social responsiveness.

Other experiments Effie Mumford had recently attempted: the establishment of a connection between serial killers and corrupt world leaders based on the shapes of their heads, hands, and feet; a scientific evaluation of the effects of rudeness in daily conversation; and an exploration to locate the gland in the human body which produces evil, a hypothesis which was impossible to prove without the procurement of a fresh cadaver.

The evidence thus far in her most recent experiment, before the unplanned murder of her test subject: In a clear case of environmental stimulus having a profound effect on a creature's day-to-day existence, the bunny seemed to enjoy most kinds of music, specifically big band jazz, which correlated with a much lower blood pressure, faster reflexes, and a greater level of human-rabbit affection. When a vinyl recording of real-life war sounds from Germany or an inaugural speech by President Nixon was introduced, the bunny became unresponsive, unaffectionate, uncoordinated, and sad, sometimes becoming so en-raged as to bite Effie's hand. Perhaps Effie Mumford was only trying to prove something she already knew: that, like all animals, she was at the whim of the general disorder and unimaginative meanness of the world surrounding her.

FOUR

In the pale green hallway of Shady Glens, the boy detective is busy counting the number of steps to his room, so that if he is kidnapped and blindfolded, he will know how many paces it will be to safety. The answer is thirty-seven. He whispers "Thirty-seven" out loud.

This is what a boy detective does: He is always counting, estimating, recording. He cannot stop himself and simply let one moment move into the next. His is a life of connections, patterns, histories, motivations. In the world of the boy detective, as in our world, there is a reason for everything. Without a reason, without a plan, without a precise count of steps to the closest escape route, there is nothing.

Nurse Eloise, one of the custodians of this wing of Shady Glens, a young woman with dark eyes, dark hair, and a bloody handprint on her uniform skirt, walks with Billy along the hallway. "You must be both very nervous and very excited to be here."

"No," Billy says, "I am nothing."

As they walk down the brightly lit tile hall, they pass a Mr. Pluto: a large, bald-headed behemoth of a man in a blue hospital gown stitched from enough fabric to make four smaller men's gowns. Billy immediately recognizes him as the Amazing Pluto!, a former circus strongman long ago convicted of several vault heists. His eyes are like small black buttons, and from his incomprehensible mumbling, it is clear that he is most definitely mad. He is brushing his bald head with a golden brush and whimpering very frantically.

"Poor Mr. Pluto, what's the matter, dear?" Nurse Eloise asks. "Did you lose your wig again?"

Mr. Pluto nods.

"He's only nervous meeting new people, the poor dear," Nurse Eloise explains. "Why not introduce yourself, Billy?"

Billy smiles at the giant, who looks away shyly.

"Oh, he's just bashful around strangers," Nurse Eloise says, taking Billy's hand and leading him to his room.

It is strange, but as the boy detective enters, he decides it is just as he imagined it would be. Although it is meant to be a residence, there is still something definitely institutional in all of it. The room is very small with faded, peeling green wallpaper and strange black spots which are growing along the ceiling. There is one window, which is barred, and no furniture save for a white wood dresser and a pale green and white bed. It looks nearly the same as his room at the mental asylum, which in the end, the boy detective finds strangely comforting.

It is a surprise when the nurse flips the light switch and instead of offering luminosity, it somehow begins snowing. Tiny white flakes begin to drift from the ceiling in powdery drifts and the nurse, her apple cheeks reddening, switches it off nervously.

"We need to repair that," she says.

The snow begins to disappear, melting into the dull green carpeting. Billy catches a single snowflake on his finger and watches it turn to tears. He looks up and frowns. "It's all right," he says. "I don't mind really."

"Well, I apologize," Nurse Eloise says, embarrassed. "Why don't I give you a few minutes to get your bearings?"

"OK," Billy says.

The boy detective closes the door of his new room and looks around. Scratching at his scars, he takes a seat on the bed which sags with dust. He sighs at an aged, sad-eyed painting of a large-headed child held along the wall in a dusty gold frame. He opens his suitcase and begins to take out some of his clothing. Finding his owl-shaped alarm clock, he winds it and sets it beside the bed. Sighing once more, he finds his newspaper clippings, the wrinkled front pages depicting his adventurous youth, and, one by one, he begins attaching them to the pale green wall:

BOY DETECTIVE HOOKS SEA MONSTER CROOKS

Children Reel In Hoax-Makers at Lake Gotham

BOY DETECTIVE SOLVES PRICELESS CROSSWORD PUZZLE

Kid Sister and Neighbor Boy Help Decipher Missing Jewel-Laden Word

BOY DETECTIVE DASHES FIREWORK SMUGGLING RING

Several Hoodlums Die in Fire

and on and on until the walls are papered with the familiar faces of the ones he so dearly misses: There is Caroline and Fenton in the beard and mustache; there is Caroline again, very young in her white dress, pointing at a crooked fireman; there is Fenton smiling as a reporter asks what his favorite flavor of ice cream is, the small soft hands of the neighbor boy holding one of his evidential drawings; there is a villain disappearing into the back of a police vehicle; there is a photo of each of the children victorious, laughing; there is the ruddy face of his sister as she sneers at a corrupt politician; there is Caroline again with the fingerprint kit, providing the daring clue to some startling case; there are her bright eyes and small ears and narrow lips; there is her figure, which now is only black dots on yellowing newsprint, only black smears on a pulp page; there again is Caroline

Caroline

Caroline

Why did you go when you did?

In the privacy of his room, Billy, terrified of all that is unknown around him, lays on his bed and closes his eyes. Like always, he begins to remember. He returns to the case of the Haunted Candy Factory, a famous one he solved as a boy, quite brilliantly. Billy stares at the smudgy newspaper clippings on the wall, dreaming of the distant memory he so happily recollects any time he is feeling so very badly.

That summer so long ago, the Gotham police had been stumped by a series of strange occurrences at the new Happy Land Candy Factory. Some unlucky kids, taking a tour of the place, reported seeing a "ghostly figure" hovering above the Chocolate Marshmallow vat, moments before several support beams fell from their necessary places and leveled the brand-new Strawberry Kisser machine, injuring a few of the children in a dangerous wave of sharp, crystallized gelatin lips. A few days later, a factory employee operating the Nougat Splashdown extruder confessed to hearing an eerie voice echoing in the vicinity of the control panel just as several pipe fittings exploded, showering workers in a detonation of dangerous sparks. An anonymous letter some time later, sent inside a foil-wrapped chocolate bar, provided the first and only clue. Billy and Caroline and Fenton stood together in the police station slowly reading it.

EVERY DEAD GHOST IN A FACTORY IS BENT

The boy detective solves things like this in his sleep. Or he used to, at least.

FIVE

The boy detective suddenly realizes that Professor Von Golum, his lifelong archenemy, is now living across the hallway from him. It is unmistakable: The Professor is a tall, narrow villain with a long face. He is wearing a sleek white robe and white pajamas. Without a welcome, he steps inside Billy's room and immediately begins snooping, laying his small, grasping fingers all over Billy's things, grinning as he remarks to himself what he finds interesting.

"Very interesting," he says, nodding. "Oh, *very* interesting."

Billy sighs and takes a seat on the bed, watching the Professor move about his room quite deliberately.

"We meet again, Billy Argo, and yet in the most surprising of places, yes?"

Billy stares down at his hands and frowns, touching his wrists.

In that moment: magic. Billy realizes Professor Von Golum is dead. He has been for some time, due to a strange accident at his laboratory involving a faulty disintegration ray and a lovely assistant who was mutilated in the catastrophe. Billy remembers this fact very suddenly, looking up in terror.

"I thought . . . I thought you had died," Billy whispers.

"I thought I had, too," the Professor says. "But here am I, sitting on this bed. What I've learned is that there is nothing in this life that does not fail to disappoint us, even our own deaths."

"Yes, I see."

"Yes, it is quite strange indeed," the Professor says and nods sadly.

"Yes. It is."

"Is it true what I have heard, boy detective?"

"I . . ." the boy detective stutters.

Professor Von Golum stares at Billy, gently touching his wrists. Seeing the scars, the Professor quietly nods.

"Oh, I see. And with the wrists, too. Well, that was brave, at least."

"Why are you here?" the boy detective asks.

"Well, as you know, I had a problem with the fairer sex. As brilliant as I was, well, I could never quite figure them out exactly. I had this one beautiful young specimen in my lab and she was very talkative until finally, I said, 'If you don't be quiet and begin undressing . . .' And she said, 'But I'm only a kid, I'm only fifteen.' And right there, I decided maybe the best way to understand these women—all these women— was to maybe try and open one up, you know, to take a look inside and see how they all work, like a time machine . . ."

Professor Von Golum gets nervous suddenly and looks around, startled.

"Did you hear that, Billy?" he asks. "The nurses are always lurking around. Do you want my advice? Keep whatever you have that's valuable with you at all times."

Professor Von Golum picks up one of Billy's sweaters and begins to try it on, admiring himself in the mirror.

"You cannot trust anyone in this place, Billy. Well, except me. We are like old friends, are we not?"

Professor Von Golum stands, walking across the room, then pulls a clipping of Billy and Caroline off the wall. He stares at Caroline, her hair short and blond, a daisy behind her left ear, the old man gumming his jaws, his beady eyes transfixed.

"Now that girl, *that* girl, she was always so lovely."

Billy grabs the clipping from the Professor, who chortles and nods, turning away quickly.

"What you need to do is to learn to trust people again, Billy. You're out in the world now. Not everyone wants to hurt you." The Professor gently pats Billy on the shoulder and smiles, his black eyes glinting. "Yes, yes, speaking of trust, listen—Perhaps this may be of interest to you. There's a fellow staying here, Mr. Lunt. He's a daft old gent, like you and me. He was a crook, though, you see—a thief, with banks, robbery, terrible stuff. He pulled down quite a bit of loot back in his time, or so he says, and he's living right here among us, sleeping in the room right next to yours, right across the hall from mine. That selfish old gent, well, he has a pile of loot hidden away, still just sitting there—a bundle from a job back in 1909, he says. That poor old fellow refuses to share the certain whereabouts of this wondrous wealth, and what I believe is, as cohorts in this facility, it ought to belong to *all* of us. And so I have been doing some figuring, and you and I as geniuses, well, I thought we might convince him, or discern exactly, where the load of said cash is hidden . . ."

Billy shakes his head sheepishly. "Please, no, sir. I just want to be left alone."

"No, eh? Well, it's your loss, Billy. Because somehow, someway, I'm going to get my hands on that lovely treasure and when it's all said and done, I'll be on the lam somewhere living like a king and you'll be still here rotting, doing paint-by-numbers with the rest of these ninnies."

The boy detective is silent.

There is an awkward pause, until the Professor speaks again: "I am going to have to destroy you now, aren't I?"

"Yes, I guess so," Billy says, staring down at his hands.

"Yes, it seems that way."

"All right."

"OK, consider yourself destroyed as soon as I am well rested."

"Yes. Fine."

Very quickly, Professor Von Golum grabs the newspaper clipping from Billy's hands and runs through the door, still wearing the boy detective's blue sweater. Within a blink, Professor Von Golum has disappeared into his room across the hall and has closed and locked his door. Billy stands, shaking his head, then sighs, returning to his suitcase to soundlessly finish arranging his things.

It is after some time, when the boy detective is nearly finished, that he finds, at the bottom of his effects beneath his clothes, Caroline's gold diary. He slowly lifts it out and then, without a thought, turns to the last entry. Billy moves his finger down the tiny white page.

It reads, in girlish handwriting:

nothing is good. nothing is ever good.

On another page, near the front of the diary, he discovers this entry:

how to begin? as usual, Billy was quite courageous today, my brother
the famous detective. as we searched through the abandoned old house
i discovered a secret passageway behind a large painting of a
pale lady; i was too frightened to enter
but Billy, like always, led the way
we crept past the rather large wooden door and
into a narrow hallway which wound downwards
there were a number of cobwebs inhabited by a variety of
long-legged, menacing-looking spiders, but we simply marched on
the three of us, Billy holding the light, Fenton mumbling, and me
looking behind for any sign of a ghost, bandit, or otherwise

unlikely villain; we then discovered a large trunk, which when opened, as you might have expected, revealed the pirate's glowing costume . . .

The boy detective places the diary under the mattress of the creaking bed. Then Billy lifts the True-Life Junior Detective kit out of his suitcase, staring at it with a remembered softness and a certain kind of disdain. It has not aged well: The corners are caved in and the cartoon boy on the cover of the box—a boy who had once been blond and whose hair is now gray and dirty—holds up a magnifying glass, discerning a secret message which will never be completely translated. The box is now old and sunken, the cartoon child small and withered, the paper having begun to turn and decay.

Billy, ignoring his shaking hands, begins to open the kit, then stops himself, and finally decides to place it in the bottom drawer of the white dresser. He closes the drawer and stares at it, behind which the detective kit lies, unopened; the boy detective can only dream of what might be inside.

We cannot blame him for putting it away. We cannot. We cannot blame him for being afraid.

SIX

The boy detective begins to pack his bag again, removing the lovely press clippings from his walls, folding them so gently, returning them to his small yellow suitcase. He is through the double glass doors of Shady Glens and walking down the street, when Effie Mumford, still in her purple and white winter jacket, comes hurrying after him.

"Where are you going?"

"I did not think I was ready and now I know it," he huffs, hurrying toward the bus stop at the end of the block.

"But wait. What about my bunny? Aren't you going to find its head?"

"I can't help you with that."

"But you said you're a detective, didn't you?"

"Yes. No. Not anymore."

"But look," the girl says, stopping, reaching into her puffy pocket, and retrieving her bright purple wallet. "Here is a dollar if you can find it."

"I don't want your money," Billy says, setting down his suitcase, breathing heavy.

"No, take it and find out."

The boy detective stares at the soft, wrinkled dollar. He stares at her small open palm, her weirdly round face, the white patch over one eye, the smashed glasses. He thinks he is staring at the picture of how his heart must look: small and sad and mashed. Billy pauses, feeling the sun beat down on his neck, the sweat on his forehead, the smell of the flowers outside—puffy and sweet—the barking of a dog somewhere, the sky looming wide open above his head, the sound of bees glowing in the very last moments of summer, and he knows if he were to keep walking toward the bus stop, he would never see any of these things again. He would never try again: He would simply walk back into the familiar, perfect world of his own death. The boy detective closes his fist around the money and smiles slowly.

"OK, yes."

"Yes?"

"Yes. I will find it. I will solve this case by the end of the week."

"Good. Thank you. Thank you, Billy."

The girl stares up at him with a grin as wide as some unnamed equatorial line, and then she squeezes his hand.

The boy detective turns, picks up his bag, and begins walking decisively back toward Shady Glens. He hurries back into his room, hoping no one has noticed his quick departure, lays his suitcase on the floor, and climbs onto his bed. He finds one of his bottles of pills, the Ativan, and takes two more than he should and very, very soon his vision begins to blur. He looks up at the ceiling and smiles, then switches on the light. He stares up wide-eyed as a hazy cloud of delicate snowflakes gently appears above his face. He is surprised to see a tall office building outside his window disappear suddenly.

At one time, in nearby New York City, a beautiful silver cathedral was built. Before long, a masked villain blew it up with an explosive device and many people were killed. We hate to even discuss it because your pretty cousin Amy, sadly, was inside. Immediately, like everyone else, she was turned into a brilliant explosion of stained glass. Tiny bits of it fell everywhere. The colorful pieces were carried into the river and disappeared downstream, turning everything they touched gray. Little children, fish, deer—anything near the explosion— became slouched and old. Miles and miles away from the lights of that great city, everyone in our town, including you, became ill, either from the colored glass in their blood or the sadness of seeing the spot on the horizon where the cathedral used to be.

SEVEN

It is later that evening when the boy detective hears someone quietly sobbing in the hallway of Shady Glens. He pulls on his blue sweater and walks out, finding Mr. Pluto lying against the doorframe, gigantic tears splashing from his button eyes, a puddle of grief already forming. Clearly, this is a man who has been very upset by something. Billy frowns at him. Mr. Pluto, wiping his eyes, smiles back.

"What is it? What's wrong?" Billy asks.

Mr. Pluto holds up a gigantic golden hairbrush and attempts to comb his hair, but it is clear: His wig is still most definitely missing. Mr. Pluto takes Billy's hand and places it along his great bald scalp, still sobbing.

"Your wig is still missing?"

Mr. Pluto nods. Billy helps Mr. Pluto to his feet.

"It's awful silly for a man your age to be wearing a wig in the first place."

Mr. Pluto begins to cry louder, banging his fists against his chest.

"Fine, yes, I'll help you," Billy says, shaking his head and sighing. Holding Mr. Pluto's hand, he walks down the hallway, searching for some clue, some evidence, some sign. He begins with simple questions, the grand tool of the boy detective, trying to establish the motive of this very minor crime. "Where was the last place you had it? Do you remember that?"

Mr. Pluto nods. He pulls Billy down toward the end of the hall to his room, where there is a small hand mirror lying beside a white Styrofoam head, the wig's resting place, no doubt. Billy bends over and slowly inspects the brush. Along the bristles is a single, small, yellow hair.

A single yellow hair.

Eureka.

Billy nods and smiles knowingly, and at once the mystery has been solved. He grabs Mr. Pluto's enormous hand and leads him down the hallway, stopping at Professor Von Golum's room. Billy squints in front of the door, peeking through the keyhole, listening to a record of strange jazzy music playing loudly inside.

It goes like this: Through the keyhole, Billy can see Professor Von Golum, lying in his bed beside Billy's blue sweater, which has been stuffed with pillows, the clipping of Billy's sister Caroline resting where the face might be—Mr. Pluto's long blond wig completes the ghostly figure's head. The Professor is romancing the imaginary composite woman, talking very sweetly, gently rubbing its arm, telling it what he most admires in this, his only companion.

"You have very good-looking teeth. No, don't talk. Just lie there and let me stare at them like that, as they are so pretty."

Billy nods and motions to Mr. Pluto, explaining with a simple pointing finger that his wig is inside. Mr. Pluto, angry, his small eyes getting big and wide, gently moves Billy aside, steps back, and knocks the door in with a single great kick. Professor Von Golum lets out a high-pitched scream as Mr. Pluto strides across the room in one step, grabbing for the Professor's throat, lifting him from the bed and choking him with one gigantic white hand. The boy detective moves to prevent certain murder, tugging on Mr. Pluto's blue gown. Mr. Pluto returns the Professor to his feet, who, doubling over, continues to choke and wheeze.

Billy takes a step beside Professor Von Golum, staring at his shoulder and the long golden hair left curled along the evil scientist's neck. The boy detective had noticed the foreign hair earlier—why? Because the boy detective's mind is always detecting; it cannot stop itself. Billy picks off the hair and smiles. Mr. Pluto turns and retrieves his wig with a snarl, pushing the Professor aside.

"Now you, you stay away from my door," Billy says to Mr. Pluto.

Mr. Pluto nods bashfully, then creeps out as quietly as he can, his enormous feet thundering down the hall. The Professor continues to choke, cursing, pulling himself upright finally. He turns and points one long dirty-fingernailed finger at Billy.

"That was an awful mistake. I tell you this. You can expect *serious* trouble from me from now on, boy detective."

The boy detective sighs and walks out, returning to his room. He frowns, then blinks his eyes, staring at the newspaper clippings on the wall, adding the one he has just retrieved:

THE HORROR OF THE HAUNTED MINE

What Lurks Inside Miller's Cave?

That evening the boy detective, asleep in this strange bed, in this strange room, wakes up to the sound of someone else's screaming. He bounds out of bed, opening the door to the hallway, his face glowing red with fear. Nurse Eloise, in her white uniform, hurries past, stopping for a moment to console him.

"It's only Mr. Lunt with his poor phantoms again."

From down the hall, he can hear the old man shouting: "Phantoms! Phantoms! Merciful lord, grant me reprieve!"

Billy closes the door, crawling back to bed. He begins to fall asleep, but soon the old man is screaming again.

"Phantoms! Phantoms! Why am I cursed so? Lord have mercy on me!"

The boy detective lays in his bed and smiles. The sound of Nurse Eloise's feet is the sound of something very comforting.

EIGHT

It is at the hour of midnight exactly when a man—appearing to be missing his head—opens his black valise. Hidden from the streetlights, he stands beneath a tree of small nesting bluebirds, his dark suit, white collar, black tie all hanging mysteriously around an empty neck. A pair of gloves suddenly appear on his hands. He sets down his suitcase, unclasps the clasps, and removes a large silver pair of scissors. Soon the shadows all along the quiet street hum with life as the scissors issue their strange racket: It seems the trees and telephone phones immediately begin shrinking and expanding with each *clip-clip-clip*. The birds, high up in the tree, begin to sing out in terror, and then, in a moment, they are deathly silent, though the night air is still thrumming.

NINE

At the bus stop, the boy detective watches in horror as a glamorous woman in a white fur coat enjoys a long-tipped cigarette. The boy detective is terrified of cigarettes: The smoke, like the malignant, vaporous claw of near-death, is enough to send poor Billy into a fit. He inches away from the woman but it is no use—like a sentient cloud of gray infirmity, it nears Billy's face as he begins to tremble and cough.

Before long, a handsome man in a blue business suit approaches the bus stop, talking loudly on his cellular phone. "No. It's just as I said, I refuse to argue anymore," he says.

Billy stares at the man's face, his fragile mind racing: *Who is he speaking with? What has he just said? Why does he refuse to argue?*

"No. No. I already told you. No. Listen. Listen. Do not fuck this up. I am warning you. Do not fuck this up for me."

Billy clamps his hands over his ears and glares upward, the advertising plastered all around the bus stop somehow echoing the same sense of doom:

1-800-WHO'S the FATHER Find Out Now
ERECTILE DYSFUNCTION?
SHOOT SOMEONE WITH A GUN AND GO TO JAIL

On the bus, the boy detective stares at his fellow passengers—shabby, strange, menacing—glowering at them all with disapproval and disdain. The boy detective thinks: *It is as if the world has lost all its manners and meaning. It is as if people have lost their minds. It is as if we are adrift in a glowing asylum hurtling through the darkness of space and there is absolutely no escape.*

During that same bus ride, the boy detective must also stop himself from trying to tie three different strangers' untied shoelaces.

At work, the boy detective is absolutely terrified. Having been hired by Mammoth Life-Like Mustache International to conduct telephone sales on their behalf, Billy sits in the drab green lobby, staring at the company's catalog, which features various styles of fake beards and mustaches:

- The Junior Executive
- The Noble Hunter
- The Mysterious Stranger

The office itself is an unending maze of cubicles through which many businesspeople and important-looking white documents are constantly crossing. Crowded around the water cooler and various desks are several attractive, well-dressed mustache salesmen, all laughing and winking and shaking each other's hands. They all have sleek expressions and very handsome, natural-looking mustaches. Above the cubicles, along a silvery wire, papers with completed orders for new merchandise are being sent along like a conveyer belt. Workers in other parts of the office take the papers and replace them with new ones, without any apparent order to their movements. It is very busy and chaotic, and this is what worries Billy.

"Billy?"

At that moment, Melinda, a handsomely dressed brunette in a professional blue suit, takes Billy's hand. Billy nods in response. Melinda wears a huge amount of makeup, her lipstick bright red and smudgy. She continues to shake Billy's hand as she goes on speaking.

"You must be Billy, am I right? Terrific! You're going to be just terrific, I can tell. This is going to work out great.

Let's go ahead and get you started with an entry-level hair-replacement product evaluation, OK?"

Like that, the boy detective finds himself taking a written exam, matching various hair products to their names, guessing at answers for the two hundred question true-or-false test:

Question #9: T or F: Toupee is French for savvy hair product.
Question #36: T or F: All Mammoth Life-Like Mustache International products are guaranteed flameproof.
Question #115: T or F: Wigs are only for women.

"Terrific! You're a natural, I tell you! It's amazing! I'm going to recommend you for an immediate interview with Mr. Mammoth. Just take a seat, he'll be with you in a minute, OK?" Melinda says.

Billy sits in the hard green chair outside Mr. Mammoth's office, his hands shaking uncontrollably. Melinda reappears, touching up her lipstick, waving the boy detective inside. Billy stands, clasping his shaking hands together, following the strange woman into the small room which is institutional-green and wood-paneled, instantly reminding Billy of the director's office at St. Vitus.

"Now as you may know, the president of Mammoth Life-Like Mustache International, J.D. Mammoth, besides being an amazing entrepreneur, world-class athlete, and noted left-hander—that's why everything in the office is left-handed, Billy—well, he was also something of a technological wizard. He passed away twelve years ago in a mysterious elephant-hunting accident right before we were federally investigated for the first time. It was a terrible year for the company and we would have been sunk if Mr. Mammoth hadn't arranged all of his future affairs beforehand. He recorded over ninety thousand hours of plans, initiatives, directives, conversations, and requests on reel-to-reel tape to be played in his future absence. Hirings, firings, disciplinary actions—all handled by a color-coded system. Isn't technology just amazing?"

Billy nods, frightened, looking about the room. A painting of Mr. Mammoth, a bald, short, round, mustached man in a suit, hangs over an empty mahogany desk. There are several giant color photos of Mr. Mammoth hunting various big-game animals—a tiger, a lion, an elephant—their eyes staring back at Billy, plaintive and dead. Melinda steps around behind the desk, silently pressing a button on a large reel-to-reel tape player, the machine green and plastic and full of dust. Melinda leans to the side of the player and begins to smile widely.

"Now, there's nothing to be nervous about. Go on and have a seat, Billy."

Billy takes a seat in a small chair, holding his hands, staring at the tape machine as it whirs to life. From its gears and sprockets, a ghostly voice begins to rise: *"Welcome! First of all, good citizen, we wish to welcome you to the world of Mammoth Life-Like Mustache International. By now, you've passed our extensive evaluation process and are about to enter the exciting world of hair-replacement telephone sales. Before you begin, we feel it's important you know the history of the company you're about to represent. How does that sound, good citizen?"*

Billy does not know if he is supposed to respond but does so anyway. "OK."

"Well, we'll be honest with you, kind worker. When we were your age, we would often sit and stare up at the ceiling and wonder, is there room for us? Is there a place where we belong? And that's when we hit on it, kind worker: mustaches. Do you know how many American men are unable to grow a good-looking mustache? Thousands. Hundreds of thousands. Some of them are fair-haired, some have low testosterone, some are victims of terrible crimes,

but all of them have a dream. The dream to look good. Slowly, our product reached the homes and hearts of thousands. Then thousands after that. Then the international market—do you understand how many beards we sell in the Far East? Now we've moved into the brand-new world of weaves, extensions, and wigs, growing to cover all of our customer's hair-replacement needs. Why? Because the world is a better place when we are all looking our best. Now, kind worker, I ask you, don't you share that dream, kind worker?"

The boy detective whispers: "Yes."

"Well, kind worker, with that, we want to wish you the best of luck here at Mammoth Life-Like Mustache International. Remember, in each of you is a little bit of me. End tape."

"Um, thanks," Billy mutters quietly.

Melinda shakes his hand once more and exclaims: "Terrific! Welcome to the team of Mammoth Life-Like Mustache International. How about we go and get you started off with something simple?"

TEN

The hair catalog of Mammoth Life-Like International looks like this:

For the Modern Attractive Male

The Junior Executive
is a real go-getter. Who gets the job done and still has time to play? Who's going straight to the top every day? Available in natural brown, blond, and red.
001-125 — $44.95

The Noble Hunter
wants to be left alone, but doesn't mind the company of a like-minded female. Beware his dead eye, once prey falls into his sights. May require out-patient surgery.
001-003 — $55.95

The Mysterious Stranger
is the guy everyone is talking about. Who walks into the party and commands attention? Who's the fellah taking you home tonight, ladies? Two pieces, custom-fit to each man's preference.
024-490 — $44.95

The Trustworthy Father
likes Saturday mornings in bed with the wife. His newspaper, slippers, a fresh cup of coffee, this guy is the one everyone turns to for answers. Just don't buy this man a tie for his birthday. Black and gray only.
009-121 — $69.95

The Nordic Prince
is dashing, aristocratic, a king among men. This is the fellah who always demands respect whether at the club or board room table. Only available in Arctic blonde.
096-065 — $54.95

The Gallant Sailor
knows the port of call women prefer. Brash, but always a gentleman, he's been around the world and knows what it takes to be captain of his own fate. Mustache and beard sold separately.
871-063 — $34.95

It amazes the boy detective that hair replacement is an actual business. It is not amazing enough, however, to keep him from wondering what he is doing there in the first place. Once he takes a seat in a small gray cubicle, Melinda hands him a phone receiver, which is connected to a large, greenish-gray computer; it is all plastic, like an appliance from the '70s, and seems strangely out-of-date.

"Terrific! How about we start you off with something nice and easy, then? Super. Have you ever used a left-handed phone before, Billy?"

"No."

"Well, you'll get used to it quick. Now, the computer here does all the hard work—the dialing and account information—all you have to do is talk. Isn't that easy? Now, Billy, Mammoth Life-Like maintains its competitive edge in the hair-replacement market by exclusively targeting the unwell and also the elderly. What happens is we buy lists of hundreds of prospective clients from credit card companies—prospective clients who are, let's just say, not healthy: cancer patients, car-accident victims, survivors of fires and other natural disasters—clients who are getting on there in years. Sometimes it takes a while before we know whether a prospective customer is dead or not, which, believe it or not, isn't necessarily a 'dead end' in itself—sorry for the pun, Billy. Believe it or not, sometimes the person who answers is also a cancer patient, sharing a hospital room. Or maybe they were in the same car accident or fire and managed to live, or maybe—maybe, just maybe—they're also getting on there in years. The important thing is not to be discouraged. This will give you an idea of what to expect while you're trying to improve the overall hair quality of someone's life."

Billy nods, staring down at the telephone receiver.

"So OK, here's a beginning script. I'll give you a few minutes to get comfortable, make a few calls, you know, just have fun with it!"

"Terrific," Billy mumbles to himself as Melinda quickly exits.

The boy detective picks up the phone and watches as the computer noisily begins to dial, its gears and sprockets turning wildly. Busying himself, his heart pounding, he nervously flips through the Mammoth Life-Like hair catalog and stares at the strange words on the salesperson script.

Out there in the world, somewhere, a lonely customer—a middle-aged widow in a yellow housecoat—answers the ringing phone, her hands weak, her eyes gray and sad. In the background, her children are screaming and fighting. The customer tugs on her stringy blond hair and black mascara streaks down her face as she stares at a photograph hanging in the hallway, a picture of her husband: a square-faced brick-mason, recently deceased.

"Hello?" the woman whispers.

"Hello," Billy whispers back.

"Yes? What? What is it?"

"I'm sorry . . ." Billy says, his breath coming quickly. "I . . ."

"Glen . . . is that you? Oh God, just say something. Please, say something . . . anything . . ."

Billy sighs, holding the phone nervously, unable to speak.

"Oh, Glen, you don't have to talk at all. I miss you. I miss you so much. Just, shhhh, just be quiet. I'm so sorry. I miss you. I miss you so much. When are you coming back? Just tell me when."

"I . . ." the boy detective sighs.

"No, no, you're right. I need to be strong on my own. I need to make it on my own."

"Yes."

"The kids, Jesus, Glen, they miss you, too. We all do. You, you would have been proud of little Leonard. He went right up to the casket and kissed his daddy's cheek and . . . Oh, Glen, what am I going to do without you? What am I going to do?"

At that moment, the boy detective remembers Caroline in her small white coffin, her long blond hair spread out like a glowing halo, the image exactly matching the Nordic Princess wig from the catalog Billy is now holding.

The customer is now crying on the phone.

Billy cannot think what to say or do. Holding the phone against his ear, he whispers, very sadly, still thinking of his sister Caroline: "I'm so sorry."

Billy hangs up the phone. He wipes many small tears from his eyes. He gets up from his desk and heads for the bathroom, falling into an adjoining cubicle before he really begins to cry uncontrollably.

The boy detective stumbles into the men's bathroom and finds another man inside, also weeping. He is drinking from a flask and wiping his teary eyes. The man is a short, greasy, round salesman with an enormous black hair piece and a tiny black mustache. He is wearing a ton of gold chains and several gold rings. The man smiles, shrugging, then offers the flask to Billy.

"This here, friend, is the only way to make it through the sob stories, day after day."

Billy frowns, backing away. The man shrugs his shoulders, taking another swig.

"We'll see what you say after a week of being here. They sign you up for the graveyard shift yet, kid?"

"No."

"Well, those are the worst. You never know what people are going to say when they're all alone in the middle of the night. You do one week of the night shift and then you'll be as lousy as me, I promise. Poor old Larry here? I worked the graveyard shift for five years straight. They say you get used to everything being left-handed, but you don't. I know that much."

Billy looks at Larry's left hand and sees the white spot where a wedding ring used to be. He notices there are green markings beneath all of Larry's remaining rings.

"Sure, well, I'm the national sales leader in this office now, you know, but it wasn't always this easy."

"I believe Patrick Vigo is the national sales leader. I think I just saw his plaque outside in the lobby."

"That's this month, kid. I'm talking for the whole year."

"But Debra Cummings was the national leader for the year. Her plaque was beside the others."

"Well, sure, you're a sharp one, huh? Well, what I mean is this *current* year. I'm not talking about the past year. The current year."

"It's better never to lie. To be honest, I don't care either way."

"Why'd you say that, kid? Why'd you call me a liar like that?"

"There's a pawn-shop ticket stuck to the top of your shoe. And all your jewelry is fake."

"Well, sure, I had to pawn the good stuff, but I got this junk because I have to keep up the image. Wow, well, that's amazing, kid. You some sort of mind reader or something?"

"No."

"Well, it's uncanny is what it is. How'd you do all that? Figure me out like that?"

"I dunno. Everyone is good at something. I'm good at finding out the truth."

"Well, you're a real danger to have around here. You're OK by me, pal. You sure you don't want a quick snortful?"

Billy stares down at the white tile floor. "No thanks. I think maybe I should go back to my desk."

"Well, OK, stay alive out there, kid. It's more than you can say for your clients, ha ha. You get dreary, you know where to find me."

Larry shakes Billy's hand. Billy slowly returns to his desk, wiping his hand on his pants.

The boy detective picks up the phone and dials once again.

Somewhere, some other phone rings. Sitting at a table, an old man with large glasses stares at a photo of his deceased wife and answers the telephone regretfully.

"Good afternoon. Is Gladys in?"

"Hello? No, no, I'm afraid Gladys isn't home. No . . . not, not anymore. Not ever again."

Billy hangs up the phone quick. He lifts it again and the computer dials the next number.

Somewhere else, on the edge of town, in a tiny, run-down boarding house, Killer Kowalzavich—a monstrous, hammer-faced ex-convict in a dirty blue torn shirt—sits in the darkness of his shabby rented room. He is shaved bald and has all kinds of tubes and devices hooked up to his person. He is very old and very sick, but still frightening. The boy detective begins: "Good afternoon . . ."

"Who is this?"

"Hello, good day; my name is Billy Argo with Mammoth Life-Like Mustache International. I was wondering—"

"Did you say Argo? Billy Argo?"

"Yes sir, with Mammoth Life-Like Mustache International. I was wondering if I could take up a few moments of your time?"

"I'd say you already took up most of the time I had, Billy Argo."

"Pardon me?"

"You took up almost all of the time I was given and now there's not much left. Don't you remember my voice, Billy Argo?"

"No. I'm sorry, I wish I did."

"Sure, sure, you and your brat sister and your little fat friend got me locked up about ten years ago. The Case of the Pawn-Shop Kidnapper? Sure, sure, the boy detective solves a string of strange, mysterious kidnappings. Sure, sure. That was me."

"Killer Kowalzavich? When did you get out?"

"Just a few weeks ago. Just in time to sit in this lousy room by myself and die."

"I'm . . . I'm sorry it ended up like this for you. I . . . I never wanted to see anybody—even you—get hurt. Only I know they would have gone easier on you if you had told them what happened to Miss Daisy Hollis. You know, they . . . they never found her."

"I told them I had nothing to do with that girl. What kind of kid-napper do you think I was? Sure, I tried to pawn the other girl's fancy belongings, but that Hollis girl, they couldn't ever pin that one on me. I'll take that, and, well, a whole string of things with me to the grave. Boy detective, huh? You wouldn't know the half of it."

"I'm done speaking with you."

"Sure, sure, but before you go, be swell and tell me, how's that sweet little sister of yours?"

The boy detective slams down the phone. He immediately begins crying. Larry crosses the aisle and helps Billy to his feet, gently rub-bing the back of his neck.

"First-day jitters is all, kid. Nothing a good night's sleep won't fix. Get a good meal and turn in early. Tomorrow, you'll be back among the living, good as new."

"OK," Billy says, and realizes he is still holding the phone.

The boy detective, at the bus stop, prevents himself from calling his parents, Mr. and Mrs. Argo. He imagines they are, at that particular moment, too busy to talk to him. He thinks his father is probably pounding a great wood table, calling out some objection in naval court, and the judge is shouting back, "Objection overruled!" His mother is either working on a new substitute for plastic or painting a masterpiece reminiscent of some Flemish work of art. He stands in the telephone booth and stares down and sees a strange brown shape near his feet. His heart stops beating: It is someone's hair. There is a clump of human hair just lying there in the corner of the phone booth. The boy detective, at this moment, thinks: *The world has gone mad. The world is broken and falling apart and completely mad.* He finds his small bottle of pills and pops three Ativan into his mouth, his fingers trembling.

The boy detective hangs up the phone and then is running awkwardly down the street, toward the bus stop, small tears streaming down his cheeks.

ELEVEN

The boy detective always returns to the case of the Haunted Candy Factory:

Caroline, sitting in her hiding spot beneath the white wood porch, wrote the clue in her gold-colored notebook again and again. It was now a bet—who could discover the meaning to the phantom's riddle first—and Billy, listening to her fuss beneath the wood slats, only laughed at her struggle, then feeling bad, he was quiet. After a good few hours, he climbed beneath the porch and took the pencil and paper from her hand, revealing:

EVERY DEAD GHOST IN A FACTORY IS BENT

which easily became the anagram:

EATING CANDY IS SO VERY BAD FOR TEETH

Caroline smiled, shaking her brother's hand. "But golly, who wrote it?" she asked.

"Who do you think?" Billy replied.

"A dentist?"

"Perhaps," Billy said. "A very mean dentist."

Caroline added: "A very mean dentist who really hates cavities."

TWELVE

The boy detective and the Mumford children are searching for clues beside their front porch. It has just stopped raining and Effie, in her purple and white jacket and her yellow soccer uniform, kneels beside her brother, Gus. Each of them is quiet, looking for some sign, some intimation, each of them caught in a strange world of curious wonderings.

"Billy?" the girl asks.

"Yes?"

"Do you think people are mostly good or mostly evil?"

"Why do you ask?"

"I'd like to know your thoughts on the matter."

"I don't know. I would have to think about it."

"I don't know the answer either," Effie Mumford says.

"It is a good question."

"Yes, I think so," the girl says.

They are both silent for a moment. Gus Mumford nods too, giving it serious thought.

"Do you think we will find my bunny's head?" Effie asks.

"I do. I am quite sure of it."

"Why?"

"The only thing all men have in common with one another is their inherent capacity to make mistakes. We will always fall short. We will always fail at our grand schemes; we can trust that there will always be a clue or a fingerprint or some sign. That is what we must now find. We must think like the criminal here: Surely it was night time when he did his terrible deed."

"Yes."

"Surely he was in a hurry, nervous that he might be caught."

"Yes."

"Then surely he must have overlooked something as he made his escape."

The boy detective pauses, inspecting a spot of dirt that is crossed with several horizontal marks, a trail of prints running under the porch. Billy follows them on his hands and knees excitedly.

"What do we have here?" he whispers.

Gus Mumford hands Billy a note which reads: *It looks like a footprint.*

"Have either of you been under the porch recently?"

The Mumford children shake their heads. Billy, on his hands and knees, crawls beneath the front porch, the Mumford children following.

"It is the footprint from a large man's shoe. It's muddy but it's clearly a man's, no? We now know our friend was under here, as I assumed, and that he is a he—yes, *he* had to hide his actions, so he chose this place. Notice how there's very little blood about. Only a speck or two there. We should continue our search."

"No," the girl whispers. "I don't want to look anymore."

"But I believe we are getting somewhere. There is more work to be done," Billy replies.

Effie Mumford nods, covering her eyes. She has silently begun crying.

"I know it's because a lot of people don't like me. That's why they did this," she says.

"What?"

Effie Mumford's eyes are wet with tears.

"It's because of how I am in school, but I can't help it."

"I know."

"I wish I was better at sports and not smart. I really do."

Billy smiles and turns. A large black automobile pulls up in front of the Mumford house. An angry-looking man begins to honk the horn loudly.

"It's my coach. I have to go to soccer practice now."

"It's all right. We will continue this later."

"OK," she says, continuing to cry.

"What's wrong now?"

"I wish my coach didn't hate me so much."

"Why do you think he hates you?"

"I make my team lose all our games."

"I see."

"He's very mean. He says very mean things to me."

The boy detective and the Mumford children hide under the porch listening to Effie's coach honking.

Beep-beep-beep.

Beep-beep-beep.

Beep-beep, but the third honk doesn't come. The fact that the sound is so loud and harsh and the third honk doesn't come causes a nerve to twitch beneath Billy's eye. The coach begins again:

Beep-beep-beep.

Beep-beep-beep.

Beep-beep, again missing the third beep. Billy's hands begin to clutch helplessly at the air. Once more, the coach hits his horn:

Beep-beep-beep.

Beep-beep-beep.

Beep-beep, and before Billy knows it, he is crawling out from under the porch.

"You two, wait here," he tells the children.

"Billy?"

Immediately, Billy decides he does not like the looks of the coach.

The man's face is large and angry with an enormous, stubbly chin. The coach holds the horn down: *Bbbbbbbbbbbbbbbbbbbbbbbbbbbbbbbbbbbbbbbb bbbbbbbbbbbbbbbbbbbbbbbbbbbbbbbbbbbbbbbbbbbbbbbbbbbbbbbbbbbbbbbbbbbbbbbbbb bbbbbbbbeeeeeeeeeeeeeeeeeeeeeeeeeeeeeeeeeeeeeeeeeeeeeeeeeeeeeeeeeeeeeeeeeeeeeeee eeeeeeeeeeeeepppppppppppppppppppppppppppppppppppppppppppppppppppppppppp*.

An intense white heat is exploding from behind Billy's eyes. It overtakes him. He looks around and sees Effie Mumford's field hockey stick lying on the front lawn: He grabs it and charges the automobile without a word, smashing in the front headlight. It breaks without much of a sound at all, just a single soft *crack*. The coach lays off the horn and is suddenly out of the car, shoving Billy. He has Billy in an awkward full nelson. Effie Mumford is hurrying out from under the porch but not before the coach punches Billy in the stomach, pushing him to the ground.

"No, no, no!" Effie Mumford shouts. "He doesn't understand."

"That guy started hitting my car!" the coach yells back. "He's crazy."

Effie Mumford helps Billy to his feet, holding his hand while he tries to breathe.

"Billy, why did you that?" she asks.

"I don't know," he says. "I don't like that man's face."

"Oh," Effie Mumford says.

The three of them are standing in the sun then, Billy doubled over, breathing heavily.

THIRTEEN

It is truly his secret weakness: The boy detective is not very daring, though he wishes he was. While he is lying in his small bed, holding his sore ribs, he hears, from down the hall in the Shady Glens television room, a theme song from his favorite television show playing loudly. The show is *Modern Police Cadet*, a black-and-white British series from the '50s. The theme song's lyrics are:

Modern
Police
Cadet
Familiar with all the latest laws
Modern
Police
Cadet
Beware criminals
Everywhere

Modern Police Cadet is, without a doubt, the boy detective's favorite television program of all time. It is a series that follows the investigative exploits of one Leopold Jones, an awkward, stuttering, nervous Scotland Yard cadet by day, who, because of his amazingly modern crime-solving skills, is allowed to work on unsolved cases by night. Billy must decide if he will go down to the television room and watch it or not. He thinks about it for a good, long minute. He imagines the thinly mustached Leopold Jones, Modern Police Cadet, working some strange case—the Mystery of the Stolen Diamond Hand, perhaps, following the clues, missing his cadet exams (as he was often apt to do), coyly admonishing the beautiful cat burglar when catching her in the end. Billy then decides he *will* go down the hall, but only to check to see if it is an episode he has watched already.

As he reaches for the doorknob, he stops, realizing there is a good chance if he goes down the hall, one of the other residents will want to talk to him about something, or will want to touch him, or worse, may try to assault him. He stands in front of the door, wondering if it will be worth it. He will stand there for more than an hour, trying to decide.

FOURTEEN

It is embarrassing to admit, but Chapter Fourteen has been stolen. We truly apologize for this.

FIFTEEN

The boy detective and the Mumford children are now playing freeze tag. It is twilight and the children only have one hour before they must be inside. Billy is frozen in a running position as Gus Mumford chases Effie Mumford around him. Just then, two teenaged boys in black dusters and black eye makeup pass. The boys are looking at each other and winking. One of the boys is rounder with a black ponytail, the other is taller with short, spiky blond hair. They push a suspicious-looking little girl's bike in between them, small and awkward and pink.

Billy stares at the bike for a moment and the strange machinations of his mind begin turning. He thinks: *!* He glares at the two boys as they pass, both of them elbowing each other and laughing. The short round one with the ponytail whispers a single unheard word to his friend and they both snort.

"You there," Billy calls out. "I'd like to ask you about that bicycle."

Billy begins walking toward the boys, pushing his glasses up against his face.

"What?"

"I'd like to ask where you got that bicycle."

"From your butt," the chubby one says with a laugh.

"Yeah, from your butt," the tall boy says, nodding.

"There's no need for that. It just seems out of the ordinary. I'd appreciate it if you answered me."

"We don't give a shit what you appreciate."

The boy detective nods. He is now quite sure these boys have stolen the bicycle but does not know what to do next exactly.

"I would only like to ask you a few questions."

"Fuck off. We're not telling you shit."

The boy detective nods, taking a step closer.

"I am trying to be polite but you are making it hard for me."

"What are you gonna do about it, spaz?"

"Please. I only want to ask you a few questions about that bicycle."

"Tough shit. We are in league with the Devil," the chubby one shouts, "we do what we want!"

"With our dark powers, we do whatever we like," the other taller one howls.

"We kill and destroy."

"We annihilate without mercy."

"We are pure evil."

The boy detective takes another step forward, staring hard at the round boy's face. The boy detective thinks: *These young hoods are only cowards and don't mean any real harm*. He thinks, *As long as I do not show my terrible, terrible fear, all will be well*. He clenches his hands at his side. He glares confidently into their small, beady eyes. But it is in that moment that a single bright red drop of blood falls from Billy's left nostril and lands on the back of his hand. He sees it, frowns, and then immediately faints, leaving his feet.

When the boy detective comes to, he is lying on his side, staring up, and mumbling. "My nose is bleeding. My nose is bleeding. My nose is bleeding." The blood is running copiously down the side of his face, dripping down the front of his blue sweater, irreparably staining it. He lifts his head and sees the two boys have disappeared and the two Mumford children are standing above him with worried looks on their small faces.

"I am OK," he mumbles. "I am OK."

"We thought you were dead," Effie Mumford whispers, holding up his head.

It is a good thing that Nurse Eloise knows how to stop a bloody nose. She has had four older brothers, she explains. She stands over Billy in the television room of Shady Glens, holding an icepack to his face, while Mr. Pluto stares at him very nervously. Finally, when the bleeding stops, Nurse Eloise asks: "Billy, how did it happen?"

But the boy detective is silent.

"I know you are embarrassed, but I'd like to know how you got a bloody nose."

But Billy only shakes his head.

"I get them when I am nervous," he says.

"Was it the two boys at the end of the block? The blond one and the short one?"

For a moment, the boy detective is a statue. Then his eyes twitch and he nods once, solemnly. Nurse Eloise pats his back and sighs, "I thought it was them. They are no good, either one of them."

Mr. Pluto stares at the boy detective and then hurries from the room, his massive steps echoing down the hallway.

"Just lie there with your head forward," Nurse Eloise says. "I'm going to do my rounds and I'll be back to check on you in a half hour." She hands Billy the television remote, which lies unused in his lap. He leans his head forward and tries to blink to keep himself from crying.

In a few moments, Mr. Pluto returns, maneuvering a small bicycle down the hallway. It is the exact same suspiciously pink bicycle the two teenage boys had been walking with.

"An act of evil is the death of wonder," the giant man whispers, his voice deep and intelligent.

Very gently, Mr. Pluto hands Billy the bicycle and then nods, holding out his fist. In this gigantic hand he is carrying an enormous hunk of human hair. It is perfectly banded together in a black ponytail. The boy detective is immediately both gratified and slightly frightened. He stands staring at the bike silently until Mr. Pluto strides off, smiling.

Nurse Eloise reappears and adjusts the icepack. "Billy, are you feeling any better?"

Billy nods *yes,* but it is not because his nose feels any better. It is because he is thinking. He is thinking that those boys may somehow be involved in the case of the bunny's mysterious decapitation. He holds his hand up beneath his chin and nods his head again, a perfect portrait of the great detective in thought, if you could remove the pack of ice that is keeping his nose from further swelling.

Ebtre

SIXTEEN

At home after school the next day, there is a telephone call from a Mysterious Stranger. Effie Mumford is eating a bowl of cereal. She has her glasses on from the previous summer, big and brown and plastic and held together with white tape, the prescription not quite right. She and her brother Gus are trying to watch a cartoon in Japanese when the phone begins ringing.

"Effie . . ." the voice murmurs. "I know what you're doing right now. I know you two are there all alone." The voice is high and sounds phony, the breath coming fast and shaky. "Come out on your porch. Come outside. I want to see you."

"No, go blow," Effie mutters, and hangs up the phone. Five minutes later, as she empties the bowl, the telephone rings again. Effie sighs and answers it, sitting in front of the TV.

"I want you to tell me a secret, Effie."

"No."

"If you tell me a secret, I won't call back."

"I don't care."

"If you tell me a secret, I won't murder you tonight."

"Fine."

"What is your secret, Effie?"

"Nobody in the whole world likes me."

"Why doesn't anyone in the whole world like you?"

"Because I'm weird-looking. Because I'm way ugly."

The line is silent for a long while.

"I'm coming over, Effie. I'm going to come over and you're going to let me in."

"Nope."

"I'm going to come over and you're going to let me in. You're going to let me do whatever I want, aren't you?"

"No."

"You're going to let me do whatever I want to do, aren't you?"

"I don't care," Effie says. "Come on over if you want."

"I'm coming, Effie. That door better be open when I come, Effie."

"OK. Fine." Effie hangs up the phone and goes over and makes sure she has locked the door.

With Gus, her brother, she sits in front of the television until it is dark and they finally hear the familiar rusty whine of their mother's car. The both lie down quickly, closing their eyes, imagining their mother and father coming in, standing over them, blinking and smiling. When they open their eyes, it is only their mother there, in her small blue hat and blue coat, her arms full of groceries. Directly behind their mother, there is the family photo on the wall, their father's head cut out, gone, completely missing.

"Effie," her mother whispers, "why are you wearing your old glasses, honey?"

SEVENTEEN

The boy detective practices his strange detective words in bed at night: he practices what he is going to say and how he should say it, and because of this, he does not sleep. It is because it is not so easy. We, like the rest of the world, expect someone who is named *the boy detective* to solve every crime, every riddle, every mystery, and it is this fear—of failing us—that forces him to lie there in his bed all night, practicing his very strange words and very dramatic faces.

In the early evening, the boy detective interrogates the two teenage boys at the end of the block. They sit on their front steps, the chubby boy holding the back of his head with a serious look of pain.

"I want to know the truth: Do either of you have any idea who killed that girl's bunny?"

"No way," the chubby one whispers.

"We did see a dead cat, though," the tall one says. "It was missing its head, too."

"Where? Where did you see this?"

"Down by the river. Right by the drain pipe."

"Where is that?"

"In the woods, behind the last house on the street. It's where the stuff from all the different gutters goes."

"How long ago was this?" the boy detective asks.

"Two days ago. It was just sitting there. It was pretty awesome nasty."

Billy stares at the boys' faces for some sign of mendacity, but there is none. He feels quite sure they are not lying.

"As I promised," the boy detective says, handing them back the small pink bike.

"Dude, it's not even ours," the chubby one chuckles. "It's totally stolen."

The boy detective chooses to ignore this and hurries down the street toward the end of the block. He follows the narrow metal gutter along the curb where it winds downward—past several small hills into the darkness of the woods, loud with the sound of the river—to the spot where all the water empties from a large silver drain pipe. There the trees are tall and close together and the prairie grass is high and green, the small silver-colored insects bright and buzzing, a gym shoe, an old dirty magazine, someone's entire book bag discarded here.

Following the soft patter of water until he is leaning over and slowly pushing the reeds aside, the boy detective discovers several large footprints, very similar to those found beneath the Mumfords' front porch. The boy detective glances up. He thinks he is being watched. There is the sound of someone breathing in the shadows. A twig snaps. A branch is quickly moved. Billy looks down and immediately something in the shallow part of the brackish murk catches his attention. It is just as the boys have said: There, along the bank, is a small white cat, fluffy and immobile. The creature's head is mysteriously missing. Billy stares at the animal, following the footprints along the river to a thicket of woods and trees.

Ahead, what appears to be a shadow—a glimpse of the shape of a man—dashes suddenly into the darkness. Billy stares and holds in a breath. Somewhere close by, a branch whispers as it snaps. He keeps his eyes open wide as he moves, trying to memorize everything as it is, then hurries toward the sound in pursuit.

Holding his hands out in the dark, pushing tree branches and waist-high weeds aside, the boy detective catches sight of a large man crossing into a sliver of moonlight. The man is carrying a rectangular valise, running in the darkness, leaping over fallen logs and woody brambles, disappearing into the shadows, then returning, his breath fast and nervous. The beams of moonlight breaking through the tops of the autumn trees are shaky. The wind whistles high in the empty branches as the moon itself peeks through like one great suspicious eye. It is then that Billy realizes he is lost. He is lost and now he has no clear sense of where the strange man might be hiding in the darkness around him.

Billy begins to turn, and as he does, he stares directly into the face of the man who is missing his head: There are no features, no eyes nor nose nor mouth nor any kind of face, only a ghostly blank space, from which a hideous voice escapes.

"Why are you following me?" the ghoul asks angrily.

The man stalks closer in his worn dark suit, and from his dark hand comes the large black valise. Quickly, the man opens the case and retrieves a pair of long silver scissors, and in that moment Billy begins to cry, backing away, stumbling into a wide tangle of brambles, falling on his side. He struggles, grasping the man's thick suit jacket, gripping at the man's wrist as the scissors move dangerously close. Terrified, Billy pulls at the headless man's necktie and as he does so, the black cinch comes easily apart. In a moment, the villain begins to howl, mortally undone. Billy holds the unknotted tie in his hand and watches in horror as the strange man begins to hiss, the ghoulish voice echoing in the woods, "What a life of woe I have led, what a life of woe . . ."

Soon the headless man's clothes begin to sag miserably, becoming lifeless, and Billy, looking down at the black tie, quickly realizes the villain has met his end. The strange man continues disintegrating, as if he has been unstitched, his black suit and shoes and pants and valise lying there unattended, a cloudy vapor rising like steam from the un- . occupied items of clothing.

The woods are suddenly silent.

When the boy detective looks around, there is no one and nothing, only the dark night as it appears in speckles and spots in the weepy corners of his eyes. He looks curiously through the strange man's belongings, and there, in one of the man's pockets, he finds a small invitation which reads:

> *Attention:*
> *We have noticed you and your work recently and liked what we've seen. Please join us at the Wax Museum at midnight this Wednesday to discuss your possible future with our most prominent organization. The museum is located in the mini-mall along Route 9. Come alone. Entertainment will be provided.*

Billy stares at the invitation and wonders. He finds two Ativan in his pocket and places them gently in his mouth. The only sound then is the wind in the trees. The only movement is the tricky light of the moon. He places his hand over his heart and feels it begin to slow down. The night blurs as he struggles to breathe. A strange hum echoes in his ears. Suddenly the world becomes shadows and he feels so very soft

and hazy.

ubjy,

It is a scientific fact: The ghost world of
Gotham, New Jersey is significant. The
decapitated brown bunny, Mr. Buttons, will
not rest until its head has been discovered
and the perpetrator of the evil act
responsible for its death has been identified.
It wanders the neighborhood looking for its
body. It decides it must find a body at once,
and hovers above a small green and yellow
garden gnome, trying the body on for size.
It is upright and uncomfortable. Next, a
stuffed toy elephant left on a neighbor's back
porch, though along the elephant's belly
is an enormous tear, right at its stitching,
which is not very becoming. At the end of
the street is a small plastic bird with wings
that twirl in the wind. Mr. Buttons cannot
fathom how this body moves and drifts back
into the darkness, tired of trying. It, like all
the ghosts of the world, is now only another
victim of malice, waiting to be saved.

EIGHTEEN

The boy detective is laying on the couch, his shoes and socks off. His therapist lights his cherry wood pipe ponderously. The boy detective has no choice: As part of his release program he must visit this strange bearded man twice a week.

"So why this need to save everyone, Billy? What's the significance of that?"

"Pardon me?"

"Let me rephrase, yes: Why this need to rescue everyone from evil?"

"I don't understand."

"In all of these memories, you are always discovering the clue or saving the day somehow. Why? Who are you trying to get validation from?"

"No one. I like solving puzzles."

"Life is a puzzle. Did you ever try to solve that?"

"Um . . . no sir."

"Tell me, what did you father do for a living?"

"He was in the military. A lawyer for the Navy."

"Interesting. Your mother?"

"She was a scientist."

"Of course. The facts. The truth. Life has very little to do with either," the therapist says, tugging on his beard thoughtfully. "What was the last crime you solved?"

The boy detective looks at his watch. "The hour is up."

"What was the last crime you solved?"

"I don't solve crimes anymore, doctor."

"Why not?"

dhvpxyl

"I'm an adult now."

"So you just gave it up?"

"Yes."

"So you quit?"

"No. I stopped."

"Why did you stop?"

"Because I'd gone off to college."

"Not because your sister died?"

"No, it was before that."

"What were you studying in college?"

"Criminology."

"Criminology? Very interesting, Billy. I thought you had given it up."

"I had."

"You gave it up because of your sister's death?"

"Yes."

"Yes?"

"Yes."

"And tell me this, I'm very interested: What happened, in your cases, when you did not succeed?"

"Pardon me?"

"When you could not solve the case?"

"We always solved the case."

"Always?"

"Always."

"You never failed once?"

"Never."

"Let me ask you about this mystery then: Why do you think Caroline killed herself?"

"I do not know."

"Is it because the world is an evil place? Is it impossible to defeat evil, in the end? Is that the lesson then: That she was simply morally weak?"

The boy detective looks at his watch again.

The doctor nods, smiling. "How is your medication working out?"

"It makes me feel slow sometimes."

"It will even out soon enough," the therapist says, still nodding. "But it won't change the feelings you have. It won't change what has happened."

"My time is up, doctor. I apologize. I must be going."

NINETEEN

The boy detective and the Mumford children are sitting on the front porch in silence.

"I don't understand," Billy whispers.

"We are not allowed to be alone with you anymore," Effie Mumford says again. "My mother thinks you might be a psychopath. She says she didn't know you were a resident across the street and everything. She said she thought you were a real detective."

"I am a real detective."

"No, like a *real* one and everything."

"But I found a clue. We will have the case solved within a few days."

"She says you can sit on the front porch and talk to us, if you like. But we're not to leave earshot, she said."

"I see."

What are you going to do now? Gus Mumford asks, passing Billy a note.

"I will go on with the investigation on my own."

It might be dangerous, Gus Mumford replies, passing him another piece of paper.

"I understand. But perhaps, if I can solve this case, your mother will think differently of me."

"Maybe," Effie Mumford says. "But probably not."

"No, probably not."

The three of them are silent for a while, until Gus Mumford asks, with another note: *So what's next?*

"Tonight, I must go to the wax museum."

"The wax museum?"

"Yes."

Be careful, Gus quickly replies with a piece of paper.

"I will. The both of you remember the cardinal rules now."

"The cardinal rules?"

"Yes, the cardinal rules. Number one: You must solve any inexplicable mystery."

"Yes," the Mumford children pledge, Gus nodding.

"Number two: You must foil any criminal caper you can."

"OK."

"And cardinal rule number three: You must always be true to your friends."

The two children raise their hands in a formal vow and nod. Billy nods in reply and they all shake hands.

"Here." Effie Mumford digs into her winter jacket and gently gives the boy detective a small silver horseshoe. "It's for good luck. I always win the science fair when I carry it."

"Thank you."

Gus hands him a small white note: *Good night, Billy.*

"Good night."

TWENTY

As the invitation described, the boy detective discovers the wax museum is indeed located in a mini-mall, directly between a Quick Stop convenience store and a Korean nail salon. It is now nearly midnight. The door to the wax museum is unlocked, and carefully, as stealthily as he can, the boy detective sneaks inside. At first it is dark, and Billy notices the interior of the museum looks as if it has been hit with a wrecking ball: Broken hunks of plaster hang down from the ceiling beside loose pipes and wiring. Very cautious now, Billy stumbles about, stopping before a large wax display entitled *Hall of Rogues*, where he reads this:

One particular series of unsolved crimes were the work of the Torso Killer of Kingsbury Run in Cleveland, which occurred during the 1930s. At the time, Kingsbury Run was a shadowy divide: a small, pock marked shanty town that stretched along the banks of the Cuyahoga riverbed. Beginning in 1934 and through 1938, Kingsbury Run was the daring stalking grounds of the Torso Killer with at least thirteen documented murders.

In 1934, famed detective Elliot Ness arrived in the city of Cleveland, immediately charged with heading the investigation of the unsolved Torso Murders. But the Torso Killer continued on with his devilish work: from January of 1936 through August 1938, eight more people would be murdered by the Torso Killer. Most of them were decapitated; their torsos and other body parts were found in the train yards near Kingsbury Run.

Finally on August 16th, 1938, the Torso Killer boldly discarded the torso of an unidentified woman at East 9th and Lakeside, in clear view

of Elliot Ness's office. Elliot Ness then arrested a suspect by the name of
Frank Dolezal for two of the murders but the suspect died in jail from
injuries sustained while he was in police custody before going to trial.

Despite the death of this suspect, Elliot Ness publicly claimed
that he solved the Kingsbury Run murders. In the end, Detective
Ness was just as tragic a victim as the poor souls who had been dis-
membered, forever maligned for mishandling of the Kingsbury Run
murders. When he later ran for Mayor of Cleveland, some voters
hung the body parts of mannequins from their trees in objection.

In the end, of course, the detective lost the election.

The boy detective looks up to see that Elliot Ness, dapper in a
pinstripe suit, his head cleaved off by a fallen arch, rests atop a dismembered Al Capone. Beside them, John Dillinger, his jaw melted to the
floor, has begun to disintegrate at the feet of Adolph Hitler, small and
lifeless and shrunken from the heat. Billy stares in the dark and regards
the wax effigies, their gnarled hands still reaching out to ring the necks
of the good and noble men of the early part of their century.

Billy climbs over piles of broken wax limbs and soiled hair, searching
for a clue, a sign, a missing puzzle piece. In a moment, there is an evil
shriek, and several black-winged bats hurry past, and Billy—terrified of
the small, sharp-eyed creatures—trips and falls, stumbling to his knees.
He feels a dull pain in the palm of his hand and notices he has cut himself somehow. The thought slowly turns in his mind—*You are no longer*
a boy. You are no longer a detective. Go back now, Billy—and then his whole
body begins to tremble. He holds his hand against his heart and now
knows what he has feared: he is once again lost. He has no idea how to
proceed—in his life, in this case, in this strange place—and very soon, a
soft fluttering of tears begin to sparkle in his eyes.

It is then that he notices the small silver horseshoe, the token of good luck from Effie Mumford, shining brightly in his other hand. All is not so dark then. With this tiny glimmer of luminescence, Billy looks up and sees the passage before him, though craggy and dark, is not impassible. He pulls himself to his feet and slowly begins walking again.

Billy stops and removes a dismembered Napoleon blocking the path, the emperor now desiccated and torn apart by rats. He turns suddenly and hears the echo of a hideous laugh. It is then that, from out of the shadows, a strange-looking villain steps, his bizarre appearance made more terrible by his troubling amusement at having found the boy detective lost and wandering about his secret lair. It is none other than the Blank, in a white mask, small black holes for eyes, a black suit and tie obscuring the rest of his body. In the dark, the strange white head seems almost to be floating.

Billy turns and faces the Blank with a frown.

"I apologize," Billy whispers. "I did not expect to find you here."

"Boy detective, it is I am who is truly surprised," the Blank says in a whisper.

"I have been away a really long time," Billy says, stepping forward. "I do not know what I'm doing here really in the first place. It was a mistake. I will be leaving now. As I said, I truly apologize."

Strangely, the Blank only nods and holds his hand out.

"No, my dear friend, it is I who must apologize," he whispers. "I have much work to do and so must end our reunion now. Again, I am sorry for this."

It is then that the fiend retrieves a dull silver pistol from a black shoulder holster. In silence, without another word, he shoots the boy detective, point blank.

TWENTY-ONE

At the hospital, the boy detective reads detective magazines. The left side of his temple has only been grazed by the bullet's path, yet his entire head has been bandaged, and so he must sit alone—no one has come to visit—staring down at his adventure stories for two days straight.

When released, the boy detective wobbles onto the bus and spills a handful of silver and bronze change everywhere, which roll like bells down the empty aisle. The bus driver groans and waves him on and Billy, his head still thoroughly bandaged, elicits many stares from the other equally strange-looking passengers. In a moment, a man in a full-size pink-and-white rabbit suit climbs aboard the bus and decides to sit right beside him.

At the empty end of the parking lot belonging to the XXX Bunny Hop XXX, the boy detective meets with an old ally, former detective Browning, who is now a security guard at a particularly pathetic strip club. He is much rounder now, his dark hair going bald, his bright blue uniform replaced by a dull maroon windbreaker. Overhead a neon sign flashes from pink to blue, the enormous shape of a voluminous woman shaking her voluminous hips up in the dark sky. The light flashes down across Billy and the former detective's face.

"I saw him with my own eyes. He is planning some sort of big caper," Billy says. "He has begun an organization of some kind."

"I don't know," former detective Browning mumbles through a mouth full of cigarette smoke. "I haven't heard anything, Billy. Though it's not like I am exactly looking for trouble anymore," he says.

"Yes, I am surprised to have found you here," Billy replies.

The former detective nods. "So am I." He itches his nose, which is round and red, and then takes another puff on his cigarette. "I thought, you know, what the heck. I've had enough of being the garbage man for the rest of the world. I did one good thing—one good thing—and that ruined me."

"You saved a boy from drowning. You saved another person's life."

"Yep," the former detective says. "But I ruined mine. After that, I was in all the papers and then people started expecting me to do that all the time. My wife, my kids—they all looked at me like I was some hero after that, which I knew I wasn't. It practically killed me. I couldn't do it again. I mean, I would drive around at night, alone, after my shift, and look for somebody to save. I never found anyone. I don't know how hard I was looking exactly, but, well, like I said, saving that boy was the worst thing I ever did."

"I do not believe that."

"It doesn't matter if *you* believe it. I've thought about it for a long time now. Maybe we only do one good thing ever, like in our whole lives. Like me pulling that kid out of the river: Maybe that's all we're capable of. Maybe some of us don't even get that. Maybe we're really pretty awful, except for once. Maybe for one brief moment in our lives where—by accident or fate or circumstance—we just happen to do the right thing, the best thing, and then, well, then we go around the rest of our lives trying to fool ourselves that what we did wasn't just a fluke or mistake. I don't know, you tell me. I'm just a security guard now."

"I don't know about any of that, Detective Browning."

"It's just Frank now. Just Frank, the guy in the corner watching to make sure you don't grab nothing for free. That's what I'm supposed to be proud of now: I stop someone from slapping some stripper's behind."

"Sir, there is no caper that you have heard about being planned?"

"If there was, I wouldn't know anything about it."

"I see. Thank you, sir."

"I got to give you credit, Billy. You still think someone is going to thank you or something, huh? That if you help enough people, it's really gonna matter? Look at me, Billy. I'm proof that good doesn't ever conquer evil."

"Thank you for you time, Detective Browning."

"Frank."

"Yes, thank you, Frank."

"No problem." Detective Browning lights another cigarette and then stares at Billy for a moment. "Hey, do you mind telling me what happened to your head there, Billy?"

"I was shot. I was shot in the head."

Former Detective Browning nods sadly in response.

The boy detective turns, and just then Frank gives a shout, hurrying to Billy's side.

"Wait a minute, just wait a minute. Look—If I show you something, will you . . . will you pretend you ain't never seen it?"

Billy shrugs, staring into the other man's face. Frank nods and digs beneath his windbreaker, pulling out a small slip of paper. *Convocation of Evil*, it reads. At the bottom is an address of a nearby nondescript hotel, and a date and time that reveal an event only two days away.

"This guy in a purple mask and cape was in here last week. He got thrown out for grabbing the girls, and, well, I found this on the sidewalk the next day."

"Sir?"

"OK, OK, I think, well, I think, they're having a convention of some kind," the former detective says.

TWENTY-TWO

The boy detective returns to Shady Glens that evening and finds Nurse Eloise in the kitchen baking a cake and, at the same time, crying. Small silver tears fall from her nose and directly into the white cake batter. She is arguing with herself. *Why is she doing that?* the boy detective wonders, as the young nurse stirs the bowl with a great wooden spoon, damp lines streaming down her soft, round face. Billy stands there hiding behind the soda machine and watches as Nurse Eloise looks up and frowns at him. She whispers, "I am tired of being hurt by people."

"I understand," Billy whispers.

"I came home last night and found my ex-boyfriend, the magician, taking all of my things. He said he needed the money for a new trick rabbit or something."

"I am very sorry to hear that," Billy mumbles, staring down at his feet.

"He stole one of my dresses for some new assistant," Nurse Eloise hisses and then continues stirring and crying.

The boy detective is surprised to receive a mysterious letter in the mail when he returns to his room. There is no postmark or address. The envelope, in small black handwriting, simply says: *To the boy detective*. Billy slowly opens the letter, slipping his finger beneath the fold of paper and tearing. Inside is a single piece of yellowed paper that reads:

XI: 5-12-15-15-2,
26-11-2 11-4-25-8 2-18-24 9-18-21-10-18-23-23-8-17 16-8?

It is a secret code, but sent from who? The boy detective thinks *Caroline* immediately, and then admonishes himself for thinking that at all. He stares at it for a few moments more before giving up, hiding it under his bed, afraid of what it may be.

Perhaps dear reader, you might help him. Match the code X1 with the decoder wheel found on the back flap of this volume.

The boy detective, in his bed, holds the bandages against his forehead and wonders if there is a test of some kind—an exam, an X-ray, a blood sample—that would reveal who is good and who is bad. That is what he would like, he thinks. It is the strain of walking around the world—down the street, riding city buses and elevators, moving from place to place to place—and not knowing who might want to destroy you, who might like to fill your heart with poison, who might rob you and stab you, who might stand above you in the dark with a tarantula. In the end, it is the invisibility of those who might really hate you that makes him so sad. He stares at the invitation to the Convocation of Evil, holding it above his face, turning it over in his hands.

In an hour, Billy strolls down the hall and is horrified to find Nurse Eloise has finished her cake: It is a red velvet cake with white frosting, in the shape of a severed bunny.

TWENTY-THREE

The boy detective, at work, mumbles into the telephone: "Yes, it's exactly that, sir, a miracle. A miracle of modern living. Hair-replacement surgery can be expensive and dangerous, so why risk it? What we offer you is quality hair replacement without the serious dangers and side effects."

The blank terror of the dial tone is the customer's only response.

Larry peeks from over his cubicle at Billy and winks.

"Billy, old pal, what happened to your head?"

"I was shot."

"Shot?"

"It only grazed me."

"Oh, only grazed, huh? Well, how are your sales going today?"

"I do not like selling people things they don't need. It is criminal, I think."

"Oh, come on now. Think about it. You're doing these people a favor. You're offering these people consolation. Conversation. You find out what they're missing, sell it to them, and they get exactly what they've been dreaming of. And you get your sales tallied. It's mutually beneficial. For instance, say an old lady lost her husband. Nothing like a brand new Princess Eternity model to help pep her up, restore her spirits and all. Say a fellah is sick, all his hair has gone. A victim of a motorcycle crash? A Dashing Gentleman mustache and eyebrow kit will do the trick. Make him feel human again. You just listen and see what they say and offer them help the only way you can: with quality hair-replacement products. If you look at it like that, it's like you're doing a good deed for all these people."

"It's not a good deed. It's not. And I know it's not."

"Well, who wants to live in a world of gloom all day? Who wants to accept the fact that no matter what we do, we're all probably going to be stabbed to death by someone we love? That to me is the real tragedy—accepting evil, accepting defeat."

"You're not convincing me, Larry."

"You've lost somebody, haven't you?"

"Yes, I have."

"Who?"

"My sister."

"You feel any better about it sitting here grieving, thinking about her all the time, talking to her in your sleep?"

"No."

"You feel helpless, powerless. Maybe this is just the kind of thing you're missing. A moment to feel a little better. A moment to feel whole again. Human. This may be the answer to that question—that terrible question: What do you do when bad things happen to good people?"

"I don't think you can buy that answer with a fake mustache, Larry."

"Well, you're the one who's got to face it, not me. Whatever you do, don't talk to any customer for more than ten minutes. If you can't sell them in the first ten, they're not buying. Good luck, kid."

Larry pats the boy detective on the shoulder once more, then crosses back to his desk. Billy picks up the phone glumly. He stares at it and, before long, realizes he has already begun talking into it.

"Yes, it's exactly that, ma'am, a miracle. A miracle of modern living. Hair-replacement surgery can be expensive and dangerous. So why risk it? What we offer you is quality hair replacement without the serious dangers and side effects."

Billy looks around the office and wonders what effect all these telephone calls are having. He closes his eyes and goes back to speaking.

When he leaves for the evening, Billy steals a Gallant Sailor hair replacement kit: The black mustache and black beard get hidden tightly beneath his blue sweater.

TWENTY-FOUR

At school, sitting in class, Effie Mumford has to hold her old taped glasses onto her face as she looks down at her American History book. Suddenly, at the back of her neck, she feels a sharp pain, and sees she has been hit by something. She looks over her shoulder and sees Parker Lane, a narrow-faced girl with blue eye shadow, glaring back. Parker Lane points toward the floor and Effie Mumford's gaze follows. It is a note, folded into a tiny white triangle, which has hit Effie in the back of the head. She reaches over, opens it up, and reads: *You're right. You are way ugly. Nobody in the whole world likes you.* She folds up the note and presses her broken glasses up against her eyes and forehead, not knowing what to do with her face.

It is the school library where Effie Mumford goes to hide during lunch period. She does not eat at school. She is too afraid someone will take advantage of her while her mouth is open and that she will eat an item from her lunch which has somehow been poisoned. Poisoning some-one does not require much imagination and she believes that, if given the opportunity, her classmates would surely take it.

It is later in the school day that she realizes today is the day of the science fair. She has nothing prepared. Her experiment having been ruined by the death of her rabbit, she walks about the small, terribly arranged exhibits—past a display for a rocket-car of the future, past a papier-mâché model of a volcano, past a bumpy bust describing the science of phrenology—to Parker Lane's prize-winning presentation, entitled, "How Water Totally Becomes Ice." Effie Mumford stops and stares, dumfounded, glaring at the horrible Magic-Markered illustra-tions, the torn and oddly pasted *National Geographic* pages, and worse, a rectangular ice cube tray from which Parker, grinning, offers samples.

Effie Mumford's small hands turn red, as does her face; what is so bothersome is the knowledge that she could have easily won if she had only tried again. It is this knowledge that makes her cry—not for the murder of her bunny, not about the enduring, pervasive insults, not because of her terrible, taped-together glasses. It is knowing that she could have done better than all of this and did not, which forces the small, shiny tears from her eyes. She has allowed herself, once again, to be defeated by mediocrity, and it is this thought—the ap-parent triumph of the uninspired and average—that truly makes her angry. Out of both rage and frustration, she purposefully knocks over Parker Lane's poorly assembled display, the poster boards crashing to the gymnasium floor as Effie runs away.

TWENTY-FIVE

The boy detective suddenly realizes it is Professor Von Golum, his lifelong archenemy, who is sitting across from him on the bus on his way home from work that evening. The Professor is out of sorts—perhaps it is his medication or the consequence of his age, but he is pressing the yellow *Stop Request* button very angrily. He is being ignored; the button does not seems to be working.

"Professor?" Billy mutters. The boy detective looks around and becomes aware that there are no other passengers aboard. "Do you want some help, Professor?"

"We demand this bus takes us directly to the Gotham City Bank. And . . ." the Professor takes a breath, inhaling through his small, skull-like nose, "the combination to the Gotham City safe."

"*We?* There is no one else here, Professor," Billy says.

"We, the Gotham City Gang, demand it. And we demand you get punished for your sniveling backtalk."

"The Gang is all dead, Professor," the boy detective says sadly.

"All dead?"

"All but you, sir."

"Chet the Blind Safecracker?"

"Yes."

"Waldo the Heaviest Man Alive?"

"Yes."

"Pete the Elastic-Faced Boy? What about Pete?"

"Pete the Elastic-Faced Man. Yes sir, dead."

"Oh God, where are we going?" the Professor asks nervously, reaching across the aisle, holding the boy detective's hand. "I'd just like to know where I'm supposed to be going."

The boy detective goes silent.

Professor Von Golum takes a seat beside him and nearly collapses. "I don't know what I'm doing with this," he says, handing Billy a small silver test tube clearly labeled *ACID*.

Billy takes the vial and stares at a small note in Professor Von Golum's other hand. It reads:

> *today*
> *go to store*
> *buy acid*
> *kill boy detective*

The boy detective holds the vial tightly in his hand and stares down at his feet, frowning.

TWENTY-SIX

At the Convocation of Evil, the schedule of events reads:

9:00-9:30: Welcome with coffee and assorted muffins and bagels
9:30-10:30: Break-out groups:
    • *Crime as Your Career: Investing for the Future*
    • *Kidnapping: More Hassle Than It's Worth?*
    • *High-Grade Explosives from Everyday Chemicals*
10:30-11:30: Featured Presentation: A Century of Madmen
11:30-12:00: Featured Panel: To Wear a Mask?
12:00-1:00: Lunch
1:00-2:00: Officers and Sub-Committee Elections
2:00-3:00: Featured Guest: Senator Jonah Klee (R-Texas)
3:00-4:00: Closing Remarks: "Our Evil Architectural Plans"

On the stage at the podium in the Van Buren room of the Gotham Hotel, the Blank is speaking. The Blank is not the name his parents would have preferred, but honestly, it is better than the one they gave him. There he stands, in his white mask, black suit and tie, the clothing giving the appearance that there is indeed a phantom's face hanging in the air above the wooden podium. He does not move his arms or gesture with his hands. He looks down at his notes and marches through his words, one after another, without much charisma at all. He is not a very good public speaker: His voice is high and weak, and he is terrified of looking up and actually seeing the audience listening.

Some of what the Blank is saying is this: "Our evil plans include world domination—as one might imagine—through the use of right angles and right angles only. We will only adhere to the highest order of very straight lines. We will not rest until we have achieved global uniformity. As you can see in my first slide"—a perfectly rectangular town with perfectly rectangular buildings appears on the screen behind him—"all other buildings must be destroyed."

The audience does not seem very impressed with any of it. In fact, they seem bored. They stare down at their feet, they whisper to one another, they sip on their complimentary cups of coffee. As a cadre of villains from near and far, they are very uninterested: Mr. Brow sighs and picks at a nail on his left hand. The Mug fills nearly two seats, his enormous shoulders crowding Tinyface Thompson, who snoozes loudly beside him. The audience—Boris the Bandit, Handsome George, Dr. Hammer—dreams of getting up and leaving, suddenly uncomfortable in their strange attire, each wishing they had not bothered to respond to the strange invitation.

The masked man behind the podium makes the tragic mistake of looking up just then and notices his audience is no longer interested. He hurries through his notes and in doing so, skips some important points. He immediately begins stuttering and, to grab their attention, he rushes to his surprise announcement.

"We have decided as a show of our seriousness, we will make another building in this very town disappear tonight."

The audience looks up. A man in a cape and mask raises his hand.

"Whoever asks a question at this point in the presentation will most definitely be asked to leave."

The man lowers his hand.

The boy detective, his face covered in white bandages and disguised with a beard and mustache, attempts to enter the strange meeting.

He creeps down the white-wallpapered hallway without incident. He finds the Van Buren meeting room and moves to slowly open the doors. It is then that he is troubled to find that the Convocation of Evil has hired its own private detective: Her name is Violet Dew and Billy recognizes her immediately. Seeing her in a white blouse and a soft brown skirt, her chestnut hair bobbing beside a dainty chin, Billy feels his heart flutter. *Violet Dew, the smartest girl in the world,* or so she, at the age of twelve, had proclaimed.

Violet spots him, smiles, and walks toward him quickly. "Stop right there, Billy."

"I will not."

"You will," she says, holding up her small left hand and pressing it against his chest. "Because I know you'd never hit a girl."

Billy nods. "Violet."

"Billy."

"Your hair looks the same," he says.

"I'm in a rut," she says.

"I think it looks lovely."

Billy stares down at her small, narrow fingers and frowns. "I thought you were married."

Violet shakes her head. "I was. It didn't go so well."

"I see."

"Did you ever . . . ?"

"No."

Violet sighs. "It's because we've been ruined, Billy."

"Yes. That's true."

Violet drops her hand and they both stare down at their feet.

"Why are you here?" Billy asks.

"I've been hired to run interference and make sure no one interrupts this meeting."

"But they are all villains," Billy says.

"You know the score, Billy. If you've got a case, take it to the police."

"Why are you helping them?"

"I'm not in the position to turn away much work these days."

"I see."

"And I must warn you that you're trespassing on private property and unless you leave, I'll be forced to call the police."

Billy nods, sizing up the threat. "Hmmmmmm," he says.

"Hmmmmmmmmmmmm," she says.

"Hmmmmmmmmmmmmmmmmmmmm," he repeats.

"Hmmmmmmmmmmmmmmmmmmmmmmmmmmmmm," she responds.

It is not over. Not quite. Billy suddenly takes Violet's hand and smiles. He holds it and stares at her and the feeling of her palm against his is warm and soft and Violet is surprised and blushes quick.

He leans in and whispers in her ear: "You wrote me a letter once."

"Billy, you said you would never mention it."

He frowns, still holding her hand. "Once we were waiting in a clock tower and there were cobwebs in your hair and I said something that made you laugh."

"Billy, please, don't."

"I am asking you for your help, Violet. I need to solve this case. If I don't, I'm as good as dead."

Violet closes her eyes. She has never looked so beautiful in all her life. "Billy, if we weren't so damn alike . . ."

"Please, Violet."

The smartest girl in the world nods and leans in, kissing his cheek.

"Thank you, Violet."

Violet smiles. "Yes—and Billy?"

"Yes, Violet?"

"Do something good, Billy. Like we used to, OK?"

It is then that the boy detective lets his true identity be known: Removing the long black beard and mustache, it becomes quite obvious he is not a villain at all. He is Billy Argo, boy detective. He steps past the young woman and gives the doors of the meeting room a dramatic shove.

The Blank is trying to remember a joke he was to make about the problem with time bombs, but in his nervousness it seems he cannot remember it. He pauses, searches through his note cards, itches his neck, searches through his note cards again, and then gives up. "Yes, well, now then, we will answer your questions," he says.

The man in the cape and mask raises his hand. "Why do all the buildings have to be the same?" he asks. "It seems kind of pointless. I mean, why bother with that kind of thing?"

"We will establish a death grip on the world through complete and total uniformity. We will start with surface structures, like buildings, and then . . . it will all be very easy."

The caped man sits down, shaking his head.

It is at this exact moment that the boy detective enters.

The Blank looks up and sees the bandaged face of his longtime adversary, then places a black hand against his white forehead in a gesture of defeat.

"Oh no. Oh, no," he says.

Every villain in the room sees the quickstepping young man moving toward the podium and draws in a breath. Certainly they remember the lad: the brash twinkle of his eyes, the nervous though intelligent eyebrows, the small blue cardigan sweater. Billy dashes down the aisle and stands before the stage, the Blank's white-faced henchmen hurrying aside. The boy detective stares up at the wood podium and then points at the masked man onstage.

"It is now over, fiend. Whatever you had planned will now come to an end."

"Ah, but it is too late, boy detective. For at this very moment, a disintegration bomb is being hidden at a secret location in town, a bomb which is set to go off at midnight tonight, a bomb with absolutely no failsafe device. Not even *you* will be able to stop it."

"I see."

"Perhaps you would like to know the whereabouts of the bomb?"

"Yes, I would."

"It is none other than . . . the bus station."

"The bus station?"

"Yes, of course—a more hideously designed building has never been raised. It is circular and asymmetrical at the same time. It is quite awful to behold. I am doing this town a favor."

"The bomb cannot be disarmed?"

"No. It cannot."

"I see."

"Any other questions?"

"I do not think so. Other than the one about whether it can be disarmed or not."

"As I said, it does not seem very likely. Even if you could, the bomb has been carefully hidden. You would have to find it first, which would be nearly impossible."

"Oh, I did not think about whether it would be hidden or not."

"Yes, it is hidden quite well. Now if you don't mind, we're having an important meeting," the Blank says.

"Oh yes, I'm sorry," the boy detective whispers, defeated. He suddenly becomes aware of the bandages on his face. He suddenly becomes aware that he is about to faint. People are staring at him, mumbling. He has failed. He will not be able to save the day. He silently apologizes to the conventioneers, as he turns and drifts through the doors of the meeting room. The convention is at once silent. A chair squeaks and the sound rises through the room like a scream. Someone begins whispering.

Everyone holds their breath, wondering what might happen next.

TWENTY-SEVEN

The boy detective and the Mumford children are sitting sadly beneath the front porch.

"But why did they kill my bunny?" the girl asks.

"I am afraid there is no answer to that question, other than what we may have already discovered: to make you sad. It is their job to break all our hearts. Theirs is a world of evil and it seems we are truly at their mercy."

Gus hands Billy a small note. It reads: *Why are we under the porch?*

"We have no way of saving ourselves at the moment. We have no way of knowing when the world of evil will find us. We have no way of knowing how to stop evil from happening, so all we can do is wait here and hide."

In the looming twilight, the sunlight dying as it makes its way through the slats in the porch, the boy detective lays on his side and, bringing thumb and forefinger together in a small circle, while keeping his other three fingers straight, he watches the shape of the shadow of his hand change suddenly. He holds his fingers against the concrete foundation of the house, imagining the head of a small shadowy rabbit, waiting there in the near dark.

Why is a mystery so terrifying to us as adults? Is it because our worlds have become worlds of routine and safety and order the older we've grown? Is it because we have learned the answer to everything and that answer is that there is never a secret passageway, a hidden treasure, or a note written in code to save us from our darkest moments? Why are we struggling so hard against believing there is a world we don't know? Is it more frightening to accept our lives as they are than it is to entertain a fantasy of hope?

Depressed, the boy detective pops two Ativan and lies in the television room of Shady Glens, watching an episode of *Modern Police Cadet*.

In this episode, titled "Evil Is Everywhere," young Leopold Jones has been double-crossed by an unscrupulous policeman named Constable Heller. Heller wears black-framed glasses and a black beard. He is something of an intellectual and argues that crime is a positive plague enacted by nature to wipe out the poor and weak. It becomes clear that the Modern Police Cadet has been tricked when, after discovering a bomb planted outside a displaced-persons shelter, Constable Heller prepares to shoot him in the back.

"I wish it could go some other way, my friend," the Constable says, then draws his small silver pistol.

Leopold Jones, Modern Police Cadet, turns, unwilling to look the villain in the eye. "If you are going to shoot me in the back, I will not give you the pleasure of watching me cower at your feet," he says, and begins walking away.

Constable Heller, in a moment of truly brilliant acting, pauses, wipes his mouth, and takes off his black-framed glasses, as Leopold continues to stride toward the police coupe, the lights still flashing bright white. Constable Heller stares at the bomb, then at Leopold's back, then at the bomb again, while a violin howls terribly. It is clear this is a moment of serious deliberation for the evil Constable. The next sound is a loud gunshot, and young Leopold drops to his knees. For some reason, the Modern Police Cadet begins smiling.

"You poor fool," Leopold says, losing consciousness. "Now you will never ever save yourself."

Although the boy detective has seen this particular episode many times before, it is still very startling when the Constable fires and the Cadet is left for dead in a ditch. But he knows that the Modern Police Cadet is not dead. Leopold Jones has studied many forms of Eastern medicine, like Chinese acupuncture and herbal botany, while serving as a science officer in Asia Minor sometime after he was separated from his division during a British mission to Burma, and he knows what specific plants can be found floating in a ditch along the side of the road in urban London that can quickly cure a bullet wound in his own back.

Billy stares at the flashing screen and wonders why nothing in his own life is ever so easy. He stands to switch the television set off, still watching as the Modern Police Cadet judo chops a great-necked thug, discovering the Constable's hideout. The Constable, in the time span of a half hour following the Cadet's near-fatal gunshot wound, has risen to be the new London kingpin. The final scene is, of course, Leopold, the Modern Police Cadet, chasing the Constable across several shadowy rooftops, until finally the evildoer surrenders. A Scotland Yard helicopter circling overhead, the episode ends with the Modern Police Cadet handcuffing the criminal mastermind and leading him away.

The boy detective wonders if the Modern Police Cadet ever feels totally alone. He wonders this and finally decides that somehow the Cadet has found a way to face the evils of the world and still live with who he is.

Leopold Jones, kissing his wife in the final frame of the show, whispers, "The world of evil is only as evil as we allow it to be," as they sit waiting at the London train station, off together for a much overdue holiday.

Billy finds himself standing there and clapping for some reason. The wing of Shady Glens is utterly silent. The entire world is quiet. Billy puts on his shoes and immediately begins running down the hallway.

TWENTY-EIGHT

En route to the Gotham bus station, the boy detective is riding near the front, directly behind the driver, silently wondering what exactly he will do when he arrives. Very soon he discovers he is again sitting across from Professor Von Golum. The buzz of traffic hums outside the window as Billy tries to speak.

"Professor?"

"Ah, boy detective. We meet yet again."

"I'd like to ask you something."

"You know you'll pay for the answer with your life."

"If that's what you say," Billy whispers.

"Your question then?"

"Why do people do evil things?"

The Professor nods, tugging on his white tuft of beard. "It is our true selves: our identities as they appear in nature. The natural world is full of disorder and so, by our flawed definition, the natural world is evil. We are immoral by design, and so when we act evilly, we are only revealing our most basic selves, the simplest, most convenient action, to fend for oneself and oneself only. To do right—to act justly, to put the needs of someone else above your own—now that is an act of true mystery. It is completely unnatural—a gigantic step beyond the jungle instincts of man and a leap into the unknown wisdom of silent grace which lurks, harbored in the small vessel of mankind, within us all."

"But why? Why did you do the evil things you did?" Billy asks suddenly.

"Ah, because I could not imagine consequences," the Professor says. "To do harm, to live through evil, is to align oneself with chaos. Now it is the same chaos which is slowly destroying me."

"Excuse me?"

"It has begun to rule my body, my health, my mind. My left hand has stopped working. My breathing comes and goes and then is lost. And I cannot remember the way to leave this bus. I've been on it for hours now and I have forgotten how to get them to stop."

"Just pull this cord."

"The cord! Yes, now I remember."

"Good evening, sir."

"Good evening, Billy."

TWENTY-NINE

At the town's bus station, there is much intrigue: Billy searches about the nearly empty waiting room, expecting the strange bomb to explode at any moment. He hurries through the aisles of seats, crawling furiously on his knees, knocking the few suitcases aside and trampling over someone's sleeping feet. He bolts down the narrow hallway, running from bathroom to bathroom. He upends garbage cans, he tears open the machines which dispense newspapers, he raises his hands and howls and pounds his hands against the large glass windows and nearly begins crying.

Then Billy turns and notices the enormous wall of small orange lockers, perhaps a hundred of them, their orange keys glimmering in their locks. Frantically, he begins to pull at their doors, one after the other—empty, empty, empty—until there, in the lowest right corner, one of them is definitely locked and definitely seems to be ticking. He places his ear against the dull orange metal and nods. He starts pulling, shouting, kicking, but the door will not budge. He looks up, the *tick-tick-ticks* still clicking along in his head. He counts quickly. There are maybe four people in the bus station at this time of night. He dashes toward the ticket booth and begins shouting, but the ticket agent is uninterested. He is a small man with glasses and has a hard time believing what he is hearing. He closes the window and disappears behind the booth and leaves Billy there shouting.

Billy continues screaming, grabbing a young mother towing a bright-faced baby in a blue stroller. He hurries them outside, leaving them standing there on the corner, staring back at the small bus station, the sounds of the city muffled and sad in the middle part of the night. Billy hurries back inside, finds a bearded vagrant, lifts him under the arms, and drags him out, depositing him on a bus stop bench nearby. The man seems both unconscious and unimpressed. Another man is sitting in the last aisle of the bus station reading his magazine. Billy approaches him. The man decides he does not believe the idea of the bomb. He licks his thumb, turns the page of his paper, and looks away. Billy stands arguing before him, jumping up and down and pulling at his own hair, but the man in a tan check suit and hat does not agree. "It is impossible," the man says. "No, I do not believe it."

The boy detective pounds on the ticket counter once more and the agent returns. He points toward the bank of lockers, the ticking very audible now—*tick-tick-TICK-TICK-TICK*. The ticket agent pushes his glasses tightly against his face, stares at Billy, stares at the lockers, and then, very professionally, closes the ticket booth, leaving a sign that says, *We will reopen in fifteen minutes.* He follows Billy outside, and with the young mother and her child, stares back inside the glass windows of the bus station, waiting. There, in the last aisle, the man continues reading his paper. He looks up at the strange people shouting to him outside and shakes his head, perturbed. He flips the page. He shifts in his seat. One second goes by.

In a moment, the bus station simply disappears. The man inside, unhappily reading his paper, also vanishes, while somewhere very near, a siren begins howling.

Flat on his back, the boy detective holds the young mother's hand and stares up at the stars, feeling as if he is somehow flying.

THIRTY

At twilight the next day, the boy detective feels obliged to help the Mumford children give a proper burial for their pet bunny. There in the soft muddy earth beneath the front porch, Billy and the Mumford children sit, hand in hand, staring down at the slight mound of earth, unsure what it is they should be doing.

"I'm sad, Billy," Effie Mumford whispers.

"Yes, I understand. It's very natural to be sad in a moment like this."

"But why did it happen? It was just an innocent animal."

The boy detective twitches his nose. "There are people in this world who mean to do us harm."

"I know," the girl says.

"Yes, but you should try not to fear them."

Gus Mumford hands Billy a note that reads: *Why not?*

"We are watching out for them. You and me and Effie, we will watch out for them together."

The girl nods silently. She looks up and smiles and Billy's heart breaks momentarily. He remembers Caroline, his sister, many months after her dove's unexpected death, hiding under the slanted white wood porch, burying her bird, Margaret Thatcher, the small pile of earth beside her white shoes, staring at the tiny grave of the stiffened dead dove.

Billy blinks, holding back the sting of tears in his eyes, and then, opening his black briefcase, presents the Mumford children with a small white and blue package. The two children open it silently, Effie removing the bow and ribbon, Gus tearing the paper very carefully, and soon they discover it is an ant farm—*Ant City!* the bright packaging reads.

"Ants," Billy simply mumbles, smiling.

"They look safe," Effie Munford says. Gus Mumford nods, staring at the small red ants hurrying behind the shiny pane of protective glass. He hands Billy a note: *We really love ants.*

Billy blushes.

"They are quite lovely," Effie Mumford adds.

Billy nods, staring down at the busy little creatures. "Yes, well, I hope you enjoy them."

It is very quiet beneath the porch then as all three watch the ants bustling about their tiny, invisible lives. Together, Billy and the Mumford children follow their movements for a while, and then the girl, Effie Mumford, stares up at him, questioningly. Her eyes have gone small with tears and her bottom lip is trembling.

"Billy?"

"Yes," he replies.

"Everyone at school thinks I'm a gaylord."

"It will be all right," he says, nodding. "It will all be OK."

The boy detective is doing his best to play Ghost in the Graveyard. He is not very good at it. He does not really understand when he is supposed to shout, "Ghost in the Graveyard!" He is tagged out by Effie Mumford three times in a row. The other children on the block laugh when he stumbles and gets dirt on his knees, but he tries not to get angry. When it is his turn, he finds Gus Mumford hiding behind a parked car and Effie Mumford pretending to be a tree. When it gets late, someone's mother says it's time for the neighborhood children to go to their homes. Billy says goodnight and returns to Shady Glens. In his room, in the dark, with the light switch on and the soft cloud of snow gently falling, Billy takes his dose of Clomipramine and lifts Caroline's notebook above his chest, quietly turning the pages. He is holding his breath. He listens carefully for a voice he might recognize, the snow drifting above him until it is no longer evening.

CHAPTER THIRTY-THREE
THE CASE OF THE
VANISHING LADY

Some frequently asked questions
regarding the boy detective:

Does the boy detective like sweets?
—No. He does not. He has a very
healthy diet and rarely eats candy.
Does the boy detective have a lovely singing voice?
—No. No, he does not.
Is the boy detective happy?
—No. He is not. He has not been happy
for more than a day or so at a time.
Why not?
—Ah. Because he is irrevocably
alone and incurably lonely.

ONE

The boy detective falls out of bed. The sight of him lying on the floor sure is something. He moans, turns off the ringing owl alarm clock, and begins dressing. All the clothes in his wardrobe are, of course, exactly the same: blue cardigan sweater, dark pants, white shirt, blue and orange owl tie. This is his uniform from when he was a boy and, when forced to buy new clothes, wanted to waste no time choosing what might look nice.

The boy detective waits for the bus, checking his watch every ten seconds. It is raining and gray. Early morning commuters stand around him, some listening to headphones, some cowering beneath their shiny umbrellas. The boy detective did not think to bring an umbrella. He did not think to check the weather. He has not checked the weather in almost ten years. If it was raining at St. Vitus, he was sent to the television room. If it was nice, he was allowed to go outside. He does not yet remember how to read the weather. He knows a lot, but he has forgotten many, many important things and so at the moment, he is getting very wet. His socks make a sucking sound as he paces back and forth. No one will share an umbrella with him, no matter how sad he makes his face look, and so he begins making a high-pitched noise like a motor boat starting. People at the bus stop slowly step away from him.

The boy detective is on the bus, staring ahead. It is still raining. People talk on their cell phones or read their magazines or newspapers. Someone famous is marrying someone else famous. Someone got a boob job. Some country set fire to another country and now they are sorry for it.

Billy sighs, touching his wrists and the bald spots on his head. He wonders if he will be fired today for some reason. He wonders if people at the office will still be nice to him. If they are not nice to him, he decides, he will stand up, shout, *I got screwed!* and never go back. Thinking about his job is enough to make him very anxious and so he pops an Ativan, covering his eyes with his hands. He peeks through his fingers and notices that a young man with a mustache has buttoned his dress shirt incorrectly—there is an extra buttonhole near his neck. Billy must then sit on his hands to stop himself from reaching for the strange man's shirt. He closes his eyes and tries not to think of the open buttonhole, but it is too much and so he stands and hurries toward the back of the bus.

The boy detective stands in front of a large skyscraper, staring up through the oncoming rain nervously. He is already hyperventilating. He does not like calling sick people. He does not like calling the dead. Businessmen hurry around him, knocking him from side to side. He imagines what would happen if the building were to suddenly fall over. He imagines the sound as the steels gives, the people screaming, the glass breaking. He gets nervous as he approaches the large glass revolving door, and waits, tries again, stops, and then—gaining enough speed and courage—he hurries through, holding his breath. The lobby is black marble, and standing among all the people, he feels like he is drowning. He is forced into an elevator before he realizes he cannot remember where he is supposed to be going. Someone is whispering in his ear, saying, "Hey buddy, can you hit thirty-five?" but Billy is too afraid to hit anything.

The boy detective, one hour later, stands in the same crowded elevator with some other very wet people, who are all sighing. Someone's collar is poking him in the eye. Someone's umbrella is stabbing his ankle. He is trying not to get upset, but this is not easy. His first thought is to strike a sharp-faced woman with bangs beside him. But he doesn't. He holds his breath again and hears the blood moving in his ears and when that clears he notices something: Someone is singing along with the elevator music, something with violins and pianos by Burt Bacharach. The voice is high and steady like a girl's. People begin to stare at him. It is a long moment before he realizes, strangely, that *he* is the one singing. He thinks that if he can keep singing, he will not punch anybody. The elevator doors open to his floor and for some reason, when he exits, he says goodbye to everybody.

The boy detective is at his desk, on the phone, selling mass-produced wigs to very lonely old women.

"Yes, ma'am. As I said, we do have that exact hair color, but not in the Young Starlet style."

Larry, from across the cubicle aisle, stares at Billy. He stands and points. "OK, kid, try this one on for size. Guess what train I took today? OK? Go on, give it a try."

Billy eyes Larry, glancing at his shiny white wing tip shoes. "You took the C train. There's tar on your shoes. I saw them paving the street over by the C station."

Billy glances at Larry's glossy black hairpiece. There are minute white feathers in it.

"Then you stopped in front of St. Franklin's Cathedral. Those are pigeon feathers in your hair."

Larry is dumbfounded and claps with amusement.

"You're amazing, kid, just amazing! How'd you know all that?"

"St. Franklin imported all white doves from Hamburg, Germany. It's the only place in the entire city that has snow-white doves this time of year."

Larry smiles, slapping Billy on the shoulder, and returns to his desk. Billy returns to the phone call.

From the salesperson script, Billy says: "Yes, ma'am. Fully flame-proof and flame retardant. Yes, of course, I think you'd be very happy with the Nordic Princess style. It's very popular with the younger set these days. Yes, I'm sure your dearly departed husband would approve. Well, yes, ma'am, you can take as much time as you'd like to think about it. I can have a catalog sent out to you today. No, I'm not sure. What other color options would you like?"

The phone gets heavier in his hand.

"Yes, it's exactly that, ma'am, a miracle. A miracle of modern living. Hair-replacement surgery can be expensive and dangerous. So why risk it? What we offer you is quality hair replacement without the serious dangers and side effects."

Billy pages through the catalog to a still photo of a female model wearing a brown wig, the Domestic Enchantress, #318.

"Yes, ma'am. No, but we do have the Metropolitan Debutante model in three different colors: summer sensation, autumn reunion, and springtime mist. No, that's a kind of platinum-blond. Yes, yes, ma'am."

TWO

The boy detective is on the bus, staring straight ahead, careful not to make eye contact with anybody. If he makes eye contact with someone and looks away first, they will own him. He does not want that to happen. Is it still raining? Yes, it is. Everyone's hair looks wet and misplaced, hanging in clumps over their foreheads and faces. It makes everyone look crazy. It is also very crowded on the bus. People are standing and talking on their cell phones or reading their evening papers and the headlines are somewhat different but still somewhat the same: Someone has called someone else a liar. Someone has made a new movie. Another building in town has disappeared without reason. Some other country is bad for doing something.

Billy sighs, touching the soft white scars on his wrists, and then looks down the aisle and sees a short, mousy-looking young woman in drab brown and pink. The lady has very large glasses on her very tiny face and she frowns as she makes her way toward an opening in the busy line of people who are all still very wet with rain.

A strange thing then happens—it is strange, yes.

The young woman looks over her shoulder, very suspiciously, looking to see where other people are now glancing. The lady adjusts her pink pillbox hat, then slowly approaches a matronly woman near the rear of the bus, eyeing the other woman's great black handbag which is hanging open vulnerably. The young woman is trying to stare surreptitiously, but great invisible dashes - - - - - - - - - - are being directed from her eyes toward the other woman's purse, and the way her narrow black eyebrows are arranged—pointed, with intent—it is clear where the young woman is looking.

The boy detective takes notice of the young woman, leaning forward in his seat. She inches her hand from her pink coat pocket toward the other lady's handbag, her small fingers, nimble and quick, reaching into the matron's purse. The young woman takes something from the purse and quickly slides her hand back into her coat pocket, concealing it. Then, turning away, she makes her way toward the exit in a hurry.

The boy detective watches the young woman's movements moment to moment, his hands clenching with impotent fury. He cannot help what he is about to do—no. He cannot help himself. A bluebird, falling from the sky, cannot stop itself from flying. A clipper ship, adrift in the ocean, cannot stop itself from floating. A magnolia, rising in the water, cannot stop itself from growing. So it is that the boy detective stands and begins making his way toward the lady thief. Just as he reaches his hand out to grab her pink sleeve, she moves and quickly gets off the bus, the glass doors nearly closing in his face. Billy follows just as quickly, accidentally stepping into a gutter full of rain. The lady ties a pink scarf around her head, ducking from tree to tree, almost disappearing in the soft gray haze. Billy catches up with her. From behind, he touches her right hand, scaring her, staring into her face.

"Excuse me, miss? Miss?"

The lady is very startled. "Yes? You . . . you frightened me."

"I believe I saw you take something from that woman's purse."

"No . . . I . . ."

Like that, the lady in pink runs off, darting between people. Dark umbrellas hide her path. Billy follows, hurrying past people on the street. The lady, out of breath, stops ahead and leans against a parked car. Her face is wet with tears or rain. Billy catches up with her and takes her hand again.

"You did take something from that woman, didn't you?"

The lady is now crying. "You. You scared me."

The lady reaches into her pocket and takes out a cheap plastic pen. She throws it down. It floats in the rainy gutter, slowly turning. Billy leans over and picks up the pen as the lady runs off, her pink scarf blowing behind her head. Billy watches, speechless, the pink scarf a dot, a speck, then gone, gone, gone. The boy detective slips the pen into his pocket, watching her disappear, and wonders what is the meaning of any of it.

THREE

The boy detective has never kissed a girl. Shhh—it is a secret. It makes him feel very bad.

FOUR

At school, Gus Mumford breaks the other children's arms. He is the best at it. He is doing it right now. *Ow. Ouch. Yikes.* He shoves Benjamin Radcliffe against a bank of lockers, smashing the boy's ear, pummeling his face into the puke-green metal door with glee. Gus Mumford does not know why he is doing this. It just seems it is what the other children expect of him and so he does it to the best of his ability.

Gus Mumford's greatest maiming—the one of which he, to this day, is most proud? Blackening both of Jeremy Acorn's eyes with a single, deftly dealt blow to the nose.

In the middle of third period—spelling, Gus Mumford's worst subject—there is a knock at the classroom door and a small creature enters the room: It is strange because Gus is unsure whether it is a girl or a boy standing there. The child's skin is bright pink and its head is almost completely bald: There is a single blond strand of hair at the top of its head and its eyelashes are long and white. When it takes off its jacket, it is wearing a small white shirt and a patterned pair of slacks. Gus Mumford twitches his nose and watches Miss Gale lead the small pink child to an empty seat at the front of the classroom. Immediately there is a crowd of whispers and exclamations, and one of the girls, Missy Blackworth, the child who is always called on first in class, says a single word that seems to speak to the entire class's feelings: "Bald."

Gus Mumford returns to his drawing—a graphic depiction of gigantic ants with swords, feasting on the various limbs of his teacher—every so often looking up from his page to stare at the back of the bald pink head before him.

At recess, in between delivering a heretofore unheard of ten Indian burns to children on the playground, Gus watches the pink child, still unsure if it is truly a boy or girl, who is sitting on the bicycle rack making a cat's cradle with a string of yarn.

Gus Mumford looks at the pink child's nose and decides it must be a male. Still, he is the most lovely male Gus Mumford has ever seen: small eyes, small lips, blond eyelashes more dainty than any young girl's.

When Missy Blackworth slowly takes a seat beside the pink boy, Gus stops punching a first grader named Clancy Seamen in the belly, turning the poor soul loose, and watches with squinted eyes what might happen next. On the other side of the playground, two third-graders quietly sit on the metal bike rack side by side, whispering to each other. All is well until Missy quickly reaches up, touches the boy's soft pink head, and runs off giggling in horror, jumping up and down, laughing as she hurries back to her circle of friends, holding her hand out before her as if it is now glowing. Gus Mumford wipes Clancy Seamen's spit off his fists and walks quickly over to Missy Blackworth. Without another thought, he breaks the laughing girl's wrist.

Gus Mumford has a secret: He has been talking. He has been saying words out loud, but only to the inhabitants of Ant City, the ant farm his neighbor Billy generously gave to his sister. Hiding quietly beneath the front porch of his house, he holds the rectangular glass metropolis in his hands and says—his voice unfamiliar and creaky—"I have a new friend at school. He thinks very highly of me." He is lying, of course, but is quite sure the citizens of Ant City will be unable to recognize that.

FIVE

The boy detective always returns to the case of the Haunted Candy Factory. He tells the story over and over and over again when he is feeling unsure of himself. Why? Because there is a beginning, a middle, and an end. He is comforted by it—the structure—knowing there is an answer to the strange question being asked.

After doing some smart sleuthing (having inspected the only clue in the case of the Haunted Candy Factory, and having deciphered its strange meaning, which seemed to suggest the villain was a sinister dentist of some kind), Billy had traced the producer of the out-of-date paper the original note was typed on to a supplier, who revealed the buyer, a Dr. John Victor, and his address. The boy detective and his sister Caroline found that it led them to an abandoned dental office, not more than a block away from the cursed candy factory.

Climbing through an open window, the boy detective and Caroline snooped around for a while, staring at the dental instruments and medical gowns overwhelmed with cobwebs.

"There's his office," Caroline said.

Immediately inside the office, the two children discovered an important clue.

"Look," Caroline exclaimed, "the ghost!"

There, lying in Dr. Victor's desk, was a large white sheet with holes cut out for eyes. Beneath the cloth, a large set of silver keys.

"Some ghost," the boy detective said. "I told you there was nothing to be scared of."

With that, the door to the office swung shut. Together, the two children rushed forward, but not in time. They heard the outside bolt being rammed into place.

"We're prisoners!" Caroline gasped.

Again and again, the Argo siblings threw their weight against the door. It was hopeless. Breathing hard, Billy and Caroline looked for another means of escape.

"The windows are all boarded shut," Billy said, blaming himself for not having been on guard.

"What will we do?" Caroline asked.

"I know!" the boy detective exclaimed. "Look!"

There in the ceiling was a large metal air vent.

"We can climb through!" Caroline happily guessed. Climbing on top of an old dental chair, Billy found the pedal that controlled the chair's height, and held it down with a discarded block of wood. With a *whoosh*, the two siblings rocketed skyward, close enough to slip into the safety of the air vent.

"Follow that light," Billy whispered. "I think I know exactly where it leads."

Within the darkness of the silver vent, the siblings crawled and crawled, soon finding their way into a deep, dark cave. At the end of the cave was a pixie-faced young girl, Daisy Hollis, heiress to the Hollis Dry Cleaning fortune. There, monogrammed on her light blue dress, were her initials: DH.

"We've been looking for you for sometime," Caroline said. "Everyone has practically given up—"

Wait a minute, no—that isn't right at all. Daisy Hollis is not part of this story.

The boy detective, on the bus, pinches himself, staring at the scars on his wrist.

Daisy Hollis? No, that's a mistake. That's not the case you're remembering.

Here's how it goes:

With a *whoosh*, the two siblings rocketed skyward, close enough to slip into the safety of the air vent.

"Follow that light," Billy whispered. "I think I know exactly where it leads."

SIX

It is not so very strange: The boy detective is going to the movies on his own. He does not want to ask any other resident to accompany him because his favorite film is playing. He does not know what the film is, but decides whatever it is after tonight—his first film alone—it will be his favorite.

As Billy's ticket is being torn, he looks up and notices the usher smoking two cigarettes at the same time. The tall, lanky fellow in the red vest and tiny red hat is none other than Frank Hartly, a fellow former child detective.

Together, the Hartly Boys—Frank and his younger brother Joe—solved many mysteries in the nearby town of Bayville, until they discovered that their father, also a professional detective, was leading a very well-organized counterfeiting ring. With their father's arrest and subsequent incarceration, the Hartly brothers forever turned away from detective work and private investigation. Billy had not heard from or seen them since, thinking they too had wanted to disappear into the quiet comfort of some semblance of normalcy.

Billy blinks, staring at the young man's face. The rugged chin and unruly head of blond hair, the chiseled cheekbones and determined eyebrows make it quite clear: This is Frank Hartly, one-half of the best boy detective team on earth, now just a clerk at a movie theater.

"Frank," the boy detective whispers. "Frank Hartly?"

"Yeah," he says with a nod, ashing on the floor, trying to remember Billy's face. His eyes squint and strain as he works to picture who Billy might be. "Who's asking?"

"It's Billy Argo. I knew you when we were younger."

"Billy Argo! I thought you were dead, man. Jesus."

"I was just out of town for a long time," Billy lies.

"I thought you had OD'd or something. Hey, did you hear about Violet Dew?"

"Yes."

"She's divorced now. It's terrible. How are you? I mean I had heard . . . Well, forget it."

"No, go on," Billy says.

"I heard your sister committed suicide and you shot yourself."

"No," Billy says, "none of that is true."

"Well, I'm happy to hear it—hey, you know who'd get a kick out of this? My brother Joe," Frank says, grabbing his walkie-talkie. He begins shouting into the two-way. "Joe, come over to the ticket booth, you're never gonna believe who's here!"

"You still work with your brother?"

"Yeah, we were lucky to find this place. Most jobs, they don't want to hire two brothers together. But we've been here about two years. Joe is assistant manager. He was always the charming one."

"So do you like this job?" Billy asks.

"It pays the bills and provides for the pills," Frank whispers, taking a long drag. "Seriously, do you know any doctors who write fake scrips? I have a Demerol habit that cannot be fixed."

"What happened?"

"I took a bad fall at the Old Mill—on a case, you know—my leg got caught in a mill wheel, slip, fall, crush. We solved the case, but the damn thing never healed."

"I am on four different medications at the moment," Billy confides.

"Painkillers?"

"Antidepression and antianxiety. If I take too many, I fall down."

"Do you have any on you?" Frank Hartly asks.

"No," Billy lies.

"Billy Argo!" Joe Hartly shouts, suddenly appearing. "Man, I was such a huge fan of yours when I was a kid," he says, shaking Billy's hand. "The Case of the Haunted Candy Factory. That's solid gold."

"It's good to see you too, Joe," Billy says.

"Well, what have you been up to?" Joe asks.

"Working."

"Oh, like on a case?"

"No, just working like you: at a job."

"Well, this job is bullshit. We were security guards at the mall here for a while," Joe says, "but they said we were way too ambitious."

"Joe shot a shoplifter in the leg. Shooting people is frowned upon," Frank chimes in.

"We weren't even supposed to carry guns."

"That's too bad," the boy detective says with a frown. "It's good that you have each other still, though."

"Yes, yes, it is," Frank Hartly agrees.

"Well, I hope you enjoy the movie," Joe Hartly says. "It's good."

"Yeah, maybe afterwards we can meet up and talk for a while," Frank adds. "We have, well, a kind of informal group that gets together— nothing serious, just some people who sit around and talk, mostly former detectives, you know. We discuss old cases and stuff. If you ever want to come, let me give you my number." He writes it on the back of the ticket stub and hands it to Billy.

"I'll give you a call," the boy detective whispers, and with that lie a silent alarm goes off in his heart.

SEVEN

That evening, lonesome, the boy detective is lying in bed counting snowflakes. He has counted as many as a thousand. He stands suddenly, awakened by some commotion outside, and looks out of the small barred window of his room. He notices the Mumford children moving in the dark, long after they should be in bed asleep. Puffy, in her purple and white coat, Effie Mumford is crouching on their front lawn beside what appears to be a large silver rocket, its nose pointed skyward. In an instant, the girl flips some silver switch and the sleek-looking missile begins vibrating, small puffs of smoke burning from its engines.

Billy places his face against the glass, holding the bars and watching as the children clap and holler, backing away slowly from the rocket as it begins to twitch and hover. Unable to stop himself, like a magnet to strange behaviors and intrigue, the boy detective begins taking notes in his small notepad:

—1:03am: Subject: Effie Mumford, female, age eleven, blond, in a white and purple winter jacket. Testing a new rocket perhaps?
—1:07am: Subject slips, falls on her backside, looks around to see if anyone has noticed. Her brother, Gus Mumford, age nine, frowns; subject pulls herself to her feet and continues watching.
—1:10am: The rocket begins to very slowly lift off from the ground.
—1:11am: Subject takes a bow, clapping for herself, thanks imaginary audience.
—1:12am: The rocket lifts off suddenly, turns hard, and crashes into the maple hanging over the subjects' front yard. The rocket explodes while

the subject and her brother run and hide beneath their front porch. The front lawn has begun to burn. Also, a small bush goes up in flames.

—1:13am: Mrs. Mumford hurries onto front porch and begins shouting.

—1:15am: Mrs. Mumford puts out the fire on the front lawn, extinguishes the burning hedge, and shouts until the Mumford children disappear inside.

—1:16am: The rocket, lying inert on the front lawn, explodes. In a report of small silvery blasts, the word "HELLO" is spelled out in glowing sparkles that soon die.

EIGHT

At work, the boy detective is busy at his desk, pretending to talk on the left-handed telephone, when a skinny, sad-eyed young man approaches and stands there staring. The young man is nervous; he looks around and very quietly leans beside Billy and whispers: "Are you the detective?"

Billy looks up. The young man's face is that of an eager, timid boy, with a pointed chin, bright eyes, and extremely narrow cheekbones. Billy leans close to answer, smiling.

"Yes. I am the detective."

"My name is Eric Quimby."

"Yes?"

"I work in the ladies' wigs division. Please . . . I need your help."

"Yes?"

"I would appreciate your candor regarding this matter."

"Of course."

"I believe I am in danger."

"Danger?"

"Yes. Take a look at this." The young man lifts his left leg and plants it on the corner of Billy's desk. Slowly, he raises his pant leg and reveals that below there is nothing left: no flesh, no bone, no skin, only empty space, the sock and shoe somehow mysteriously staying in place.

"I am afraid this may be a medical condition," Billy whispers, trembling slightly.

"No, no, I'm sure it's something more sinister."

"Why do you think that?"

"Look here, I received this," the young man says, and hurriedly removes a small white card from his suit coat pocket, handing it to Billy.

Billy stares down and reads: *MARKED BY THE ARROW: YOU.*
"Where did you find this?" he asks.

"I don't know. It just appeared in my back pocket."

"It is very strange."

"Yesterday it was my upper leg. Then the knee. Then the ankle. Today the whole foot. I have no feeling down there. It's as if it was never there. I'm very concerned about it."

"As you should be."

"A strange woman in a mask put the card in my pants pocket. I was on the bus and she approached me and a few moments later it was there."

"She wore a mask?"

"Yes. Black, like you wear to a masquerade. And she was wearing long black gloves. It was frightening."

"I see."

"Perhaps it was foolish to mention it to you," the young man whispers, and glances about the office quickly. "But I'm afraid tomorrow I'll wake up and there'll be nothing left."

"I understand. It is very serious."

"Maybe I should not have bothered you," the young man whispers. "No, no, I don't think we should have spoken." He then hurries away, disappearing behind a row of cubicles in the back of the office. The boy detective nods carefully and returns to his calls, frowning at the spot where the young man's shoe has left a strange mark on a stack of mimeographs.

"I would like a wig—a blond wig, if you have one—right away."

"We have over thirty styles and colors," Billy reports sadly.

"I need a wig that's long, so people don't recognize me. Do you have something like that? For people when they want to hide?"

"Perhaps it might be easier to choose if I send you a catalog."

"No, no, I need one as soon as possible. Today, if I can."

"I see."

"Which one do you recommend?"

"The Young Starlet is very popular."

"I want something very plain. Very plain."

"Perhaps the Nordic Princess model."

The line goes quiet for a moment. Billy can hear the woman sitting there, breathing.

"I'm waiting for a taxi. I'm moving out today. I need it very soon."

"Well, perhaps I might call you at some other time . . ."

"I'm in this apartment all alone right now. Please don't hang up on me."

"OK."

"My roommate thinks I should call the police. I don't want the police involved."

"Perhaps I should call back—"

"I was kidnapped. They took me to a factory. Then they let me go. That was three days ago. I can't stay here. I can't go anywhere. I don't want to be alone."

"I'm . . . so . . . I . . ."

"I should have listened to my parents. I'm never coming back to this town again."

Billy hangs up the telephone, finds a Seroquel, and pops it into his mouth.

At work, just before he leaves, the boy detective slowly strolls past the ladies' wigs division. Among the darling models of glossy hair and expressionless Styrofoam heads, the office cubicles are mostly empty.

In the background, one of the cleaning ladies has begun vacuuming. There, Billy finds, beneath an empty desk marked with Eric Quimby's name on a small gold placard, a pair of black socks heaped clumsily into a pair of brown dress shoes. Examining the soft gray seat, Billy discovers the same small white card, the message, *MARKED BY THE ARROW: YOU.* Sitting there and looking up, he sees the telephone on the desk is lying off its receiver and that, according to the signal light, a call is on hold. Billy holds the phone to his ear and presses the receiver.

A strange, metallic voice sings in a whisper directly into his ear: *"It's always twilight for lovers . . . It's always twilight for love . . ."*

Frightened, Billy returns the receiver to its cradle and backs away, stumbling over the cord from the vacuum cleaner, hurrying into the quiet solace of the elevator.

As he catches his breath, he notices a darkly dressed woman in a blue velvet dress, dark high heels, and a black mask standing beside him. He does not move. He begins to count, closing his eyes, his fingers pinching the sides of his legs until the elevator rings and the doors part open. Rushing past, Billy turns to see the small wood-paneled box is now empty.

On the bus ride, he tries to convince himself he did not see what he has seen. When he places his nervous hands within his coat pocket, he finds a small white card that he does not recognize. It reads: *IGNORE WHAT YOU THINK YOU NOW KNOW.* He leaves it on the plastic seat beside him and hurries off at the next bus stop.

NINE

It is perhaps the most terrifying unsolved case of all time: the Phantom Killer of Texarkana. From February 22 through May 3, 1946, a strange killer held the small town of Texarkana, Arkansas in a grip of fear, murdering five people and assaulting three others. The first victims were young couples, attacked while parking at the Lover's Lane section of road near Spring Lake Park. The fourth couple was attacked in their home, ten miles northeast of the town.

The strange occurrences began on February 22, 1946: Nineteen-year-old Mary Jean Larey and her boyfriend, twenty-four-year-old Jimmy Hollis, were parked on a dark road, ending their date. Suddenly, their kisses goodnight were interrupted by a gigantic, ominous shadow that belonged to a man in a bright white hood. The man moved slowly, tapping a gun against the window of the car, demanding that the couple get out. He first beat Jimmy unconscious with the pistol and then terrified Mary, pressing the barrel of the gun against her soft cheek. Luckily, a car light soon appeared and frightened the enormous hooded man off, thereby saving Mary and Jimmy's lives.

At first, the incident was considered the work of a transient and was ignored, but then on the morning of March 24, two police officers discovered the body of a man lying in a parked car on the side of the road; it belonged to twenty-nine-year-old Richard Griffin. Some distance away from the automobile was a second body, the man's girlfriend, Polly Ann Moore. Both victims had been murdered by a shot in the head from a pistol, a .32 caliber, the same gun Mary Jean Larey and Jimmy Hollis described in their encounter with the fiend.

On April 13, the bodies of fifteen-year-old Betty Jo Booker and

*her boyfriend Paul Martin were discovered, once again shot with a .32
caliber pistol. Betty Jo had also been molested and bound to a tree before
being shot. Police were sure of the connection, but unsure how to resolve
the identity of the killer or the motive for his actions. After the local
press dubbed the murderer the "Phantom Killer," residents of the town
became tremendously fearful, afraid to leave their homes after dark.*

*Starting April 14 and continuing through May, the streets of
Texarkana were like a ghost town. The Phantom Killer eluded police
for nearly a month, committing his final murder on May 3, 1946,
striking the home of Katy and Virgil Starks.*

*The Phantom Killer was never caught, and disappeared as
mysteriously as he had arrived, leaving many to wonder why he had
appeared in the first place. Why had he done what he'd done? Why
had he gone mad with such criminal brutality at the sight of love?*

The boy detective reads this in his therapist's waiting room in a
magazine entitled *Crime Psychology: A Satisfactory Study*. He sets the
magazine down as the therapist calls his name.

The boy detective is now lying on his side on the large brown vinyl
couch. The therapist is watching and taking notes. He interrupts
whatever Billy is saying and Billy sits up.

"Billy, I want you to be honest and tell me something."

"OK."

"Why do you think your sister killed herself?"

"Pardon me?"

"Why do you think Caroline killed herself?"

"I don't know."

"What do you mean, you don't know?"

"I mean I don't know. I don't know *everything*."

"So it's a mystery?"

"Yes."

"But I thought you never failed to solve a case?"

"We never did."

"Not you and your friend and your sister, just you. I thought you never failed to solve a mystery."

"I didn't."

"Well, it seems to me you're avoiding the greatest mystery of your life: why your sister killed herself."

"No."

"Perhaps, for some reason, you think you know the answer already."

"No."

"Perhaps you think it was you—that you were the reason. That somehow you were to blame."

"I . . ."

"Did you love your sister, Billy?"

"Yes, of course . . ."

"Did she love you?"

"Yes. I am sure of it."

"Is that why you feel responsible for her death? That if you truly loved her, you would not have left her alone? That if you truly cared for her, she would not have died? That love—like you—never fails?"

"I am leaving now, doctor."

"You can leave if you like, Billy, but we both know that won't change anything."

"I'm leaving anyway."

The boy detective, abandoning his shoes and socks in the office behind him, runs so fast his tears fall sideways down his narrow face.

As you may have noticed, it seems there have been an extraordinary number of conjoined twins born in our town. What seemed like a strange fact at first was later revealed to be the result of years of improper disposal of medical waste. It is not so unusual to see two or three sets of these twins shopping at your local grocery store on any given day. What is out of the ordinary is to see someone standing behind you in line, a soft red mark along the side of his or her head, a wound that suggests the terror of separation, a medical procedure which is hardly ever successful. Most with this curious affliction choose to die as they were born: as one. In our graveyards, we have arranged special plots for the proper interment of these unlucky people: a long rectangular gravestone that recalls a strange double life, revealing a partnership that, living past death, gives us an unlikely cause to be envious.

TEN

The boy detective is on the bus again, staring ahead, almost asleep. It is still raining. The bus is again crowded. People are again standing and talking on their cell phones or reading their papers. Like that, Billy notices the lady in pink at the other end of the bus. She has her hand in another woman's pocket again.

Billy stands and begins moving toward her, slowly. The lady looks up and notices Billy and what he is noticing. She becomes flush, grabs her own pink purse, and hurries toward the exit. Billy follows, hopping off the bus in a crowd of other commuters, as the lady runs away.

In the rain, Billy follows, catching her, grabbing her hand. The lady squeaks, trying to pull free. "Please . . . wait . . . please . . ."

The lady drops her pink purse, spilling it as she struggles to get away. Hundreds of pens, pencils, paper clips, tissues, lipsticks—all stolen items—fall out. Billy lets go of the lady's hand to help pick up the mess. When he looks up, the lady in pink is gone once again. Along the wet ground are more of her stolen goods: office supplies, napkins, a small white wax paper–wrapped sandwich, an apple, and laminated ID cards—dozens of them, photos of all kinds of men and women. Billy smiles, finding several more, all from the same company, ELECTEC, then an ID of the lady in pink. Beneath her drab, small face is her name: *Penny Maple*.

The apple and sandwich seem to point to the fact that perhaps she is only now going to work. A cleaning lady? Are her pink clothes a uniform perhaps? Maybe she is heading to her job right now?

Billy excitedly shoves everything back into the purse. In this moment, he decides he will return the purse to her and try to ask her to please stop stealing.

ELEVEN

The boy detective enters the small silver office building and sneaks past a snoring guard into a waiting elevator. When the elevator doors open, he can hear the sound of a vacuum running. He follows the sound and slowly sneaks around the corner of a small green cubicle and finds the lady in pink, now in a pink cleaning smock, leaning over a small white vacuum, running it back and forth, dancing to her headphones, shouting along loudly. It is impossible not to smile, seeing her: eyes closed, feet tapping in place, yelling louder than the vacuum cleaner.

In a moment, the lady stops vacuuming and begins dancing with a tall silver coat rack. One of its rungs holds a suit jacket, which is swaying back and forth in time. Then the lady grabs a handful of files and tosses them up in the air. Finding a chair, she sits and spins around, pounding her feet on the top of the desks. Like that, she has climbed up on a conference table and, her face all red and nearly out of breath, she slides down the table, scattering an enormous pile of recyclable paper.

If somehow, through science or magic, we could discern an X-ray of Billy's heart just then, it would look like a lovely, perfectly shaped balloon—the kind sold on Valentine's Day in the comical rounded heart shape—growing larger and larger, filling his chest, his eyes, expanding to the size of the room, as the lady swings her hair around, still dancing. Perhaps it would look like this:

Billy smiles, genuinely moved. He forgets himself and starts clapping.

The lady turns, dropping her headphones, startled. She falls off the desk and hurries for the exit. Billy pleads, running after her, calling: "No, wait, please, wait . . ."

The lady nimbly runs into the office stairwell. Billy follows only a few steps behind, but once inside the stairwell, the lady in pink is gone, and there is absolutely no echoing sound of retreating feet to relate where she might have escaped to. A door slams and locks somewhere in the stairwell and Billy stops, calling over the railing: "Wait! Please wait!"

The boy detective holds the pink purse, smiling sadly. He hears another door slam somewhere and shakes his head. He leans over and leaves her identification badge on the stairs; keeping the purse, he heads back to the elevator once again.

On the bus home, he holds the purse in his lap and wonders why he did not simply leave it there.

TWELVE

The boy detective is lying in bed, thinking about kissing Penny Maple.

> *Penny Maple*
> *oh, Penny Maple*
> *Penny Maple*
> *oh, Penny Maple*
> *Penny Penny Penny Penny Penny Penny Penny Penny Maple*

He is thinking this: *smooch-smooch, kiss-kiss*. He is imagining what her small pink lips might feel like next to his. He is lying in his bed and imagining these things: what her ankles look like naked and the soft smell of her hair beneath her hat. He is holding her purse and he is becoming overwhelmed and he begins kissing the soft fabric. He cannot stop himself. He smells her flowery perfume and discovers a pink scarf inside the purse and he begins kissing that, too. Very soon, he is kissing everything—the pillow, her purse, the scarf. He is lying under the covers and practicing every kind of kiss he knows.

On his own, Billy has developed nearly forty kinds of kisses. Each one is scientific, with its own place and purpose. Tonight he practices the first ten he knows in this order:

1. Eskimo
2. Closed-eyed
3. French
4. Slow-breathing/fast-breathing
5. The Cary Grant

6. Nibble-kiss

7. The Venus de Milo

8. Fish-kiss

9. Top-lip kiss

10. Bottom-lip kiss

The boy detective opens his notepad and begins to plan new ways of kissing—methods that are untamed, wonderful, never before considered. The boy detective is suddenly afraid that kissing might always remain a mystery to him. He sits up in bed, wondering how Penny likes to be kissed, and whispers her name again and again like a song:

Penny Maple
   oh, Penny Maple
Penny Maple
   oh, Penny Maple
   PennyPennyPennyPennyPennyPennyPennyPenny Maple

   Penny Maple
   oh, Penny Maple

   Penny Maple
   oh, Penny Maple
   PennyPennyPennyPennyPennyPennyPennyPenny Maple
Penny Maple
   yes, Penny Maple
you are Penny Maple
   your name is Penny Maple
   PennyPennyPennyPennyPennyPennyPennyPenny Maple

Penny Maple

    yes, yes, yes, Penny Maple

Penny Maple?

    oh, yes, Penny Maple

    PennyPennyPennyPennyPennyPennyPennyPenny Maple

Penny Maple

    oh, no, Penny Maple

Penny Maple (Maple, Maple)

    oh, Penny Maple, yes, yes, yes

    PennyPennyPennyPennyPennyPennyPennyPenny Maple

Penny Maple

    oh, go now, Penny Maple

Penny Maple

    you are the only Penny Maple

    PennyPennyPennyPennyPennyPennyPennyPenny Maple

Penny Maple

    oh, look out, Penny Maple

Penny Maple

    PennyPennyPennyPennyPennyPennyPennyPenny Maple

    You scared me, too.

THIRTEEN

At school, Gus Mumford has written a note for the strange bald boy sitting before him. While Miss Gale posts enormous mathematical enumerations on the blackboard, Gus Mumford gathers his courage, folds the small scrap of paper into itself again and again and again, then—as gently as he knows how—flings the note against the back of the child's strangely pink neck. *Oh no*—he has projected it much too hard. The paper ricochets off the soft bald head and falls there, between his feet. The boy blinks, turning around in his seat, his nearly nonexistent blond eyebrows lowering into a frown, his mouth a stab of red sadness. Gus Mumford is unsure how to proceed and simply lowers his head to his desk, pretending he is now mysteriously dead—perhaps it is scurvy or impetigo or the black death.

The boy reaches down and grasps the paper lightly with his small pink fingers. Slowly in his lap, he unfolds the note and begins reading. The note is simple, only four words: I LIKE YOUR EYELASHES.

The bald child turns around in his seat once more and smiles, blinking at Gus Munford sitting behind him. But Gus Mumford, notorious bully of the third grade, is too afraid to lift his head to see. The bald boy turns back around, tears a corner from his notepad, and begins composing a reply. Within a few moments, he has finished; he folds the note up into a perfect white triangle, waits for Miss Gale to continue with more of her useless enumerations, and turns quick, with finesse, simply placing the note on the very edge of Gus Mumford's desk. Gus, peeking from between his fingers, grabs the note dizzily and begins reading it, hidden between the open pages of his mathematical primer. The note is equal in its simplicity, but the handwriting is soft and looping and pretty: I LIKE YOUR EYE-LASHES AS WELL.

We are amazed at how a few short words have such a profound effect on our friend, Gus Mumford. His face goes red and warm and he hides the note in his pants pocket, afraid that the contents of his secret correspondence might somehow be revealed. What to do now, though? A reply to his reply? Is this how it is done? How are friends made? He does not know. He has never passed a note across class to someone before. He has held their faces against dead birds, wire fences, the hardwood floor of the gym, but never has he been so intimate with a child his own age as this moment here. Before he can consider a proper course of action, the bald child turns again, in a whirl, and deposits a second note on the corner of his desk. Gus Mumford is more than a little surprised. Perhaps the other boy has made a mistake. Perhaps he has changed his mind and realized he did not care for Gus's eyelashes at all. With less enthusiasm, Gus Mumford slowly opens the note in his lap.

It says: I KNOW YOU ARE SMART.

What occurs now is certain dread: It is Gus Mumford's most hidden shame, most hidden secret, and here this small creature—this stranger—has so easily discerned it within a matter of a few short days, the admission bright red on Gus Mumford's face. Yes, yes, he is smart—smarter than the smartest child in class by books and books and years and years—but to consider the thought, to accurately grasp the notion while watching Gus Mumford force-feed a smaller boy the end of a length of worm, it seems near to impossible.

Gus Mumford stares down at the small, daintily written words and sighs, knowing any friendship with this child has now been lost, any hope of camaraderie has been dispelled with the apparent knowledge of his most vicious secret, and so he resumes his position, resting his face in his folded arms. Miss Gale ruminates on the potency of addition and subtraction, the sounds hanging in the air like a wordless dirge. If Gus Mumford was capable, surely he would cry, but as a bully he has not the capacity for it, and instead sniffles his nose, unsatisfied with the incompleteness of this, his most sad facial expression. It is then that, as a complete surprise, the bald boy turns around once again in a flash, and when Gus Mumford peers from above his hands, he sees a third and final note sitting there. Quickly, without regard for Miss Gale's prying eyes, Gus opens the note and stares at the small curves of the words, his face still flush, his nose still twitching.

It says: YOU ARE NOT A VERY BELIEVABLE BULLY.

FOURTEEN

At Shady Glens, the boy detective leaves his room during Bingo Hour—an hour when he usually tries to avoid entering the hallway—because he has heard that the lovely Nurse Eloise has baked a gigantic buttercream cake, which is one of Billy's favorites. It is shaped like an enormous Eiffel Tower. In the white-tiled boredom of the television room, Nurse Eloise welcomes him and carves him a large piece.

"I've got some wonderful news, Billy. I've gotten back together with my boyfriend and we're going to Paris next month. His magic show has been booked there for four weeks, so I thought we should all celebrate. I know you like buttercream."

"It looks lovely."

"The only rule is that you eat it here with us, Billy," she says.

Billy turns and watches the other lunatics eating: Mr. Pluto is wolfing the treat down with his enormous fingers, smashing it into the monstrous cavity of his mouth; Professor Von Golum is stabbing another resident in the neck with his fork; Mr. Lunt is sleeping, his bearded face resting atop his slice. Each of them has somehow found a new way to be very, very disgusting. Billy smiles and decides he is not too hungry.

He hurries back down the hall and returns to his room.

In a moment, there is a knock at the door. He opens it and finds his slice of cake with a napkin and a glass of milk sitting there.

It is so beautiful he almost cries. He decides Nurse Eloise is the nicest person of all time. The boy detective drinks the milk and gently wraps the cake up in the napkin, deciding he will keep it for work tomorrow, when he knows he will be feeling bad, indubitably.

* * *

As the boy detective is lying in bed, he turns the light switch on and soon it begins snowing. The tiny flakes glitter down all around and disappear as they touch the tile floor:

snow	snow	snow	snow	snow	snow	snow	snow
snow	snow	snow	snow	snow	snow	snow	snow
	snow	snow	snow	snow	snow	snow	
		snow		snow		snow	
		snow				snow	

Following the snow as it drifts down with his eyes, Billy notices his arch-foe, Professor Von Golum, curled beneath the bed frame. Though the old man is asleep, there is a length of shiny wire twisted in his hands, the murder weapon held close, at the ready.

"Professor, may I ask what you are doing down there?"

"I was planning on strangling you as soon as you went to sleep."

"I see."

"Perhaps it was poor planning, but I could not stay awake. It is very comfortable under here."

"Would you like some help out from underneath?"

"No. No, I'm all right. I'll just stay here, if you don't mind."

Billy sighs, turning on his side.

"Professor?"

"Yes?"

"May I ask you a question, sir?"

"Yes, but know it may be the last question you ever ask."

"Have you ever been in love, sir?"

"Oh, my poor, poor childish detective. Surely you must know by now. Love is the invention of man. It does not exist. It is a fairy tale designed to keep order. Imagine how we as humans would behave if we freed ourselves from the idiocy of that one particular idea: what a wonderful world; what a world of absolute possibility."

"I think I may be in love, sir."

"May I ask how you know? How can you *prove* it? You are a detective, no? Where is the evidence? What clues are you basing this foolish assumption on?"

"I don't know, really. It just occurs as a feeling in my hands and behind my knees."

"But can it be placed in a bell jar? Can it be seen under a microscope? How can something as invisible—as insubstantial—as love ever hope to last?"

"I cannot stop thinking about kissing her."

"That is chemistry—or biology—it has nothing to do with hearts and flowers and the like. Do not be confused by what the natural world knows: We are all, in our own way, completely and totally alone. If love is real, it is a complete and total failing of the intellect. It is utter self-destruction. It is pandemonium."

"Yes, thank you, sir."

"It is my pleasure, Billy."

In the near dark, the boy detective finds his bottle of pills and quickly swallows one Ativan, holding his breath until he is sure the villain has crept out. He looks up in wonder as the soft haze of snow drifts down.

FIFTEEN

It is past midnight and the boy detective is watching the Mumford children again. The houses on the small street are quiet and still, their lights having been turned off for the evening. But there is Effie Mumford, in her purple and white jacket, kneeling beside another amateur rocket, this one very slim and golden, her brother Gus looking quite sleepy in pajamas, sitting on the porch. Billy notes in his notepad:

—12:10am: Subject, Effie Mumford, prepares for second rocket test. Subject and her brother, Gus Mumford, both wearing pajamas.

—12:11am: Subject ignites rocket.

—12:12am: Rocket does not lift off ground: the fuse seems not to be working.

—12:13am: Subject, Effie Mumford, stands the rocket, inspecting the firing mechanism.

—12:14am: Subject kicks the rocket, knocking off the nose-cone: the rocket sparks and explodes, knocking the subject off her feet.

—12:15am: Rocket shoots directly up into the sky, leaving a long, silver trail of sparks: Subject, Effie Mumford, and Gus Mumford clap wildly.

—12:16am: In the dark sky, the rocket explodes. In a flash of blue and white sparks, a message is spelled out which, noted here, reads, "ANYONE OUT THERE."

—12:17am: Very quickly, lights in neighboring houses switch on. Mrs. Mumford opens the front door and begins shouting. The Mumford children are hurried inside.

SIXTEEN

In the dark, the boy detective lies in bed, staring at Caroline's diary.

i may have made a terrible mistake:
forgetting that i was not a true detective
forgetting i was not my brother, Billy
failing to remember how i was no genius
or failing to remember how i was not so very smart
or so very
useful on my own
i have stumbled upon something i do not grasp;
nothing makes sense without him
and worse, it seems all my
days go by without an end to this mystery
there is no hope of reprieve
do i dare tread into the dark again on my own?
do i dare walk unescorted once more into evil
all i hear are the whispers of my doom
at night, as i lay in bed
in quiet voices, i am often reminded of
the silent immovability of the dead, while the
stiff hands of those ghosts, murky, floating underwater, reach out to me
you will never know the terror of doubt, Billy
you will never know the terror of being without you

Billy gets up, goes over to the dresser, opens the bottom drawer, lifts out the detective kit, then sits on the bed, peering at the aged box.

He cannot get himself to open it, not even when there may be a mystery somewhere in this very world—at this very moment—afoot. Like that, with his sister's diary in his hand, he begrudgingly falls asleep.

Billy, in a dream, descends slowly into a dark and mossy cavern, past the signs that mark it. Holding a flashlight, he climbs further and further, listening to someone crying. At the bottom of the cave, through the dark, Billy can see his sister Caroline, still a young girl. In a white and yellow dress, she cries, "Help me, Billy."

Billy approaches in a hurry, and suddenly a horrible ram-horned, claw-fingered demon leaps out from the darkness, howling.

The boy detective wakes up to Mr. Lunt's screaming. Billy sits up, covered in sweat, still holding the diary, which he stares at, confused, as he sets it beside him on the nightstand. He turns and hears Nurse Eloise in her squeaky white nurse shoes march down the hall.

"It's only a dream, Mr. Lunt, dear, it's only a dream."

"Phantoms! Phantoms! I seen them! They're coming! They're coming for *me*!"

Billy lies back down, pulling the pillow over his head. He considers the bottles of pills beside his bed. It is only a moment later when the owl alarm clock begins ringing.

SEVENTEEN

The boy detective, at work, flips through the Mammoth Life-Like catalog and notices the model for the Metropolitan Debutante looks very much like the lady he has seen on the bus, the lady in pink. With his pen, he draws a small scarf over her head and then a small set of eyeglasses over the woman's face.

"Hello," he says to the catalog. "I am sorry for scaring you away again."

At lunch time, the boy detective goes to the office kitchen to retrieve his piece of buttercream cake, but it is gone. He stares at the spot in the refrigerator, the blue napkin lying there empty, a few golden crumbs hidden in its folds. He turns and begins to look around the office: Someone else has eaten it—he is sure of it. The boy detective has a reasonable suspicion that the culprit is Tad from accounting, but he is too preoccupied to bother tracking him down. His medication does not seem to be working very well today; he cannot concentrate. He returns to his desk and sighs. He is supposed to be making calls, but he ignores the phone and instead stares at the drawing of the lady in pink.

"Someone ate my cake," he says to the picture.

The picture seems to smile empathetically.

"I know. These people are savages."

The picture cheers him to go on.

"Some of them are OK."

The picture seems to tilt an ear closer to him.

"With you, I feel very comfortable," he says. "With you, I feel I can say anything."

* * *

The boy detective is on the phone later that day: "Yes, it's exactly that, sir, a miracle. A miracle of modern living. Hair-replacement surgery can be expensive and dangerous. So why risk it? What we offer you is quality hair replacement without the serious dangers and side effects."

"What's your name, again?"

"Billy, Billy Argo. Mammoth Life-Like . . ."

"Billy, I want you to listen to me: I just lost everything I had in a fire. It's like I wasn't even supposed to be alive and yet here I am."

"I see."

"It's all gone. My whole life. Everything."

"Yes."

"I lost my wife. I lost my wife. I lost her, too."

"I am so sorry, sir . . ."

"Billy, I did some awful things. I made some awful mistakes. I want to apologize to her right now and I can't. I want to tell her how sorry I am. Do you think she still might hear me? Do you think?"

"I do not know," Billy whispers.

"Billy Argo, my greatest fear is to die alone."

"Noted."

"Billy Argo, now you tell me your greatest fear."

The boy detective is quiet for some time. He holds his breath and listens to the sound of the other man crying.

"I am afraid of not knowing the answer to something."

"I don't understand," the man says.

"I am afraid that when the time comes, I won't know the answer to the question someone is asking."

"Oh," the man says. "That's very understandable."

"Yes," Billy adds, "love is one of the questions I do not even know how to begin to answer."

After that phone call, the boy detective hides in the washroom, crying in front of the dirty mirror. He washes his face again and again in case someone walks in and wonders why he is only standing there, sobbing. He finds a Seroquel in his pocket and takes it, drinking a handful of water from the sink.

At the end of the work day, the boy detective once again passes the ladies' wigs division. He glances at Eric Quimby's desk and sees the small gold placard has mysteriously been changed: It now reads *Penelope Anders*, and there is no mark of the previous occupant's presence. Billy hurries back to his desk, collects his things, and just then his telephone begins to ring. He answers it quickly and a high whine hums through the wires.

The voice, strange and metallic, begins to sing: *"It's always twilight for lovers . . . It's always twilight for love . . ."* Billy slams down the phone and gazes around the empty office, then hurries toward the elevator. The device is slow to arrive at the boy detective's floor. He is looking around nervously, panicked. He thinks he can hear someone walking slowly up the stairwell. The elevator draws near, the golden needle above the entrance to the machine rising, indicating it is now only a few floors away. Right then the stairwell door opens and a strange masked woman in a gray flannel skirt approaches, stops, stares at Billy, then places a hand beneath a plastic flower pinned to her blouse. Immediately the flower begins glowing.

In that moment, Billy is stunned.

He begins backing away, pressing the call button to the elevator hurriedly, as the masked woman approaches. The villain does not speak, only steps slowly forward to follow as Billy struggles to escape, crashing backwards into a tall golden cigarette ashtray. The masked woman aims the flower, which shoots an invisible malignant ink and which vaporizes the ashtray from existence. Billy howls with fear, stamping his feet. As the masked woman moves very close to Billy, the elevator chimes, the mechanical doors open, and Billy rushes inside, securing a narrow escape. When the doors shudder closed, the masked woman makes a final attempt, the stream of acid hissing through the panels, before the machine rattles downward, ending her attack.

In the lobby, the boy detective hurries outside and finds a strange-looking delivery van parked at the curb, idling. Inside the gray vehicle are four well-dressed women, all wearing black masquerade masks. Billy stumbles to a halt as the van pulls away and, in a glimpse, he catches the faded lettering of the rear door: *Property of Gotham Amusement Park*. In his notepad, Billy makes the appropriate marks and wonders onto what strange villains he has stumbled, and upon what nefarious scheme.

EIGHTEEN

Safe at Shady Glens: The boy detective is attempting to watch an episode of *Modern Police Cadet*, but the television room is much too noisy. Why? It is because Mr. Pluto is crying. Professor Von Golum is pacing in front of the television screen, shouting something angrily. Mr. Lunt, in the orange chair beside Billy, is snoring loudly. Each, in his own way, is destroying Billy. Why? The boy detective is getting very agitated, having never seen this episode of *Modern Police Cadet* before. He is unsure where it fits into the nearly seven years of the program's history. In the show the Cadet is wearing a black tie, which usually signifies an episode from Season Two. However, the Cadet is driving the police coupe instead of riding as a passenger, which signals it is the program's very last season. He is also wearing a silver badge—which to the discerning eye means he has already graduated from the Scotland Yard Academy—but his partner from the first three seasons, Benny, a wise-cracking street-tough detective from Edinburgh transplanted to the strange world of London crime, is riding beside him. More disconcerting than all that, the Modern Police Cadet's flat is totally foreign: The Cadet seems to be living alone, no university textbooks from his second-season wife, Trish. Additionally, the Modern Police Cadet is kissing some strange woman, a brunette with very long hair, and because the noise in the television room is so loud, Billy has no idea why any of this might be happening.

Professor Von Golum hisses something at him and he tries to look past and it seems, on the TV, the Modern Police Cadet is now proposing marriage to this strange woman, placing a gigantic ring on her finger. In the next scene, they are actually getting married—the woman in a pretty white dress with a gray veil, Leopold Jones in his cadet uniform, walking down the aisle—and now Billy is pushing Professor Von Golum aside, placing his ear against the television screen.

The boy detective thinks, *Is this woman a spy from the London mob or a plant from ORACLE, Scotland Yard's enemy organization, perhaps? How will Leopold Jones fare in love with someone I have never seen before? How will it all be resolved by the end of the hour?*

Before Billy can discover the answers to these important questions, the show is over and the credits are rolling.

NINETEEN

The boy detective sits on the porch as the Mumford children prepare to test a third rocket, their flashlights flashing in the dark. It is late and the neighborhood is sound asleep, the streetlights flickering solemnly at the end of the narrow street. The Mumford children in their pajamas hurry back and forth on the lawn making final preparations: Gus Mumford in blue, Effie Mumford in purple to match her winter jacket.

"May I ask what is the point of your experiment?" Billy calls out in a hushed voice.

"We are trying to prove that people are social beings coerced by society to be distrustful of one another even though we are all naturally fond and curious of one another. I have it all here in my notes," Effie Mumford says, passing Billy her notepad. "It is my new experiment for next year's science fair."

"Very interesting," Billy says. "And how do you mean to prove that?"

"With this rocket, like a message in a bottle adrift at sea, we are attempting to gain the attention of some other human being. Our first two attempts were, for various reasons, unsuccessful. But the sky is clear tonight and we think we have solved our problem with the firing mechanism."

We have definitely solved the firing mechanism problem! it says in Gus Mumford's note.

"Are we ready?" Effie Mumford asks.

Everyone nods. Billy smiles as Effie Mumford holds the silver launch device in her hand.

"We will begin the countdown. Launch in 10-9-8-7-6-5-4-3-2-1. Launch!" When she presses her small fingers against the silver button, the rocket quickly ignites and shoots deftly through a clearing in the trees straight into the plains of the high night sky. In a moment, the rocket explodes, and in large silver letters a single message becomes brilliant and clear: *HULLO, ANYONE OUT THERE.*

"We misspelled 'hello,'" Effie Mumford whispers, making a note of this in her notebook.

Billy glances up at the sky again and very slowly the silver letters begin to sparkle and fade, and fade, and fade, and soon they are only a glimmer of floating black paper and smoke.

"Now what?" Billy asks.

"Now we wait," Effie Mumford whispers, leaning her elbows on her knees.

"Wait for what?"

"For somebody to reply."

"I see."

The trio sit on the front porch, staring up at the night sky, the stars doing their best twinkling, the moon a quiet coin in a dark fountain, the Mumford children watching and waiting and slowly getting drowsy. Effie Mumford leans against the railing, her eyes fluttering, Gus Mumford has tightened himself into a small ball, and Billy, head growing heavy, begins to drift away, all of them quiet and content beside each other on the Mumford's front porch.

In our town, we feature a variety of adult-
themed bookstores; we think you may be
familiar with the kind. Along the narrow
and dusty aisles are thousands of doe-eyed
women caught in the most mysterious
of poses. Why are there so many terrible
places like this in our town? Because the
heart is terrible—like a rotten tooth, it is
small and soft and weak. It has a terrible
requirement, and that terrible requirement
is mystery. For example, there is one
particular magazine in one particular aisle
in one particular dirty bookstore in our
town called *Girls in Turtlenecks*. That is all
there is: shot after shot of blushing gals in
tight-fitting turtlenecks, naked from the
waist down. We stare at a copy and feel flush.
And somehow, silently, we know the truth:
Airbrushed and honeyed, they are still no
match for the feeling we get waiting to kiss.

TWENTY

In the morning, the boy detective thinks he sees the lady in pink as he is riding the bus. She is a lovely woman in a pink hat hurrying down the street and then—*poof*—she is gone like a dream. Looking out the window, he is surprised when the Sterling Tower, the tallest building in our town, likewise disappears.

Moments later, as the bus moves past the fallen industrial sites toward its destination downtown, the boy detective begins to once again remember the Case of the Haunted Candy Factory. At his best, at his smartest, at his most daring: He returns to remember what he once was—the boy with all the answers, not a miserable young man who is obviously failing, quite miserably.

Following the light through the air vent, the two siblings found themselves directly on the catwalk far above the candy factory. Below them, two gunmen were jimmying the Grape Dynamite machine.

For a second, the two gunmen stared up in disbelief at Billy and Caroline.

"The boy detective!" one of the gunmen snarled. "So *you're* the snooping pests we've caught!"

There was a strange rumbling from within the tunnel behind the opened vent. A skinny man, breathing hard, huffing and puffing, crept out. The boy detective and his sister recognized him almost instantly: the strange bearded dentist, John Victor, their number-one suspect.

The dentist glared at the boy detective.

"What are *those* two doing here?" he asked.

"That's for you to discover," the boy detective retorted.

"How did you ever escape?" the dentist asked. "Those doors were locked!"

"The only tool a good detective ever needs is ingenuity."

"You may have discovered I was the culprit, but it looks like your ingenuity has all but run out."

"We better get rid of these kids right now," one of the gunmen muttered, drawing his pistol near.

"Not so fast!" came a voice just before the factory lights flooded on. Within a moment, the gunmen were surrounded by armed policemen. Flashlights and sirens filled the scene with brightness.

"Just in the nick of time!" the boy detective and his sister shouted with surprise. Daisy Hollis hugged them as well, thanking them for a job well done—*No*.

No.

That is wrong again.

Daisy Hollis was already dead then. Not dead, but missing. Indefinitely. Her remains had never been recovered. The only victim of the Pawn Shop Kidnapper never to be found.

Daisy Hollis did not have the chance to be hugged by anyone again.

Daisy Hollis.

It is a terrible thought. It is a terrible thought the boy detective does not like to consider.

TWENTY-ONE

At recess, Gus Mumford does not punch anyone in the guts, he does not hurl smaller children through the air, he does not poke anyone in the eye: Today he is a lamb. He sits swinging beside the small bald boy, both of their feet dangling in the air. Neither of them speak. In their silence, more than a dozen secrets are shared. Gus Mumford smiles as the other boy smiles and blushes as he blushes. He watches the fold of the other boy's neck and the dimples in his cheeks. He likes the shape of the boy's ears, small and like seashells. He likes how he smells, like powder and fall leaves. He knows he cannot put into words all the thoughts he is thinking so he does not write, he only watches and hopes that the other boy does not suddenly turn to vapor and vanish. When the bell begins to ring, marking the end of recess, the small bald boy quickly rises, takes Gus Mumford's hand and without a word, gently presses Gus's forefinger against his long, pale eyelashes. Look, look, there is one now stuck at the end of his finger. Gus Mumford stares at it and beams. He watches it as all the other children hurry past, disappearing back inside, his heart light and glowing.

At school the following day, Gus Mumford is alarmed to see the seat in front of him is empty. He looks around the room nervously, staring up at the clock, turning to watch if Miss Gale is going to explain, but no. The school bell rings and class is started. Miss Gale asks the class to please take out their spelling workbooks, and *still* the seat before him is unused, the soft bald scalp now a soft fuzzy glow of a memory. Gus Mumford panics and a voice somewhere in the back his throat begins to gurgle. He raises his hand and, as is the case, Miss Gale ignores the small, prodigious fingers there waving so near her face; instead she calls upon Arthur Allen who, out loud, perfectly spells "hemorrhage." Morning classes continue like this: Gus Mumford growing frantic, stirring in his seat, scratching at his desk, watching the classroom door for some signal, some sign, until finally the lunch bell rings and the third-graders, in a uniform burst of chaos, scuttle to their brown-bag lunches. Gus Mumford, hands nervously balled into their most comfortable form—fists—stalks up to Miss Gale's desk, slamming a single note hard against the wood, glaring up at the dark-eyed woman who has, for so long, offered only question, question, question after question, the answers of which Gus Mumford already knows. Here, scribbled dramatically in pencil, is a question Gus Mumford would like to ask, and after Miss Gale's eyes dart down to read it, she is truly surprised by what is being asked, and so, forgoing her usual treatment of the boy, answers rather affectionately: "Oh, he's ill again, I'm afraid."

Gus Mumford's face does not change. He mumbles a small sound—like the saddest sigh of all time, ever, escaping from a weak heart several thousand miles away—and then, after the sound has risen and dissipated, his head grows heavy and hangs down, and Miss Gale's cruel hand is somehow gentle on his neck.

"He had to go back to the hospital. I don't think he'll be rejoining us, I'm afraid."

It is that day that nearly every third grader in the world gets crippled. The poor young dears must bear the brunt of Gus Mumford's unending rage, and he works his way through the playground at recess, torturing, assaulting, maiming. Blood, tears, broken fingernails line the jungle gym, four-square court, sandbox. Boys, girls, small, short, tall, lanky, skinny, fat. Charlie Evans sipping his milk through a straw loses a tooth as he is smashed in the face by what may be either a wrecking ball or Gus Mumford's right fist; Lindsay Scottworth somehow loses a pigtail; after that sad day, it seems poor Bobby Cohen will never walk in a straight line ever again.

TWENTY-TWO

Hidden beneath the front porch later that afternoon, Gus Mumford holds the prominent citizens of Ant City close to his heart, whispering, "Now I have nobody. Now I have no one." He lays there staring at the strange movements of his remaining, segmented friends, quite sure that in their cavernous exploits they are attempting to spell out a message, which, in the boy's mind reads: *WE STILL LOVE GUS.*

TWENTY-THREE

At work, the boy detective is wary: He watches for signs of the masked women. Throughout the day, he looks for a sinister shadow creeping down the aisle between cubicles and is relieved when it is only the youth from the mailroom delivering that week's new mail. Everything seems to be going fine until Billy returns from the washroom and finds that a small business card has been left for him on his seat. As expected, the card reads: *BEWARE: YOU HAVE BEEN WARNED.* Quickly, he disposes of it, running it through the paper shredder. The rest of the day is spent waiting to take his next pill and listening for strange footsteps creeping from behind the curtain of impending doom.

Another strange message has arrived for the boy detective; he discovers the white envelope beneath his door upon returning to Shady Glens that evening. Billy looks down the hall, but no, there is no sign of who may have delivered it. It is again, addressed, in small black handwriting, that simply says: "To the boy detective!" but now an exclamation point has been added. Billy gently opens the letter, slipping his finger beneath the fold, glancing at the marks in the shadowy hallway light. Again, inside is a single piece of yellowed paper which simply reads:

D-11
9-16-19-19-6,
23-19-12-8-26-12, 16 21-12-12-11 6-22-2-25
15-12-19-23.

The boy detective stares at the note, turns to see if he is being watched, then gently folds it and hides it under his bed.

Dear reader, here you can help the boy detective. Match the code D11 with the decoder on your ring to help solve this mystery.

After midnight that evening, when he knows he will not be able to rest, the boy detective pulls himself to his feet, puts on his cardigan and tie, and goes off in pursuit of the cause of his coworker's mystery. He hurries off toward the bus stop, knowing the abandoned amusement park will be the destination of this late-night search. As he waits for the bus, he wonders. He wonders if the young lady in pink might be on the bus tonight. He is disappointed when it arrives and he sees it is almost completely empty and no one is wearing pink.

TWENTY-FOUR

The boy detective suddenly realizes Professor Von Golum is sitting across from him on the bus. Though it is quite late and the old man, as a matter of his age, should be back at Shady Glens resting in his bed, it is only a moment before the Professor stands, retrieves a silver raygun from inside his white hospital robe, and points it at Billy menacingly.

"It is all as easy as this," the old man mutters. "You will be felled, at last, by my immobility ray."

Billy's heart goes cold in his chest.

"Any last words, detective?" the villain asks with a sneer. The town lights flash by their faces as Billy deliberates. The boy detective nods then, opens his mouth, and, instead of speaking, leaps, knocking the weapon from the old man's clawlike hands.

"Oh God, you broke my wrist," the Professor gasps, holding the fractured limb to his chest. "Oh God, I think you really did."

The bus driver, now aware of the conflict, hits the brakes, the two combatants falling atop one another, and Billy, securing the raygun, dashes off the bus, his heart pounding, his hand sore, his red face showing his grave embarrassment.

TWENTY-FIVE

It is through the abandoned amusement park that the boy detective
creeps. Having done his best to ignore the mysterious incident of the
young man who disappeared from the Mammoth offices; having tried
to disregard the certainly nefarious threats of the masked women who
quickly escaped into the van marked with the faded letters "Property
of Gotham Amusement Park," Billy quietly steps forward. He follows
the strange darkened path past the Jolly Roger roller coaster—now only
a wire catastrophe, its schooner-shaped cars leaning crowded against
a crushed snow cone machine—then past the great Unicorn Carousel
—the gentle animals now mostly dismembered, their horns having
been stolen by mean-spirited vandals long ago—further still past Dead
Man's Curve—with its ornate miniature Studebakers wrecked upon
one another—to a spot deep inside the park where he stops and listens
to the strange recording of a high-pitched voice he now recognizes:
"It's always twilight for lovers . . . It's always twilight for love . . ."

The sound echoes from the Twilight Tunnel of Love rising ahead,
the daring shape of a man-made mountain overgrown with false ja-
ponica and ivy, a glowing red heart still active, twinkling with sequins
above the narrow cavelike entrance.

Quietly, he hustles over the fallen red velvet ropes, over the sturdy
chain-link fence erected to prevent exactly this kind of trespass, and
into a lovely swan-shaped car, the ride still cycling, whether by mystery or malice or simply wind, the crooner's voice growing louder as
the opening approaches and the ride jerks and jolts Billy into absolute darkness.

From out of nowhere and lit only by the enormous holes which have grown along the opening of the man-made mountain, a silvery cupid's arrow hurtles toward Billy's head. He ducks and the cherubim's pointy arrow narrowly misses his neck. The ride bustles along up and over a pink-colored waterfall, crashing down past Lover's Leap. A pair of gigantic mechanical lips open and close up ahead as the swan-shaped car draws deeper into the cave. Hurrying off the ride, he finds a small, dimly lit catwalk. There in the dark he can hear the sounds of people at work: the shuffling of feet, the subdued tone of mumbles so familiar to his own work environment that creeping through a small opening he is not surprised to find a very familiar-looking office—gray cubicles, greenish carpeting, and a small army of well-dressed and professional-looking women, some in business suits, some in skirts, all in black canvas masks. Billy, spying from behind a row of empty desks, listens as the strange creatures answer their ringing phones, the hum of the Tunnel of Love's theme song still echoing from above somewhere, barely audible among the busy jostling of confidential whispering, pencils on papers, fingers on typewriters.

From what he can tell, it is indeed an office of some kind, and what these masked women are selling is a kind of uncanny extermination service. The paperwork piled high in stacks beside Billy makes it clear: They are in the business of making other people disappear. Two of the lovely masked henchwomen walk past Billy whispering, their soft black high heels marching away. Billy creeps down the empty aisle and stops, finding himself staring down at a pair of glossy black Mary Janes. Looking up, he sees a masked woman in a blue suit who immediately begins shouting. The boy detective discovers he is carrying Professor Von Golum's immobility raygun and, without hesitating, presses the snub nose of the weapon against his adversary's neck.

"Who is in charge of this nefarious scheme?" the detective asks.

"That would be Margaret," the masked woman whispers. "But she's in a meeting."

Forcing his quarry through what looks like a lobby, the boy detective thrusts open a meeting-room door and aims his weapon at the tall masked woman at the head of the table.

"What kind of sinister plot is at work here?" Billy asks.

The masked woman, Margaret, rises and tilts her head back, laughing.

"There is nothing sinister here to speak of," the masked woman says, suddenly standing. "What we do here is a professional service for our paying customers."

"I do not understand," the boy detective says.

"We vaporize people."

"You *vaporize* people?"

"Using a totally scientific approach, we are fashioning a world free of puzzling personal relationships, where one's heart is never broken, where a harsh word is never spoken. At your inclination, people who hurt you are simply made to disappear. The mysterious, bewildering nature of love is thus made predictable, tempered, and pleasing."

"I see."

"For once, this complicated problem of human emotion is solved quite easily—with an end to the grave panic of unrequited desire and the indecent butterflies of high anxiety."

"I like the butterflies," Billy whispers.

"Pardon me?"

"I *like* the butterflies."

"The world must come to understand that love is chaos. We have found a simple solution to a mystery that for centuries has been mankind's undoing."

"I believe you have made a terrible mistake here," Billy says, shaking his head. The room is very silent then. He pushes his bifocals against his face and frowns. "What you're doing seems very awful to me."

"Well, you're a weak fool, obviously. Prepare to be easily forgotten," Margaret hisses. She turns to two of her masked cohorts and points at the boy detective angrily. "Doris, Veronica, please show our guest here how quickly we do away with unwanted annoyances."

The boy detective feels himself begin to tremble as the room starts to spin. Doris, her name monogrammed in cursive white on her gray dress, seems to be the tallest in the room full of masked women. She nods and stands, clutching at the fake purple flower pinned near her bosom, taking aim on Billy's stricken face. Veronica, another underling with dark hair in a brown business suit, her name also stitched in cursive letters, follows the order, but then stops.

"Pardon me, Margaret?" Veronica whispers, her hand raised nervously. "I was wondering . . ."

"Yes?"

"I don't feel very appropriate doing this."

"Excuse me?" Margaret asks.

"Well I just don't feel it's all that appropriate just vaporizing anybody. I mean, well, some of us have been talking, and well, we think . . . we think what we're doing may not be absolutely right."

"Pardon me?" Margaret asks.

"We think maybe we made . . . some mistakes here," another masked woman in beige whispers. Her name, stitched in white lettering, is Gayle. "Like a month ago. The man with the beard. That . . . was a terrible mistake."

Nearly all of the masked women begin to nod their heads.

"And the woman, with the long red hair. That was an awful mistake as well," Veronica says.

"I don't recall that particular case," Margaret says angrily. "I don't recall *any* mistakes."

"Then there was the pet dog. I believe that was our fault," Gayle says.

Margaret's hand begins to curl up into claws.

"We just don't like what's been done. We just didn't know how to mention it to you," Veronica says. "But we don't believe we ought to do this anymore."

The boy detective begins to nod, too, and slowly begins to lower his weapon.

"You don't like what's been *done?*" Margaret whispers. "You think this is all a *mistake?*"

The masked women all nod their heads slowly, turning to each other in agreement.

"You weak fools," she says. From above the din of the bustling office, Margaret stands. "You're all fools," she whispers. "Terrible, spineless, fools. I'm not sorry for what I've done. The world is utter chaos and I refuse to live in that way." Margaret then opens her purse and lifts out a glowing white plastic flower.

"No, please," Billy says. "Put that down."

"No."

In a flash, Margaret the masked woman raises the plastic flower and, amid shouts of protest, fires the strange vanishing ink upon her own chest, so that immediately and without ado, she vaporizes. It is very awkward for all the masked women as the puff of smoke, their former friend, escapes into the air. Billy does not know what to say or do. After that, it is very, very quiet in the room.

TWENTY-SIX

The boy detective waits beside the Mumford children, watching as the sky turns from a blanket of blue into a cloud of sparkling light. It is so very late, but still they watch and wait and watch and wait, Billy telling them about his strange adventures, the mysteries and clues leading up to him solving his favorite cases—the Haunted Candy Factory, the Phantom Lighthouse, the Singing Diamond, the Unbreakable Safe. When he is finished with his stories, they all look up and suddenly the night sky is a fading blue and black canvas of twinkling silver stars. Very soon, Mrs. Mumford brings them hot cocoa and asks if they would like some blankets and everyone shouts *Yes!* She takes a seat beside them on the porch and tells Billy she is glad he is out there watching over the children. Immediately he blushes, but in the dark no one sees it. Mrs. Mumford sits beside her children and Billy under the blanket and all four of them stare up at the sky, waiting for some kind of reply.

That evening, after the Mumford children and their mother have fallen asleep near Billy's feet, a single burst of blue-white fire explodes in the sky. With a powdery burst of sparkles, comes a single response: *Y-E-S*. Billy hurries off the porch and, searching through his pockets, finds Professor Von Golum's immobility raygun and fires erratically into the sky. Just as the outlines of the single letters begin to fade, the strange ray surrounds them with a momentous glow, and they stay: fixed, frozen, temporarily unbroken in the air. Billy nods and, making sure the Mumford children and Mrs. Mumford are safe, rushes across the street to Shady Glens.

TWENTY-SEVEN

The boy detective walks down the short hallway of Shady Glens, past Professor Von Golum and Mr. Pluto, who are both wearing Billy's clothes. There is the Professor in the blue cardigan and there is Mr. Pluto wearing one of Billy's orange owl ties. They are both grinning, their teeth gray and crooked.

Professor Von Golum whistles, winking at him. "See that, Mr. Pluto, old boy. There, in front of you, is a genuine specimen: a true-life, yellow-bellied coward in the flesh. Look, look what he did to my arm!" the Professor howls, his bandaged left wrist hanging fractured by his side.

Billy walks by silently.

"Go on, boy detective, give us your wittiest response. I am daring you. Go on, Billy, please surprise me. Go on, say *anything*."

Billy ignores him, walks into his room, which is unlocked. His room has been ransacked. He sighs, staring into his closet. It is evident that all of his other clothes are now missing. All he has now is what he is wearing. In this moment, he considers suicide, then decides it would only be worse if he tried but failed again.

TWENTY-EIGHT

What the boy detective does is this: He crosses his small, dusty room and holds the lady's pink purse in his hands, staring down at it. With it next to him, he does not feel so bad about everything. He smiles, thinking of the look on her face as the lady in pink danced. He decides that tomorrow he will find her, without fail. Without fail, he will find her and return the purse to her and ask if perhaps they might talk about something very nice. He will ask if she is maybe not doing anything else that evening, and, well, maybe if she would . . . He does not know the words he will use, but decides he will ask her something and hope that she will then smile in return.

The boy detective says his prayers and whispers goodnight to his owl alarm clock. He does—honestly, every night. He says it like this: "Goodnight father, goodnight mother, goodnight bedroom, goodnight Mr. Owl Alarm Clock," like it is a first, middle, and last name. He switches on the light and immediately it begins snowing. A soft white haze fills the room, as Billy, thinking about the lady in pink, soon falls asleep.

It is not long before he is awakened, as the boy detective is every night, by Mr. Lunt's screams.

This time, however, he jumps out of bed and follows the sound down the hall to Mr. Lunt's room before Nurse Eloise can arrive. He throws open the door, switches on the light, and catches Professor Von Golum and Mr. Pluto, both dressed up as ghosts in sheets, standing over Mr. Lunt's bed, moaning quietly. Professor Von Golum howls and tries to run past Billy. Billy grabs the sheet as the Professor heads into his room. Mr. Pluto only stands there, grinning. Mr. Lunt, an old frightened fellow with a droopy white mustache and wrinkled white pajamas, looks up, shaking.

"My Lord! I thought for sure it was that no-good ne'er-do-well partner of mine cursing me from beyond the grave, trying to find out where I had hidden our last bit of treasure from a vault robbery back in ninteen-ought-nine!"

Billy shakes his head, angry, turning off the light, dropping the sheet, heading back to his room.

It is at that moment that the owl alarm clock begins ringing.

TWENTY-NINE

The boy detective, at work, is having a hard time concentrating.

"Blah, blah, blah-blah-blah-blah, blah, blah, a, blah."

"Blah, blah, blah-blah-blah-blah, blah, blah, a, blah."

"Blah, blah, blah-blah-blah-blah, blah, blah, a, blah."

"Blah, blah, blah-blah-blah-blah, blah, blah, a, blah."

The only thing he can think of is the lady in pink: her face, her eyeglasses, her small hands. He says her name to himself again and again: Penny, Penny, Penny.

In the bathroom, he winks to himself and says, "Hello, Penny. Penny, my name is Billy. It is a pleasure meeting you, Penny," before Larry enters and asks him exactly what he thinks he is doing.

THIRTY

A surprise: The boy detective is on the bus again. Like always, it is raining, but let's pay no mind. He is looking for the lady in pink. She is not
on the bus. He gets off at the next stop and waits and hops onto the next
bus that comes. He searches and searches and she's not on this one either. Billy gets off the second bus and stands again, waiting in the rain.

The boy detective gets on and off buses all night: climbing aboard
a bus, looking for Penny, then hopping off. He looks more and more
sad and disheveled as the hours pass. His owl tie is wrinkled and hanging lopsided around his neck. The owl tie has all but given up.

Finally, Billy gets on a bus and Penny is there, sitting by herself,
a lovely blur of pink staring out the window sadly. Billy takes out her
purse and hands it to her. She slowly takes it, very, very nervously. She
gets up to run off, but Billy stops her.

"Please, wait . . . I won't tell anyone. I won't tell. You can trust me."

Penny nods. Billy sits beside her, silently, for a long time. Then after
many, many quiet moments, Penny speaks in a whisper. It is clear she is
trying to shout, but the sound of her voice remains only a quiet peep:
"You . . . you scared me."

"I'm sorry."

"You scared me very badly. You shouldn't go about grabbing at
people. They might have a good reason for what they're doing."

"I'm sorry."

"Well, I could call the authorities on *you*! Grabbing people like
that. I could. I really could. But it's none of my business what you do.
I mind my own business. I mind it. I think you should apologize to
me. You really ought to."

"I'm very sorry."

The lady nods. Billy sits beside her silently for a long time again, and then the lady speaks, whispering, looking at the pink purse.

"Thank you for returning this to me. I'm sorry I shouted at you."

"Shouted?"

"I'm sorry I raised my voice. It's just that this purse means a lot to me."

"It's very . . . pretty."

"I . . . I don't own any other color clothing. A pink purse is hard to find."

"Pardon me?"

"I . . . I don't own any other color clothing."

"Besides pink?"

"Pink and brown. They're my favorite colors."

"They're very . . . pretty."

"Why did you follow me?"

"I . . . I don't know. I saw you and . . . you look . . . My name's Billy."

"Pleased to meet you. I'm Penny."

"Hello."

The two of them sit in silence for a few moments. Penny itches her nose and then whispers:

"I . . . I went four days without speaking to anyone this week. My longest record is thirty-one. Thirty-one days without talking to anybody."

"Thirty-one days? That's an awful long time."

"I don't like talking with people. You never know what they're thinking."

"You're like me," Billy says.

"I don't know. Maybe. Do you like jigsaw puzzles?"

"I love jigsaw puzzles."

"So do I. Ha."

When the lady laughs: *enchantment*.

Billy nods and smiles. "Maybe, maybe you'd like to go somewhere with me, to sit maybe. We don't have to talk, specifically. We can just sit somewhere, a diner, a café, anyplace. Would you like to go somewhere with me?"

"My sister goes with men to nightclubs. She wears black lipstick some nights."

"We could go to a nightclub if you like. It might be too late now though, maybe."

"I think . . . I think I'd like to go somewhere with windows."

"Windows? OK, I think I know a place."

The boy detective and Penny sit across each other in a small yellow diner, staring down at their coffee. Outside it is sunny. People walk past the windows, heading to work. Billy and Penny whisper very strange secrets to each other:

"My sister is a pianist and named her dog after me."

"I had a sister," Billy says. "She . . . she died a long time ago."

"Was she pretty? I think she would be very pretty."

"Yes, she was. And smart. She loved animals too. She's been gone for more than ten years now."

"Well, I like animals too, but I am allergic to most kinds. I had a cat but it left me."

It is then that the boy detective notices that Penny is wearing a wedding ring.

"Are you—are you married?"

With this, Penny, upset, runs out of the diner. Billy stands, watching her go. She has left her purse and jacket and scarf. Billy only wavers there, staring at her things, perplexed. Penny slowly returns, creeping back to the table. She sits down, straightens her glasses, and begins speaking, staring at her coffee.

"I'm sorry. It's just, my husband . . . my husband was in a horrible automobile accident. He's . . . he's . . . he's been dead a long time, but . . . it's still upsetting."

"I'm sorry."

"OK."

"OK," the boy detective repeats.

"Yes, well, yes."

"Maybe I should . . ."

"Would you like to know why I took all those pens?"

"All right."

"I don't know why. I really don't. There is something wrong with me."

"It's OK."

"No, no. I'd like to ask you something."

"OK."

"Do you think there's any way for people to stop themselves from doing bad things?"

"I . . . don't know."

"Because I don't think so. I don't see a way."

"I don't know what to say to that."

"I should go home now."

"Would you like to meet sometime and talk again?"

"I don't know."

"Well, could we maybe meet here again, some night?"

"OK. Only please don't scare me again. I didn't like that."

"OK."

"Billy?"

"Yes?"

"Are you going to tell the police what I've done?"

"No."

"Thank you, Billy."

Penny and Billy sit across from one another, staring silently.

"May I walk you to the bus stop?" he asks. "We can walk past the park."

"OK. If you like." She laughs, nervous. "But do not try and kiss me."

In our town, there is a secret spot where you can still see the stars at night, believe it or not. It is the only spot like that left, unclouded by the rumbling factories, uninhibited by the dwindling skyscrapers rising nearby. It is a good place to go to walk and talk in whispers. Following the little hill that rises from the park to a small clearing which overlooks the statue of the armless general on his bronze steed, most of us later remember this spot as the first place we knew we might be in love.

CHAPTER THIRTY-FOUR

THE CASE OF THE GHOSTLY FIGURE

What is the boy detective's greatest fear?
The bus driver: impolite passengers.
The mailman: attack dogs with hideous fangs.
The police chief: masked men in dark alleys.
The schoolteacher: children with weapons.
The banker: counterfeiters.
    Definitely counterfeiters.
The rocket scientist: The deathly quiet of
    outer space.

ONE

It is one month later and outside it is raining. It is perfect now, the rain, because it is a good reason for the boy detective and Penny to sit a little closer—but they do not touch. At the bus stop, on the street corner, beneath a faded red awning, Penny and Billy stand beside one another and smile at each other silently, happily, their hands almost, almost touching. They are barely speaking. Together they are trying hard to think of something funny and smart to say, but somehow they are so nervous they cannot, and yet their silence is perfect—it is the perfect silence of anticipation, the anticipation before the very best kiss ever.

It is a month of these moments: riding beside each other on the bus late at night, after Penny has finished her job cleaning the small white offices, after Billy, his owl tie loose around his neck, waits for her at the bus stop. He thinks of a knock-knock joke but then forgets it by the time Penny arrives and they sit beside each other, riding to the diner where they will drink many cups of coffee and stare down into their mugs, droplets of rain falling from their noses. Once—at the perfect, exact time—Billy catches a drop with the tip of his finger as it gently runs from the soft end of Penny's eyelashes, and that touch is enough to make each nearly panic with love.

On the bus route home, it is still raining—because it is *always* raining —but these two hardly notice now. Inside, beside one another, Billy and Penny smile silently, listening to the sound of their slow breathing. Their knees are almost touching—they are so close to touching. Billy and Penny laugh nervously and when finally it happens—when their knees finally touch—losing their breath, they must laugh to keep from kissing each other madly.

It is the first touch and so it goes: Billy goes to take her hand suddenly, the thought of her hand so close it is killing them both, but Penny pulls away. His hand touches her wedding ring accidentally, and she pulls her fingers back as if burned.

"I'm sorry. I shouldn't be so jumpy," she says.

"No, no, I'm sorry. It's only . . . your hand is so small sitting there. It looked lonely."

"Ha, ha," Penny chortles. "You are trying to seduce me."

"No," Billy says with a red face. "I would never . . ."

"I am sorry. I don't know why I said that."

"No, no, I am sorry."

The boy detective and Penny sit, side by side, terribly sad and terribly frightened. They cannot go on much longer like this, they are both sure of it. Penny stands, pulling the signal for the bus.

"Good . . . goodnight, Billy."

Penny shakes Billy's hand and hurries off the bus. Billy watches her through the window. He stares down at his empty hand. He stares at it like it has somehow lied to him.

TWO

At Shady Glens, the boy detective walks past Mr. Lunt's room. Within, Professor Von Golum and Mr. Pluto are standing over the old man's bed, trying to hypnotize him with a gold pocket watch, dangling it back and forth, whispering to him gently.

"You're getting sleepy, my dear friend, very sleepy . . . Now tell us the whereabouts of that treasure. Yes, yes, my dear old friend, just get that terrible burden off your chest . . ."

Billy shakes his head and continues into his room.

Billy lays in bed, smiling, staring up at the ceiling.

"Goodnight, Penny."

He suddenly must kiss his pillow for some reason. He does, and then, embarrassed, does it again.

"Goodnight, Penny."

The boy detective begins laughing uncontrollably. He begins jumping on his bed, too happy to ever sleep again. He considers taking a pill to calm down, perhaps an Ativan or Seroquel, but decides he will not. He switches on the light and the snow falls voluminously across the floor. Billy lays there and makes angels with his arms and legs. He feels the soft flakes melting on his face and begins counting until he has reached one million. It is the first night in many months that he does not dream terrible dreams.

THREE

After school, a girl with a brown ponytail and blue eye shadow is climbing into a van. The teachers are milling around the parking lot, standing by their cars, smoking, and so they ignore what this particular girl is doing. The girl stops for a moment and looks at the van. It is black and there is dirt all along the fenders and wheels, but it looks all right. A man in black, whose face is mostly hidden by shadows, is driving. He is whistling. He is pointing at the girl and she is smiling. The girl closes the door and the van pulls away. Suddenly, somewhere, someone begins screaming.

FOUR

The boy detective finds the Mumford children busy at work on a new experiment underneath their front porch. As they wait for the school bus to arrive, Effie Mumford operates a large, portable silver tape player, busily recording the sounds of the morning: the bustling of their movements and the treble of their soft breathing. Gus Mumford is, for some reason, closely watching a compass, the magnetic needle ticking north predictably.

"What is all this?" Billy asks, crawling beneath the wood slats.

"Do you believe in ghosts, Billy?" Effie asks in a whisper.

"Pardon me?"

"Do you believe that after you die, there is some other world or something? Or is it all black?"

"I don't know. I don't know what I believe. Why do you ask?"

"I have decided I would like to know, either way, which one is real."

"I see. You may find it harder to prove or disprove than you think."

"It just seems very unlikely to me that we somehow go someplace else," the girl continues. "It is very, very hard for me to believe that there is some other world, and yet there just doesn't seem to be any conclusive evidence on behalf of an argument *against* believing," Effie Mumford says, still whispering.

"You may be right."

"What do you imagine happens?"

Billy thinks for a moment and says, "I'm afraid that when you die, you simply cease to exist. Like a candle being blown out. You are gone, completely."

"And the flame from the candle goes where?"

"Nowhere. It just goes very dark."

Gus Mumford then asks, with a note: *But what of ghosts?*

"Perhaps it is only wishful thinking on our parts," Billy says. "Perhaps we have only invented this idea to comfort ourselves."

"Wishful thinking," Effie says with a sigh. "Yes. But I just do not like the idea that when I die there will be nothing. It seems very anticlimactic. It seems very disappointing."

"Yes, it does."

"I would like to believe there is a place of some kind where you meet people who have died—famous people, presidents, scientists, everyone you love—but that does not seem reasonable."

"It does not," Billy says in agreement. "So how do you plan to investigate?"

"My plan is to record sounds from various locations around town and then analyze the evidence. I am quite sure that I will be able to find something of a conclusive nature, either way."

"I see. May I ask why you are making a recording underneath your own front porch?"

Effie Mumford is quiet for a moment, then slowly points to the soft mound where her poor bunny, Mr. Buttons, is buried.

"Of course," Billy says, nodding.

"Also, Gus said last night he heard footsteps on the porch."

Gus Mumford blinks, handing Billy a note which reads: *There were definitely footsteps.*

"Any results as of yet?" Billy asks.

"No, not from under here. We did discover something strange on the tape we made near the abandoned cave on the other side of those factories."

"What did you hear?"

Gus Mumford holds up a small note: *A girl's voice.*

Billy squints, reading the short sentence. "A girl's voice?"

Gus nods and hands him a second note: *It sounded like she was singing a lullaby. It was creepy.*

"I can imagine," Billy says.

"There are some places that just harbor supernatural activity," Effie Mumford adds. "Very old houses, recent crime scenes, the Bermuda triangle, for instance. We think perhaps it may be caused by magnetism. Gus is using a compass to test that theory."

Gus Mumford holds out a small compass, the narrow needle ticking back and forth, always leading north. He hands Billy a note which reads: *All is normal here.*

"Why this sudden interest in the goings-on of death?" Billy asks, pulling himself to his feet.

The Mumford children are silent and then Effie, looking up, answers with a frown. "A girl from my school, Parker Lane, was kidnapped yesterday."

"Kidnapped?"

"Someone put her in a van and just disappeared."

"And you have reason to believe she is already dead?"

"She is the most unlikable person I have ever met. I think for sure someone would have killed her by now."

"I see."

"I mean, if she was murdered by someone, you would have a hard time blaming them."

"Yes, I understand. But still, I hope you find she is alive and returned to safety," Billy says. "If you discover anything conclusive with your experiment, please let me know."

"We will," the girl says and returns to her recording.

FIVE

At work, at his desk, the boy detective is talking on the phone. He is scribbling Penny's name over and over again in his salesperson script. Larry peeks over from across the aisle and smiles.

"Yes, it's exactly that, sir, a miracle," Billy mumbles. "A miracle of modern living. Hair-replacement surgery can be expensive and dangerous. So why risk it? What we offer you is quality hair replacement without the serious dangers and side effects."

"Oh no, poor kid. You've got a girl on the mind, isn't that right?" Larry asks.

Billy blushes. Larry pats him on the back.

"The only advice I can offer is this: Maintain an air of mystery. Women love it. Tall, dark, mysterious, that's me. Keep her guessing is what I always say."

Billy nods and blushes again. He picks up the telephone to begin his next sales call, but Melinda leans over his cubicle and smiles awkwardly.

"Billy, I need to speak with you for a moment."

"OK."

"I'd like to talk to you about your performance here at Mammoth so far."

"OK."

"You've been here two months now, yes?"

"Yes."

"We think you're doing a terrific job, but we've decided to transfer you to evenings."

"Evenings?"

"Yes. The graveyard shift."

"The graveyard shift," Billy says with a sigh.

"The truth is that it has always been our most profitable market, the late-night time slot. It's the time when the infirmed and the grieving generally tend to reminisce, and a voice—a tender voice—can work wonders for their self-esteem. We think you've been doing a great job on days and want to give you an opportunity to continue to grow in our organization. The night shift means more responsibility: You'll be on your own here, no supervision, no one standing over you—just you and your customers, all night. What do you think?"

"What if I say no?"

"This is really less of a request and more of an assignment. I'm only asking because I felt like framing it as a question would you give you the feeling of empowerment, a necessary element in maintaining a terrific sales team."

"Terrific."

"Terrific, you'll start tomorrow night."

"OK. Great."

Melinda smiles one more stiff smile before she hurries off, disappearing back into her office. Larry saunters over, frowning, shaking his head.

"That is the look of a condemned man. You got the graveyard shift, huh?"

"Yes."

"It's not so bad. If you don't mind talking to ghosts."

"Ghosts?"

"Sure, sure. Half of them are in some morphine-induced haze where you can practically hear the heart monitor beeping in the background. *Beep-beep-beep*. The other half, the widowers and survivors of whatever car crash left them standing, well, all they can think about is 'How come?' How come they're still alive and their other half isn't. They're good as dead themselves. All of them trapped in that vast profundity, asking the same question, trying to solve the same great mystery of life and death. Pretty easy sales either way, though, buddy."

"I don't think I want to talk to ghosts."

"Good luck, pal."

Billy, at his desk, finds an Ativan and carefully places it on his tongue. He swallows and stares at the telephone, hoping it will explode suddenly.

The office is completely empty and dark that following night. It is silent. After the cleaning lady in her powder blue outfit appears and then disappears, there is no one else around. Billy, sitting in his black office chair, wheels himself up and down the aisle. He times himself as he does a lap of all three aisles. His best time? Four minutes, eight seconds. He flosses his teeth with the corner of a piece of paper. He puts his feet up on the desk. He stares at the telephone and then at the clock up on the wall, waiting, waiting, waiting.

At work later that night, the boy detective is speaking to a customer. The customer, apparently, no longer has a face.

"No, sir, I'm not sure exactly how that works, with the bandages. But I'm sure there must be some way to properly attach it."

The customer is a victim of a horrible automobile accident. "Well, like I said, pal, it's the loneliness, to be honest, looking like this. That's what really hurts. The skin graft ain't nothing next to being stared at and eating in restaurants all alone. *Table for one*, there's the real brain damage, you know? I can't tell you the last time I talked to a girl, let alone, well, you know, held her hand, if you know what I mean. I think you do. But now, let me ask you this, buddy, did you say you have a beard to go along with everything?"

"Yes, sir, we do."

"Well, the mustache and the beard together, that's what I'd like."

"Would you like it rush-delivered at a minimal cost?"

"No, no rush. I've got plenty of time here. All I got is time."

"If I may have your address then for delivery . . ."

"It's the hours sitting in the dark alone like this that get me. If you see what I mean."

"Yes," Billy whispers, closing his eyes.

"They said they only give me a 10 percent chance. That's what I keep thinking over."

"Pardon me?"

"The doctors. They only give me a 10 percent chance that I'll make it. That's what I don't like. Waiting here alone, trying not to sleep because I'm afraid I won't ever wake up in the morning. I don't mind dying, I don't. I just don't want to have to go through it alone like this."

"Please, sir, let me send your order out rush-delivery as a courtesy."

"If you like."

"It's the least I can do."

"Do you mind staying on the line for a while, talking? I mean, I'll buy something else. Maybe a wig, or something for my sister."

"Yes," Billy whispers. "I can speak for a few more minutes."

"I don't sleep so well."

Billy nods to himself in agreement. Like a phantom, he has almost disappeared, the man's faraway voice a single, sad thread keeping Billy attached by the ear to his own body. He lays his head down at his desk. For a moment he is asleep, the phone beside his ear uttering a soft, gentle buzzing.

Suddenly, from the corner of his eye, he sees a strange shape looming. It is a figure. In the shadows of the office it moves, creeping from cubicle to cubicle until, near the lobby, Billy hears a door slam. He sets the phone down on his desk, quietly walks down the aisle, past the modern-looking lobby decorated with enormous advertisements for hair-replacement products, and finds the door to the stairwell open. "Hello?" he whispers, terrified. There is no reply. Staring at the partly open door, he notices some fingerprints, black, very small, right along the edge of the doorframe. Small fingerprints. *The fingerprint set.* A shudder runs past his heart and travels throughout his entire body. The fingerprints slowly fade and then disappear completely. He whispers, "Caroline," though he does not quite know the reason. Dizzy, he grabs a stapler from the receptionist's desk and raises it over his head. He opens the door and shouts, waiting for the strange figure to leap out. Of course, there is nothing. Or at least we think it is nothing. Holding his breath, Billy hears the soft sound of someone's breath as they make their way back into the shadows of the office building.

In our daily newspapers, there are
professional services that advertise unique
abilities to speak with the deceased. You
may find their ads beside descriptions of
missed connections and rebuilt automotive
devices. Their offices contain no furniture.
They are silent gray rooms where, along
the floor, there are dozens and dozens of
radios from nearly every country in the
world, or so it seems. It is in these strange
offices that a professionally dressed woman
will ask you where your loved ones lost
their lives, and, gazing among the rows and
rows of oddly shaped radios, she will nod
silently and then point. "From Iceland,"
she will say. "Everyone who dies in Iceland
ends up here." You will hold your ear up
to the crisscross pattern of the radio's
speaker. She will utter a word or two and
then switch the switch. Soon, you will be
surprised to hear a familiar voice speaking.

SIX

The boy detective is daydreaming as he rides the bus back to Shady Glens that morning.

Hidden beneath the Argos' front porch, the three children, Billy, Caroline, and Fenton, were all huddled around the True-Life Junior Detective kit.

"Oh, you're doing it all wrong," Caroline muttered, unhappily tugging the fingerprint set from Fenton's small hands.

"No, this is how it says to do it on the box," the chubby boy in his red beanie replied.

"Look, no, it's all over the place now. Billy's going to get mad."

It's OK, just be more careful with it, Billy says, sitting there on the bus.

"See, Billy can't be mad at me. We're best friends," Fenton argued.

"Well, he was my brother before he was your friend."

"That doesn't mean *anything*. He didn't ask to be your brother. It just happened that way. He *chose* to be my friend."

Caroline straightened her dress and crossed her arms over her chest.

"That's it, I'm done playing with you, Fenton. You hog the fingerprint ink."

"I won't hog it anymore."

"No, I'm going to go ride my bicycle alone."

"Don't go, I'm sorry," Fenton whispered.

Don't go, I'm sorry, Billy whispers.

"No, I'm going to play by myself," Caroline muttered.

"Please, don't leave," Fenton begged.

"Sing the song then."

Don't make him sing the song, Billy says.

"Please, don't make me sing the song."

Fenton grabbed Caroline's hand and frowned.

"Then I'm going inside."

"OK. All right." Fenton, sitting cross-legged, held one arm over his head and one to his side. *"I'm a little teapot, short and stout, here is my handle, here is my spout . . .* Will you let me use the fingerprint set now?"

"Fine, I guess."

Billy shakes his head, smiling.

"Can I tell you both a secret?" Fenton asked.

"All right."

Yes.

"I wish Billy were my brother. I wish I was in your family."

"But you're not," Caroline whispered, haughtily shaking her head.

"I know. But I wish I was. I really wish I was."

Billy smiles and says, *Well, if it's so important to you, we'll just say you are from now on.*

"OK, thanks, Billy."

"Well, he really isn't."

He is from now on.

"He is?"

Yes. All three of us will always be friends, we will always be together.

Billy looks up suddenly and sees he is talking to an empty aisle of seats. He glances around the bus and frowns. The bus squeals to a stop and fills with eager, fresh-scrubbed office workers. The day-dream is gone.

SEVEN

At school that day, Gus Mumford draws a picture of his teacher, Miss Gale, being eaten alive by deadly snakes. A cobra goes right for her jugular vein; a rattlesnake gobbles up her left leg. Gus Mumford hates the sound of his teacher's voice, the way she tilts her square-shaped head on her long prim neck when she asks a question to which Gus Mumford, of course, already knows the answer. By now the young lad has nearly given up. He no longer even attempts to raise his hand. Instead, he stares down at the strange drawing on his desk, wondering if perhaps if it would ruin the composition if he were to add a great green boa constrictor.

At recess, Gus Mumford notices Missy Blackworth, her red hair dappled with sunlight, while she tries, as secretly as she can, to pass out a number of small notes. From his spot at the top of the jungle gym, Gus Mumford sees the girl hand one to Judy Alexander, the tallest girl in the grade, one to Patrick Arlington, the shortest boy in the grade, and one to Cecil McAbee, perhaps the chubbiest boy ever. Gus Mumford squints his eyes and watches as Missy Blackworth hands a note to nearly all of the third graders, including Portia Orr, the girl who frequently urinates while sitting at her desk. Gus Mumford hurries down the monkey bars and across the small expanse of the schoolyard, knocks Cecil McAbee to the ground, and tears the small correspondence from his chubby white hands. He holds the note close to his face and reads the writing, which is small and dainty:

THANK YOU
FOR ATTENDING MY BIRTHDAY PARTY AND
MAKING IT SUCH A SPECIAL OCCASION

The message is followed by Missy's curly inked name. Gus Mumford growls, crumples up the note, and stomps off in a rage toward a trio of unsuspecting seven-year-olds, who, seeing the bully's shadow drawing near, immediately begin to scream.

In the classroom once again, Miss Gale decides to test the third grade's vocabulary. Vocabulary is, without a doubt, Gus Mumford's best and most favorite subject. Having given up on speech, the boy has simply fallen in love with the sight of the written word and decides that if he knows the answers he will at least try to offer a response to his teacher's simpleminded questions. Miss Gale takes the class vocabulary workbook from her desk and cocks one narrow eyebrow, smiling coyly.

"Now, class, who can tell me the meaning of the word 'pugnacious'?"

Like a flare, Gus Mumford's hand rises deftly into the air. Clearly he is the first, his limb waving back and forth right in front of Miss Gale's desk. It is as though the boy is invisible, however, as if the appendage belongs to some small, contentious phantom: the fingers waving back and forth do nothing to summon the teacher's attention. Finally, Miss Gale calls on Walter Scott, who mumbles, "Um . . . does it mean furry?"

"No. Not quite, Walter."

Alisha Bell is called on next. Since she wears glasses, she is often mistakenly assumed to be intelligent. Her glasses, in Gus Mumford's mind, have given her an unfair advantage.

"Yes, Alisha? Do you have a guess?"

"Is it . . . um . . . really ugly?"

"No, not quite, dear."

Arnold Reyes raises his hand slowly, lacking any kind of confidence whatsoever.

"Arnold, yes?"

"Is it a color?"

"No. No, Arnold. Any further guesses?"

Gus Mumford nearly dislocates his shoulder, waving his hand in front of the teacher's face so rapidly.

"Well, class, it means someone who likes to fight."

"Ohhh," the class responds, nodding slowly.

Gus Mumford hisses like a snake, banging his forehead against the desk.

"All right, class, what about the word 'bellicose'?"

Gus Mumford's hand is the only one in the air now. He peeks around the room and grimaces, waiting for Miss Gale to finally give in and call upon him.

"No guesses, class? No guesses at all? That word also means someone who enjoys fighting."

Gus Mumford's arm falls from the space above his head as if it has been cut off.

"All right, class, how about an easy one? Who can tell me what the word 'irate' means?"

Everyone's hand reaches quickly toward the sky. Gus Mumford shakes his head at the imbecilic arms in the air and decides he will no longer try. He glares around the room and takes note of who dares to answer. But there are just too many to count for reprisals. He squints his eyes and notices just then Judy Alexander's long arm raised in the air beside him. From elbow to wrist, there are a number of coarse red spots, blighted and puffy. Gus Mumford turns his head and sees all of the other arms waving in the air are also speckled with soft red rashes. He lowers his face into the corner of his arm and holds his breath, breathing against his shirt collar as infrequently as he can.

EIGHT

Outside it is raining; the boy detective and Penny smile at each other silently, still not touching. Billy, in his blue sweater, and Penny, in her pink hat and brown dress, smile down at their feet, unable to look at each other or even speak. Beside Penny on the bus again, Billy thinks about making a bold move—trying to hold Penny's hand—but for whatever reason, he cannot work up the courage to make such an attempt.

Billy and Penny smile at each other silently from across the booth of the small yellow diner. The table is littered with coffee cups and opened sugar packets and small plastic creamer containers. Carefully, Billy moves these items aside, making a path. Slowly, Billy goes to take Penny's hand and she lets him hold it this time: finally.

It is silent for a long time. Penny blinks, takes off her glasses, and then says, "I think I would like it if you would come to my place with me."

"You would?"

Billy's heart begins pounding loud in his ears.

"Yes, I am having a hard time concentrating on anything. I was almost fired for daydreaming tonight. I was reprimanded for mopping a businesswoman's shoes. So I . . . I think you should come over right now."

The boy detective stares down at the small woman's hand in his own and nods happily.

"OK. Yes."

Billy and Penny hold hands tightly on the bus. This grandness—this deep gladness, this fissure of pleasure—is nearly the greatest joy he can remember in his adult life.

It is raining when Billy and Penny walk up the small brick steps toward Penny's apartment. Her heels click noisily as she fumbles through her pink purse for the key. Billy can hear his heart beating loudly, ticking like a clock—*tick-tick-tick*. They stop, Penny standing higher on the steps, and stare at each other seriously. Penny's brown eyes disappear, hidden as she lowers her head in shame.

"I'm sorry, Billy. I thought . . . I thought I was ready."

Penny begins crying and leans over and kisses Billy's cheek nervously. She turns, unlocks the door, and runs up the steps. Billy catches a fading glimpse of Penny's white ankle and pink shoe as the door swings closed behind her. He sits on the steps and stares back over his shoulder at the building, frowning. He looks down at his hand, which is, once again, empty.

The boy detective is feeling badly as he rides the bus home that morning. Imagine this is how he feels exactly:

dancing dancing dancing   dancing dancing dancing
scissors scissors scissors   heart   scissors scissors scissors

NINE

It is time to play word-association with the boy detective. His therapist reads the word and then writes down Billy's answers.

"OK, Billy, how about: *island?*"

"Counterfeit ring."

"Um, OK. Good. *Mountain?*"

"Smugglers."

"OK, right. How about: *ocean?*"

"Ocean?"

"Yes. *Ocean.*"

"Um . . . spy submarine."

"Uh-huh, OK, OK. *Painting?*"

"Missing."

"All right. Umm. OK. How about this one: *happiness?*"

The boy detective frowns, tapping his forehead. The therapist repeats again: "*Happiness?*"

"Did I say 'front-page' already?"

"No, you did not."

"OK, then, front-page."

"What do you mean by 'front-page,' Billy?"

"Having your picture on the front page of a newspaper."

"Oh, yes. Yes, I see. And how about this last one: *fear?*"

"Fear?"

"Yes, Billy: *fear?*"

"Fear . . ." The boy detective is silent, and then, without a thought, he simply says, "Death."

The therapist nods and says, "Billy, I want you to think seriously about what that means."

"I do," Billy says. "I think about it a lot, sir."

"I want you to consider why you're afraid of death. I think it is because you consider it a form of failure, a mistake, something that can somehow be avoided. And yet it remains as the one mystery that unites us all: Rich and poor, young and old—all of us, one day, will die eventually."

"I do not like to consider that."

"Why?"

"It is very uncomfortable for me to think like that."

"Why?" the therapist asks.

"Because," Billy whispers. "Because there is no answer to that mystery."

"It is that exact reason why we need to think about it, Billy. It is the last thing in this world that gives us cause to dream."

"I must be going, sir," Billy mumbles. "My time is up."

"How is your investigation going?"

"Which investigation?" Billy asks.

"The investigation of your sister's death. Have you figured anything out yet?"

"Thank you for your time, doctor. I will see you next week."

TEN

At work, the boy detective momentarily shirks his duties and, discovering that the foreign cleaning lady Lupe has a small portable television set on her cleaning cart, watches TV for a better part of the night.

At first, Lupe will only watch her strange foreign soap operas, *Amor con Sangre* and *Las Muchachas Son Enfermas*, but after some convincing, Billy and his new friend sit on the green carpet and view *Modern Police Cadet*. The boy detective has already seen this episode. It is, without a doubt, one of Billy's all-time favorites, entitled "The Séance Killers," which concerns a dastardly criminal plot to rob a circle of well-off but aging socialites who are fond of spiritualism and the occult. Originally airing during the late '50s when the fear of devil-worshipping hoodlums was popular, there is one particular scene Billy really enjoys. In it, a lovely dark-haired beauty in a black turtleneck with a silver pentagram hanging around her neck, black mascara carefully painted in a sinister, nearly-Egyptian design, leads a séance in the great gaudy hall of one of the richer socialite's mansions. Around the enormous table, old men in monocles and women with cat's-eye glasses mutter silent incantations, holding hands. Mysteriously, the table soon begins to float and a strange violin hisses from somewhere above the gathered party's heads. Not so very far away, two lean men in black masks run down the long, impressive hallways of the mansion, filling their bakery sacks with silver candlesticks and jewelry. As soon as the two burglars have made their escape, the violin music falls silent, the table once again becomes stable, and the merry old widows and widowers clap their hands happily.

What happens then is that the bandits attempt to discover the whereabouts of a reported diamond necklace worth several thousand quid. It belongs to a rich old dame who, impressed by the first séance, decides to hold another. During the course of the séance, the diamond necklace is stolen and one of the attendees of the spiritualist get-together, a millionaire named Mrs. Dabny, is somehow murdered. The Modern Police Cadet makes short work of the case, revealing the miniature tape recorder beneath the table, which, set by a timer, issues its strange hissing; also, the nearly hidden wires that are used to help the table levitate; and finally, the ghostly footprints, which of course are nothing more than flour from the bakery.

What is truly brilliant about the episode is that after the ruse has been exposed and the murder solved, the Modern Police Cadet discovers that one of the guests at the séance, a thin blond girl who sat beside her haughty-looking aunt, has been dead for at least ten years. The episode finishes with the Modern Police Cadet catching sight of the girl in one of the ornate mirrors in the mansion's hallway. The sight of the small waif in her dress, walking alone down the hall, is enough to make Billy quite terrified. When he looks up from the small television screen, he notices he is holding Lupe's hand very tightly. He apologizes and hurries directly back to his desk.

After midnight, when the cleaning lady has gone and most of the world is, at that moment, happily dreaming, Billy, his head resting on his folded arms, is quietly muttering to himself in his sleep. The office is empty and very dark. Suddenly someone whispers back. Billy lifts his head and looks out into the shadows. He feels a thousand eyes staring in return. He glances over his shoulder, imagining who might be standing in the dark beside him. It is then that he hears the strange whisper from down the aisle again, perhaps rising from one of the offices. The voice is very high and weird, its warbly words hanging in the air for a moment and then disappearing. Billy stands and realizes he is holding a dead phone in his hand. He places the phone on its receiver and, as quietly as he can, creeps toward the sound, holding his breath, wondering what in the world it might be.

Along the aisle and down the hallway, Billy finally pauses outside a vacant office. He presses his ear against the wooden door and hears the voice one more time, a few of its unfamiliar words slowly making sense. He closes his eyes and makes out a single word—a small gathering of letters—which escape from behind the closed door: *Hello,* the mysterious voice says.

"Hello?" Billy mumbles.

Hello . . .

Billy runs from the office and presses the elevator button again and again and again.

Out on the street, at the newsstands, are the morning newspapers, which Billy reads, waiting for the bus to arrive, standing in place, stamping his feet. All of the newspapers seem to mention the same things: Two more office buildings have disappeared overnight and the girl named Parker Lane is still missing. The boy detective studies the girl's black-and-white picture and wonders if, like Effie claimed, the girl is already dead.

cvengrf,

ELEVEN

The boy detective is walking up the hallway of Shady Glens that very morning. The giant, Mr. Pluto, in his blue hospital gown, is standing guard in the middle of the hall, and refuses to let Billy pass. Billy tries and tries, taking a quick step to one side, a dash to the left, but Mr. Pluto is simply too big and will not let him through. Billy shakes his head, takes a step back, and smiles. He quickly digs into his briefcase and returns with a long black sample wig, handing the hairy prize to Mr. Pluto. Mr. Pluto stares at the tag which reads *Modern Empress: For Sales Use Only, Sample*, and claps happily, moving down the hall toward his own room and a mirror, finally allowing Billy to pass.

Hurrying past Mr. Lunt's shabby green room, Billy sees Professor Von Golum in white pajamas, standing over a prostrate Mr. Lunt, severely choking him. Billy shakes his head and stares, folding his arms over his chest disapprovingly. Professor Von Golum looks up, sees he is being watched, and stops, embarrassed, immediately trying to lie to Billy.

"The poor old fellow was choking . . . Isn't that true, my friend?"

"Yes, *you* were choking me."

Professor Von Golum snarls and runs out, dashing past Billy, slamming the door to his own room.

The boy detective is in bed later that day. Someone knocks at the door. He does not recognize the knock. Billy sits up, concerned, then calls out: "Yes? Who is it?"

Mr. Lunt enters, old and sad, his long beard a puff of whiteness above his brown robe. He grimaces as he approaches on two wood canes.

"I come here to thank you for your kindness with those heathens. I'm not a very polite sort of man, so it took me some time thinking before I realized I ought to thank you properly," he says.

"OK," Billy replies.

"I'm not the kind of fellah to go on and on with a lot of fancy words. I never had much use for talking. I can tell you're the same way."

"Yes, sir."

"Well, I come to find out I got no one, no one at all. And there's this business of my treasure. Seeing as I've come to find there's no one I can leave it to, I've decided I'd give you a chance with it. You've been kind to me and I want to pass it on, but not for nothing. You'll have to work for it the way I did."

"OK."

"So what it is, is a riddle."

"All right."

"I'll recite it, and if you're smart, you'll be able to figure out where the treasure is buried. That's the only help you'll get with it."

"All right."

"So here it goes, then: 'At the beginning of a silver line and the end of another made of twine, if you have old lungs, the treasure you will find.' That's it. You take some time to think on it."

"OK. Well . . . thanks?"

Mr. Lunt nods once more and then turns, ambling with some struggle down the dim hallway. Billy lies back in bed. Then he sits up and stares across the wall at a clipping of Caroline.

The boy detective thinks: *I wouldn't have anyone to leave anything to either, I'm afraid. But if it's his wish for me to find it, I will.*

He begins scribbling down the riddle on some paper with a pencil, scribbling and scratching it out. Finally, Billy takes two Clomipramine and sighs, closing his eyes, soon falling asleep.

The boy detective, in a dream again, descends into the cavern, past the now-familiar signs. Holding a flashlight, he climbs deeper and deeper, listening to someone crying. At the bottom of the cave, through the dark, Billy can see a girl in tears, but it is not his sister this time. It is Daisy Hollis, the missing kidnapping victim, a lovely blond teen in a dirtied white ball gown. Her hands are tied and she looks roughed-up. She has a white sweater on with a monogram, *DH*, etched in gold cursive.

"Help me, please, anyone! Please, help me!"

"Where's Caroline? You're not her. Where is she?"

"I don't know. Please, please help me."

Billy begins to untie Daisy's hands. She is still crying. A horrible growl like a jaguar echoes through the cave. Billy looks up, terrified.

"What? What was that?"

"It's . . . it's what brought me here . . ."

"Here, we have to hurry."

"No, it's too late," Daisy cries. "It's too late for me."

The horrible ram-horned, claw-fingered demon leaps out from the darkness, howling.

The boy detective awakes with a shout. He is covered in sweat. He pulls himself out of bed and inches across the room to the dresser, opens the bottom drawer, and pulls out the detective kit. The corners are all worn, all bent, all oddly angled. He notices his heart is still pounding. The cartoon boy looks sad and unfamiliar. Billy closes his eyes and feels the cardboard with the tips of his fingers, listening to his pulse pounding loudly somewhere within his ears. There is dust along the lid, and something else. Something like an invisible magnetic field, the childhood implements echoing in far-off whispers. Billy opens his eyes and decides not to open the kit. He puts it back in the drawer and turns on the light. He opens another drawer, finds Caroline's diary and fingerprint set, and climbs back into bed.

Billy stares at Caroline's last entry in her diary:

how can anyone in the world believe in good anymore?

On the fingerprint set is a label which has been perfectly typed and reads, *Property of Billy Argo*, but the Billy is crossed out and has been replaced by *Caroline* in a handwritten cursive.

"What happened?" Billy whispers out loud. "What happened to you, Caroline? Why? Why did you go and do it?"

He looks closely at the diary once again and makes a strange discovery: There is a small white torn corner, bound just behind the last page, evidence of a missing entry. He frowns, running his finger along the tear.

It is then that Billy hears a ruckus in the hallway. He opens the door and sees two paramedics wheeling poor Mr. Lunt out. It is obvious: The old man is dead. His face is very calm and very happy. Across the hallway, Professor Von Golum in his white robe and Mr. Pluto in his blue gown watch as the old man is wheeled away.

"Look at him, the fiend," the Professor mumbles. "There is the look of the dead, all right. Quite happy to take his secrets with him, happy to have thwarted his fellow man. Lousy old fool! Now nobody will know the truth of it!"

Mr. Pluto nods, hanging his gigantic head low.

"In the end, it seems we have only been bested by that one adversary slightly more cunning than Man, the one no mortal has ever dared to truly comprehend: our dear, lifelong companion, Death."

Billy closes his door and lays in bed. As the dark arrives, his hands make strange shadows above his bed.

He makes a bunny.

He makes a dog.

He makes a horse.

He makes a crocodile.

He makes a ghost.

TWELVE

At school, Gus Mumford is the only child in class. From his seat directly in front of Miss Gale's desk, Gus turns around and sees for himself the classroom is entirely empty. A bit of dust blows about the corner of the room. As the clock strikes and the final bell rings, Gus places his hands on his desk and stares questioningly at Miss Gale's taut white face.

"It seems it will only be you and me today, Gus," she whispers. "All of your other classmates have come down with a strange rash, which circulated at Missy Blackworth's birthday party, to which, I conclude, you were not invited."

Gus Mumford sadly shakes his head.

"We will, however, continue on with the lesson as planned."

Gus Mumford nods, and in that moment something wonderful dawns on him: There are no other students present, no one else to raise their hands, no one else who could possibly attempt to answer any of Miss Gale's unintelligent questions. The boy sits at his desk grinning, his eyes wide with delight. Cracking his knuckles, he then flexes and relaxes his fingers, readying his hand to be raised and—finally— seen. So happy is the child that if we were to listen close, perhaps we would be able to hear him giggling to himself.

Miss Gale stares down at her geography book seriously and then begins the day's geography lesson.

"Now, class, who can tell me where the Capital of the United States is located?"

Gus Mumford decides the woman at the front of the classroom has been defeated. There is no one else she can call upon, and so the small bully decides he can take his time. He glances around the room, yawns, stretches his arm, and then slowly, languorously raises his large-knuckled hand.

"No guesses, class?"

Grinning, Gus Mumford flicks his fingers right before Miss Gale's face, tapping his other hand on his desk.

"No guesses? The answer is Washington, D.C."

Gus Mumford's hand comes crashing down like a meteorite.

"Now who can tell me who Washington, D.C. is named after?"

Gus Mumford decides not to stall this time. Immediately, he raises his hand and lunges forward, nearly leaving his seat.

"No guesses? He was the first president of our country. He said, 'I cannot tell a lie.' Do you remember who that was, class?"

Gus Mumford, snarling, whips his arm back and forth.

"Class, the answer is George Washington. Do we all remember him?"

Gus Mumford drops his arm. He stares at his hand, wondering if it is somehow not real.

"Now, class, who can tell me what river did George Washington cross on his way to victory over the British?"

Gus closes his eyes and places his face in the crook of his arm, too angry to begin crying.

On the school bus, hidden back in the very rear seat, Gus Mumford raises both arms in the air and starts howling. The happy noise of after-school conversations soon dies, as all the other children turn and stare at the boy who will not, cannot, stop shouting. The sound, in their minds, reminds them of their frequent nightmares: the depiction of a deadly fall off a very dangerous cliff.

* * *

It is the very same day that Gus Mumford makes another terrible discovery: Secreted beneath the front porch, the boy finds that all but one of the proud inhabitants of Ant City have mysteriously died. The remaining fellow, a bright red and spunky arthropod, busily shuffles the corpses of his unmoving citizens, carefully constructing grave after grave after grave. Gus Mumford stares at the carnage and begins howling once again.

THIRTEEN

At work, the boy detective and the cleaning lady, sitting in the dark on the plush carpeting of the office, silently watch a television show about unsolved cases.

On the show, an older B-grade actor in a black suit and tie speaks directly to the camera, smoking a cigarette and looking back over his shoulder at the city of New Orleans. The actor, the host of the show, says: "One of the most bizarre unsolved crimes concerns a killer known as the Axeman of New Orleans. From newspapers at the time, similar killings were described early in the year of 1919. The victims, as the murderer's name suggests, were always assaulted with an axe. The front doors to some of the victims' homes were also sometimes split open with the same weapon. The Axeman of New Orleans was never caught, though his crimes ended as strangely as they began. To this very day, the killer's true identity is still a mystery."

Billy and the cleaning lady glance at one another, then around the great, empty office.

The actor continues with his story: "It seems the Axeman of New Orleans drew many revelations from pulp stories concerning Jack the Ripper. Like that other famous murderer, the Axeman penned frightening letters to the city's various newspapers, often asserting he was a demon of some kind. On March 13, 1919, a letter allegedly written by the Axeman was published in the city's newspapers, claiming that he would commit a murder just past midnight on the night of March 19, but strangely, or so the missive said, he would avoid any location where jazz music was being played. On that bizarre evening of March 19, 1919, every one of New Orleans's dance halls was full of people, while bands played jazz music at gatherings at thousands of homes around the city. More odd, perhaps, was the fact that, as promised, there were no killings that evening."

At the end of the program, Billy returns to his desk, thanking Lupe for sharing her small television. He stares at the phone, suddenly afraid to speak to anyone for quite a while. Instead, Billy tries his hand at solving Mr. Lunt's riddle. Throughout the night, the single light above his desk flickering, Billy attempts to discover the secret to the old man's clues—now his final words—a mysterious glimpse of someone Billy barely knew. Billy lowers his pencil for a moment and wonders: *Without death, there is hardly any threat strong enough to truly appreciate human life.* He thinks: *I am as good as dead—too afraid to live, only waiting, never taking a risk—I am as good as dead already.*

Billy pops an Ativan and feels its effects quite quickly. He spins around in his chair, around and around and around, and the next thing he knows, he is

FOURTEEN

Again, returning from his job, the boy detective discovers some strange new commotion at Shady Glens. As breakfast is being served and beds are being made, the hospital staff is surprised to discover that Professor Von Golum disappeared sometime in the middle of the night. His clothes and personal effects have all been removed and a single note, left posted on Billy's door, provides the only clue.

> *Billy,*
>
> *I have deduced that it is the unknown which, in the end, sustains Life and since I am so nearing the termination of my own, I have decided to embark on one final adventure—better that than to die in the safety of deathly boredom. I must salute you for years of superb opposition. You remain, to this day, my greatest foe.*
>
> > *Yours truly,*
> >
> > *Prof. Josef Von Golum*

Billy stares at the note a moment longer and then crumples the paper into a ball and throws it as hard as he can down the hall. Within a few seconds, the object explodes in a flash of green fire and cloudy, phosphorous smoke.

Mr. Pluto begins to cry softly, staring at the vacant room. The giant lowers his head and says, "Our worlds are so momentary. We are alone all our lives and then go off that way as well."

Holding Mr. Pluto's hand, the boy detective walks to the small park, past the statue of the armless general. The two sit on a park bench, not speaking for a long time. It is a day where the sun has returned, but only temporarily: a soft white dot in the sky hanging there familiar and lazy. The gloom of the end of autumn is momentarily cast away as the two men sit, watching the children in their winter jackets chasing the pigeons. They sit and stare for quite a while until Billy says, "I have never been very strong nor brave. I would be quite happy to know someone who is."

The giant nods.

"I would like to be your friend. I would like to be your friend because I would like to be remembered fondly by someone who knew me."

The giant nods again.

"Would you like to be my friend?" Billy asks.

Mr. Pluto nods once more and, patting the boy detective on the shoulder, says, "Before you came to Shady Glens, I doubted I would have a friend ever again."

"Well, I am glad that has been settled."

"Yes. Yes, I am very glad."

An inquisitive pigeon comes pecking near their feet. Mr. Pluto reaches into the pocket of his large overalls and, smiling, drops three small crumbs of bread at the cooing bird, which quickly gobbles them up.

"Well, what would you like to do now?" Billy asks. "I am free all afternoon."

"I have never been to the museum. I have been too afraid someone would laugh at me. Would you like to go there with me?"

Billy nods and the two march off toward the art museum, a strange-looking white building which rises before them a few short blocks away.

Stumbling into his room later that afternoon, the boy detective receives another secret message. It is like the others, in a white envelope with simple black handwriting. Opening it, he finds a similar code:

K-24
15-22-25-25-12,
14-15-5-14-16-14-17-14-15-5-14!

Billy's nose twitches. There is something about this third message, unlike the two others—perhaps the strange symmetry of the coded words rising like a wonderful little pyramid—that makes Billy decide to sit down on the dusty spring bed and, with a pen and pencil, begin to solve the secret message. It does not come easy at first. But when he discovers the pattern, the message quickly reveals itself. He stares down at the words and does not like what he has discovered—no, not at all. He crinkles the paper up into a ball and hides it beneath his mattress.

Billy lays in bed wondering who might have sent such a thing. *Why, why, what is the meaning?* He scrambles and takes the last of his Clomipramine. He stares at the vial of pills sadly and searches for his bottle of Ativan. It too is empty, and Billy decides not to ask Nurse Eloise for any more. He decides he will face the world of mystery now on his own. Thinking once again about the message now balled under his mattress, Billy turns on his side and stares at the newspaper clippings of Caroline and Fenton on the wall, wondering.

FIFTEEN

In the twilight just before evening, the boy detective is surprised to find both of the Mumford children standing among the graves of the Gotham town cemetery. Effie Mumford in her purple and white winter jacket, black headphones clamped over her ears, holds a large microphone raised between her hands, aiming the device at a large gray headstone near their feet.

"How is your experiment going?" Billy asks with a small smile.

"The dead are quiet tonight," the girl says. "All we have recorded so far is a strange sound coming from that mausoleum over there. We thought someone was singing, but then we heard the record skip."

"I see. Perhaps someone requested that a certain song be played over and over again after their death."

"Gus ran away from it at first."

Gus Mumford, in a hat and scarf and holding a small silver compass, nods, embarrassed. He hands Billy a note: *It most definitely sounded like a ghost.*

Billy smiles. "I understand," he says.

"What are you doing here?" Effie Mumford asks.

"I do not know, really. I saw the gates and decided I would walk inside. I have not been here in quite a while."

"Do you know anyone who's buried here, Billy?"

Billy stares across the great wide expanse of gray headstones and frowns.

"Yes, I am afraid I do."

Without a word, Billy heads over a small green hill, down a stone path, to a large grave marker, the two Mumford children following, both holding his hands now. There, at the end of the little path, is an enormous slab of stone which reads, *DAISY HOLLIS, beloved daughter*. Billy lowers his head and whispers, "If you've come to find a ghost, this is as good a place as any."

"Who is it?"

"A young girl. But she is not in there."

"Why not?" Effie Mumford asks.

"The body, sadly, was never found."

"Oh, that is terrible," Effie says. "I bet she is a ghost just waiting to be seen."

The wind whips through the empty trees, howling behind their backs then.

"Perhaps," Billy says. "Perhaps, all this time she has been patiently waiting."

It begins snowing. This makes it seem like all the gravestones are somehow frowning.

SIXTEEN

At work that evening, the boy detective sits at his desk, staring at Caroline's small gold diary. He flips through it for a moment, then picks up the phone and calls his parents.

As the telephone on the other end picks up, he knows immediately it is his father who has answered. He can tell because he recognizes the sounds of his backyard, and from his father's labored breathing he knows that he has been practicing karate, breaking boards with his bare fists.

"Father . . . it's me, Billy."

"Billy, my boy, how have you been?"

"I . . . I have some questions I'd like to ask, Dad."

"Well, sure, of course, of course. What's the matter, son?"

"Well, I guess I was looking through Caroline's diary, and there's a page missing."

"Didn't we talk about how that wasn't a good idea, you ruminating on these kinds of things?"

"Yes, I . . . I don't know, I . . ."

"Well, you know how I feel about you dwelling on the past. Let me ask this: Have you been exercising?"

"No, I mean, I . . . I was thinking . . . about Caroline, right before she died."

"Oh no, Billy, it's not healthy for you to be still focused on this. Did you read that last book we sent, *Grief Is OK*?"

"No, no, I can't read those books anymore. I just need to talk with you about this. I need to know what happened."

"Well, it's not a good time. Your mother and I . . . well . . ."

At that moment, Billy hears the crackle of electricity and imagines the fizzy tang of test tubes bubbling, as Mrs. Argo suddenly picks up the extension.

"Billy, this is your mother. This is a very bad time, darling."

"But, I—"

"Your father and I are having a rough time now, dear. We're talking about getting a divorce. It's very tense here. He's out in the backyard breaking boards all day."

"Well, if I was *allowed* in the house, but it isn't my house, is it, darling? I only worked my whole life—"

"Please, listen, I need to speak with you both about this," Billy says.

"That's not going to be helpful right now, Billy. Your mother, she's . . . she's contemplating becoming a painter and leaving me for an ambassador from Zaire."

"But please, listen, I need to know."

"You're an adult now, Billy," his mother says. "Part of being an adult is dealing with the terror of being an adult and not knowing what might happen next. Maybe the doctors misjudged you. Your father and I weren't quite sure you were ready—"

"Mom, Dad."

"No, ands, ifs, or buts, Billy. You'll get through this, champ, I promise. Keep your chin up and sail straight ahead, partner."

"But Dad—"

"We'll speak again soon, my boy."

"Goodbye, Billy."

Billy hangs up the phone and stares at the diary. He flips through the pages and comes to a page with some clippings pasted on it. There is a photograph of all of them so young—Billy, Caroline, and Fenton—all smiling.

Billy places his finger on top of Fenton, slowly, sadly tapping. He stands, carrying the diary, leaving his desk.

SEVENTEEN

On the bus, the boy detective opens his briefcase, then stares at the closed diary and Caroline's fingerprint set.

There again is the label which has been perfectly typed and reads, *Property of Billy Argo*, but the *Billy* is crossed out and has been replaced by a handwritten *Caroline* in cursive. Beside the label is a small black thumbprint that belongs to Caroline. He stares at the small formations of ridges, and remembers the subtle softness of each one.

The boy detective stands on the front porch of a small yellow house and rings the door bell. The porch creaks as he waits. An overweight woman in a yellow housecoat answers. She is wearing furry blue slippers. She stares into Billy's face and is nearly speechless, her eyes going wide, her lips fluttering.

"Is that you, Billy Argo? Is that really you?"

"Hello, Mrs. Mills."

"He'll be . . . he'll be so happy to see you."

At that moment, like most moments, Fenton Mills is lying in bed. He is massively overweight. His room is like an eight-year-old's: Pennants of sports teams are posted on the walls, comic books are strewn wildly across the floor. There are newspaper clippings from all of the boy detective's cases pinned to all the walls. Fenton's mother calls from the other room, excitedly, "Fenton, Billy Argo is here to see you!"

Billy enters Fenton's room, very slowly. He stares at his old friend and smiles a small, nervous smile.

"Fenton," Billy says. The other young man does not respond. He is enormous, in large white and blue pajamas, lying in a small white bed. He is deeply embarrassed of his large size. His little blue eyes dart about the room nervously, terrified to glance upon his old friend's face.

"Billy," he replies finally.

"I believe you've been sending me letters of some kind."

"I don't know anything about that."

"You haven't been sending me secret messages?"

"No, I haven't."

"Nothing about 'Abracadabra'?"

Fenton's large, round face goes soft. He nods as his eyes get cloudy. "It was the only way I knew you'd answer me," he says. "I tried forever to get ahold of you. Why didn't you ever call me back, Billy? I called you in the hospital! I even went there, but they said you didn't want to see me. How come?"

"I . . . I couldn't see anyone. I didn't want to see anyone. I'm sorry."

"Do you have any idea what happened to me? Look at me for God's sake, Billy."

"I'm . . . so sorry."

"You wouldn't even talk to me at the funeral. I tried to talk and you wouldn't even talk to me. Until you blamed me, Billy. You fucking *blamed* me."

"Fenton, please. I need you to forgive me."

"Why should I? You're a real asshole, you know that? You've made me feel like shit, because I thought I had done something wrong or something. You said . . . you said it was my fault."

Billy winces, his heart pounding, his ears ringing from the unfamiliar-sounding curse words.

"I needed someone to blame. I couldn't figure it out any other way."

"She just didn't want to grow up, Billy. None of us did. Well, except you maybe."

"Look, I brought you this," Billy says, digging into his coat, pulling out the diary. Billy takes a seat on the edge of the small bed. "I thought we might like to look at it together."

Fenton stares at the tiny gold book then holds it to his chest, his eyes twinkling.

"Is this hers?" he asks. "Wow, this is nice, man. I've missed you, Billy. I've missed you both so badly."

The two men hold hands, then hug.

Billy closes his eyes, nearly crying. "I brought you something else," he says, drawing away. Billy opens his briefcase and retrieves the fingerprint set, then hands it to Fenton.

"I know she'd want you to have this."

"The fingerprint set. That was hers, Billy. That was her thing."

"I know. She stole it from me. I think she'd like it if you held onto it."

"Look, there," Fenton says. There is a big black fingerprint on the case which still looks wet with ink. "That was her fingerprint. I remember the day she did it."

"I remember, too. I remember everything like it was yesterday."

"Me, too, Billy. Me, too."

The two young men are silent for a moment.

"Do you know I kissed her once?" Fenton asks.

"You did?"

"She kissed me, I guess. We were in junior high school. She said she just wanted to get her first kiss over with, so . . ."

"She never told me."

"She made me promise I wouldn't tell anyone. That was one of her two conditions before she kissed me."

"What was the other one?"

"That I would never try and kiss her again."

"Did you?"

"Every day." Fenton looks up, sad, his large eyes blinking with tears. "Why did you leave me alone like this?"

Billy looks down at his feet. The room is suddenly silent.

"Billy, why?"

"I guess it's hard to see you without thinking of her."

"It's hard for me, too, Billy."

"I know." Billy folds his hands in lap, words winding hopelessly through his head. *What to say now?* He searches, then stutters, and finally asks, "So, how have you been, Fenton?"

"I'm not doing so good. I mean, I don't do anything. I sit up here and read comic books. I had a job at the copy place for a while, but it didn't work out. I had a line on a job in the city as a clerk, but I turned it down. I didn't want to . . . I didn't want to be around all those people, looking the way I do."

Billy nods. "You probably should try to leave your house sometime. It'd be good for you to get out."

"Yeah. I don't know. It's scary out there, Billy."

"It's probably scarier up here alone by yourself."

"Yeah. So do you think we could, you know, I could visit you sometime?"

"I think you have to. I need to know there are people like you in the world still."

"Yeah, well, thanks . . . for everything," Fenton says, holding up the fingerprint set. "I mean, thanks for coming to see me."

"It's OK," Billy stands, pulling himself to his feet. He pauses in the doorway, staring down at the gold diary. "Fenton?"

"Yeah?"

"I want to know. What . . . what happened to Caroline before she died? Why did she get so sad?"

Fenton nods, sadly. "She tried to solve some case all by herself. But I guess she couldn't do it. She . . . *we* . . . weren't as smart as you."

"That's not true."

"No, it is, it is. It didn't bother us, though. We didn't want to be smart. We were just happy to be around you. But you left—you had to, Billy, you did, you did—but she couldn't accept that. She couldn't accept that it was over, you know: being kids. If you're looking for a reason, that's about as—"

"No, no, I know. I guess I was hoping there was some . . . some secret, perhaps. But thank you, Fenton, for everything. For looking out for her. For this. Thank you."

Billy hugs Fenton once more and Fenton smiles, his cheeks reddening, hugging him back. "The only secret she ever told me was the one you already know."

"Which secret was that?"

"Your secret word, 'Abracadabra,' the one about the dead dove. That's the last thing she told me, that story, about you and her burying the bird under the porch."

"Thank you, Fenton. We'll see each other soon."

Quietly, the boy detective leaves.

On the bus, the boy detective stares down at his hands, frowning. The small houses and trees of the town flash by like very old dreams.

EIGHTEEN

The boy detective and Penny stare at each other across the coffee shop booth. Billy's eyes are small and tired-looking. Penny goes to touch his hand and he smiles, pained, staring far away. In a booth beside them, two loud women exchange gifts.

"It's lovely, just lovely."

"I thought you'd just love it. Well, happy birthday."

There is a small, pink glass bird in the woman's hand.

Penny eyes the gift with envy. She turns to Billy, who is lost in his thoughts, and frowns.

"Do you want to leave, Billy?"

"No, I'm sorry. I'm terrible company tonight. It's my fault, it's me. I keep, I keep thinking about terrible, terrible things."

"Is it your sister?"

"Yes."

"You miss her very much. It's very nice to miss someone so badly."

"Yes, but it's . . . the way she left. I can't make it make sense. I don't think I'll ever know why she did what she did. It's this unsolvable mystery to me."

"Maybe start small then."

"Start small?"

"With mysteries you know you can solve."

"Like what?"

"Like . . . like small, easy things. For instance, why does it rain sometimes?"

"Well, evaporated moisture builds up in the atmosphere and—"

"That's very good. How about: Why is the sky blue?"

"It's the sunlight and clouds reflecting off the surface of the water all over the world, which really—"

"OK, OK. Now something very difficult, a very hard question: Will you please come home with me?"

Billy looks up, sad, disbelieving.

The boy detective and Penny are running hand in hand. They stop outside Penny's building, nervously staring at one another, catching their breath. Penny suddenly lunges forward and kisses Billy on the mouth. Startled, he kisses back, and they run up the steps, hand in hand once again.

In the hallway, outside her apartment, Billy and Penny kiss desperately as if they are both lost in outer space, somehow struggling to breathe. Penny stops and smiles, then says, "Please, wait. It's been a very long time for me, since I . . . well . . . please, please . . . please don't laugh at me."

"I wouldn't, I wouldn't ever."

"OK."

They resume kissing as Penny unlocks and then opens the door.

Penny flips on the light. The room is completely crowded with hundreds and hundreds of pink shoes in shoe boxes, pink dresses on hangers, pink hats, pink jackets in bags—all stolen merchandise—thrown about madly. Penny pulls Billy down onto the couch, which is covered with pink shoes and clothing. Billy opens his eyes and looks around, shocked, but smiling.

"You, you stole all of this?"

"Please—you said you wouldn't laugh."

Penny and Billy resume kissing. Penny begins to undress, unbuttoning her blouse. Billy stops after a moment, holding her by the shoulder.

"But *all* of this? You stole all of this?"

Penny sits up, upset, and covers herself.

"Please, you said you wouldn't."

"But why? Why do you do it?"

"Most of it is from strangers, women, on the bus or train. Some of it is from stores, too, I guess. I don't do it to be mean. I can't help myself."

"But why? Why do it at all?"

"It started after my husband died. He was a Naval officer, you see. He was away for weeks, sometimes months at time. When he died, he was in another country. He was decapitated in an automobile accident, and another woman—some woman I never met—was in the passenger seat holding his hand when it happened. The woman, she also died. But, but he . . . he was with another woman, in his final seconds, seconds he should have been thinking of . . ." Penny looks away, her tiny face reddened with shame. "Those moments were taken, stolen from me. I don't know why I started. Afterwards I began stealing shopping bags, purses, anything, from women I didn't know, women who were total strangers to me."

"I think I understand, maybe," Billy says, wiping her tears with his hand.

"I'm sorry," she says. "I'm so sorry."

Billy and Penny kiss again. Penny pulls away, crying into her arm.

"I'm sorry, too. I'm sorry for you, too, Billy."

Billy and Penny sit on the couch, side by side, staring out, straight ahead, holding hands, both on the verge of sobbing.

"We both need to start small," Penny says. "Me, only stealing very tiny, inexpensive things. You, only solving very simple, uncomplicated mysteries."

Billy nods. Penny kisses his cheek very tenderly. As she opens her hand, she reveals the small glass bird, stolen from the women at the adjoining table earlier that night. Billy sees it and begins smiling. They stare at each other for a long time.

When they kiss, they kiss slowly.

NINETEEN

The boy detective lifts his head from his desk and realizes he is two hours early for his shift. He also notices that he is mumbling on the phone to somebody. Larry peeks over from across the aisle and smiles.

"Yes, the Nordic Prince is one of our most popular styles," Billy whispers into the phone.

"OK, kid, try this one. What did I do last night, after I left here?" Larry asks.

"It's quality hair replacement without the surgery."

"Go on, guess. What did I do?"

"I don't know, Larry. I have no idea."

"I'm a conundrum. You think you know me? It's *impossible* to know me. I'm like a black hole. Scientific standards do not apply to me."

Larry returns to his desk. Billy stares at him, nodding.

"OK," Billy whispers to himself. "Start small. Start small."

The boy detective watches Larry as the older man gets up, winks at him, and skips off to the bathroom. Billy stands, slowly following. As he walks inside, Larry is at the mirror, washing his face. The boy detective watches him for a moment, smiling. Larry stops and pulls out his flask, takes a drink, then offers some to Billy.

"Well, Billy, my boy, how about a little pick-me-up? I had this woman today who lost her arms and legs and still thought a wig was the right option, do you know what I mean? These poor, lonely hearts, they practically kill me. Thank God we're here for them, eh, Billy?"

Billy waves off the drink. He walks over and points at Larry's middle, thinking: *Larry's shiny gold belt.*

"Um, Larry?"

"What can I do for you?"

"I was wondering . . ."

"Yep?"

"Larry, are you right-handed or left-handed?"

"Right-handed or left-handed? Right-handed, of course. Look at me, I *wish* I was left-handed. I've been working in this madhouse for twelve years, trying to get used to all the left-handed nonsense: scissors, telephones, door knobs, staplers . . ."

Billy nods and points at Larry's belt.

"I must say it's a pleasure to meet you, Mr. Mammoth."

Larry's round face goes ghost-white.

"You got it wrong this time, kid. If I was only so lucky to be that rich bum . . ."

"It's your belt, Mr. Mammoth. You put it on left-handed."

The man's round face goes red. "No," he whispers.

"Yes."

"Oh God, Oh Jesus—you got me, kid. Good grief, you really got me now, kid."

Larry removes his hairpiece. Without the black toupee, it becomes obvious he is indeed Mr. Mammoth. Billy smiles widely as Mr. Mammoth happily shakes his hand.

"Twelve years of hiding out. Twelve long years . . . Well, the game is up, isn't it? What are you, kid, a Fed? Insurance investigator? Detective from the Better Business Bureau?"

"No," Billy replies. "I just sell hair."

"You tell anyone yet? Let the Feds in on what you know?"

"No."

"So blackmail is your game, kid. Very smart, very shrewd. Maybe we can come to some sort of deal."

"But I don't want anything. If you're wanted by the law, it's out of my hands, I think."

"Well, at least let me explain my side, kid, before you go calling the cops on me. Maybe I can convince you to change your mind. Sure, sure, when you see the scope of it, maybe you'd like to get cut in on some of it."

"I don't think so."

"OK, but let me tell you—it all started right before my likely incarceration for tax evasion, which the Feds had me on for sure. Right before they set the hook, I had the second biggest idea of my life. The first being, well, this," he flops his hairpiece about. "Well, before I'm sure to get sent away, I got this brainstorm to record all my ideas and then fake my own death, which works out great. First I fire everybody. I get a new staff, who don't know me, and I just sneak in at night, work the graveyard shift, record what I want done, and no one is the wiser."

"So it's you I've been hearing at night?"

"Yep. I sneak in and record a new tape and then disappear before anyone's the wiser. Because now I'm just a lowly salesperson, without a care in the world. More than ten years of that, masquerading as a nobody—can you imagine?"

"I cannot."

"But the real brainstorm was this: Sitting here night after night, talking on the telephone, talking to all these people, nobody buying anything, finally, I come to this conclusion—everybody is unhappy for the same reason. Somewhere in their scrawny little brains, they all know they're already dead. They're working some two-bit job, they're married to someone who ended up a bigger disappointment than they could have ever dreamed, they owe bills they can't pay—so I figure what these people need is a new start, a whole new beginning. That's

what we're really selling here, Billy: a cheap version of hope. The hope
for people to start over, you see? That wearing this stupid thing is going to give them the life they've always dreamed of. That's what people
need. They really need some reason to believe what's going to happen
next is going to be better than what they've already seen," Mr. Mammoth whispers, shaking his hairpiece. "This is that reason. It's quite
a nest egg now, this business, believe me. If you're inclined, perhaps,
well, an arrangement of some kind can be made?"

"I don't think I ought to, Mr. Mammoth."

"God, that's what I love about you, kid: a heart of gold, a real heart
of gold. Your integrity is amazing. If I could only find a way to buy and
sell *that*. But . . . well, that was never my strong point, now, was it?"

"It doesn't seem so."

"You've done the right thing, kid, the right thing. To be completely
honest, I'm tired of hiding out here, this place is like a prison to me.
The poor schleps on the phone, the sob stories, they're killing me.
You're on salary from now on. Salary and a vacation, how's that? This
kid here has a heart of gold. Sure, sure, twelve years, twelve years of
all those sob stories, and no one but the boy here had any idea how to
save *me*."

As they slowly step from the bathroom and approach the lobby, Melinda appears, staring at them both. "What's going on here?" she asks.

"All this time, all this time, she never knew, kid. It just kills me."

"Melinda, it looks like this man has something to tell you,"
Billy says.

Mr. Mammoth smiles, placing his hand on Melinda's shoulder.
"You've got the run of the show from now on. That prosthetic limb
idea I heard you talking about? It's a keeper. A keeper, I tell you."

"Wait a moment, what's happening here?" Melinda asks.

"Billy solved a mystery. A great one."

"Wait a minute, what mystery?"

"The one about where you go when you die—ha ha. Go on and tell her what the answer is, Billy."

"Excuse me?"

"Where do you go when you die? Ha ha. Go on, go on and tell her, Billy."

Billy smiles. "You become a little voice in someone's ear telling them that things will be all right."

TWENTY

The boy detective cuts out a newspaper clipping of a headline and photograph of Larry being arrested, which reads, *MAMMOTH FRAUD*.
Billy pins the article to the wall next to his other clippings. He sits on
the bed, takes out a pad and pencil, and tries solving Mr. Lunt's riddle,
scratching and writing.

Silver line, line of twine, old lungs. Silver line, line of twine, old lungs.
Billy sighs, scribbling out one word after the other. He smiles, talking
to himself, trying to solve the riddle. He taps the pencil against his
forehead, then pauses, pressing his fingertips against his cheeks. He
grins even larger, surprised to find himself smiling.

One of our town's greatest attractions was
the Tiddlywinks, a family of dancing bears
who performed in our vaudevillian concert
hall around the turn of the century. The
three bears all wore blue tutus and were
tame enough to dance with courageous
strangers. When their owner died, a man by
the name of Morgensten, the stewardship
of the creatures was left up to the town
and, unwisely, the mayor decided to return
the animals to the wild, relocating the
bears into the woody forest surrounding
the outskirts of our small city: a very
bad mistake indeed. Unable to fend for
themselves, the family of bears, still in tutus,
rampaged down Main Street and later had
to be shot. A bronze statue was erected and
placed with their remains in the center of
town. It is a strange sight now, the three
of them there, dancing on clawed tiptoes.
It is what we see when we imagine what
the afterlife must be like: our happiest
triumphs, our most sincere moments, stolen
from the seam of our lives, a respite just
before the onset of imminent tragedy.

TWENTY-ONE

On the bus, Penny eyes a woman's expensive-looking handbag. She makes her way over and carefully reaches in, stealing the woman's pink eyeglasses. Penny slips them into her pocket, smiling, pleased with herself. She inches away to the other end of the bus, sees a lady with many white and pink boxes and shopping bags. Penny stands beside the woman and looks down into the largest of her paper bags.

Inside: a lovely pink pillbox hat.

Penny looks at it, very excited. She reaches down, darting her hand, as the bus moves, but the lady inches the bag further away. Penny discreetly reaches down a second time while a burly man with a large mustache across the aisle watches her. Penny notices and pretends to be straightening her nylon. The burly man goes back to reading his paper. Penny reaches a third time, grabs the hat, slips in into her bag, and heads for the bus exit. She hops off, smiling madly.

It is raining on the street, *Oh no*. Penny, beaming, hurries down the sidewalk, around a corner, and into an alley. She opens her bag and looks at the hat, very happy. Suddenly, someone grabs her hand. She looks up. When she does, her tiny heart breaks. *Oh*. It is Billy. He looks very disappointed. He lets go of her hand and frowns. Penny gets very nervous. She immediately begins muttering.

"I . . . I only found this, here. It's . . . it's not stolen."

"I don't think so."

"But it was here, I only found it."

"I was on the bus. I saw what happened."

"Oh. I see," she says. She looks down at her feet, her bottom lip trembling.

"I . . . maybe I should . . ."

"I don't know how to stop," she says. "It just seems impossible for anyone to be good, don't you think?"

"What?"

"It seems impossible for anyone to be good in a world like this, Billy."

Upset now, Billy begins to back away.

"Billy, wait, please . . . don't leave me . . ."

Penny kisses Billy. He kisses back, but very sadly.

"Please . . ." she whispers.

"I believed in what you told me. I was starting small."

"Don't give up because of me. You can find an answer. If anyone can, you can. Just please, don't be discouraged because I was weak. Please don't give up because I'm a thief."

The boy detective shakes his head.

"You stole my heart . . . worst, worst of all," he says.

Billy and Penny kiss again. It is brief and then over and then only a sad memory.

Billy stumbles out of the alley. His teeth are chattering, his hands shaking. In the darkness there, Penny lowers her head and begins to sob, softly.

TWENTY-TWO

The boy detective is on the bus crying. The people sitting beside him do their best to ignore him.

TWENTY-THREE

At work, the boy detective is distraught. He sits with his head folded into his hands. The papers and catalogs on his desk are spotted where tears have landed. At the moment, he is crying on the telephone to a customer, mumbling about losing Penny.

"I do not believe I will ever meet anyone like her again. All is lost," he says.

"I have been married three times now and I'm thinking about trying it a fourth time," the customer replies. "You have to believe this is not the end, but a brand-new start maybe."

"Yes, well, thank you very much for listening."

"Well, thank you for the discount on the Sympathetic Vamp wig. My boyfriend was just talking about me trying a new look."

"It's my pleasure. Goodnight."

Billy hangs up the phone; as soon as the next customer answers, he begins crying once again. He searches through his briefcase, then his pockets, then the filing cabinet, and remembers that all of his vials of pills are completely empty. Why has he done this to himself? Why has he decided now, of all times, to try and be bold? Billy begins to pound his head against the desktop until the sounds of the office have disappeared, his vision now soft and blurry.

Billy, sadly shuffling home in the morning, catches sight of Gus Mumford sitting on his front porch, waiting for the school bus. Billy takes a seat beside him. In the young bully's hands are the remains of Ant City, a dirt and sand metropolis of mass graves, a lone red citizen still marching there, constructing and rearranging his fellow townspeople's tombs.

Gus, staring up at Billy, hands him a note which reads: *Ant City is now a graveyard.*

"That's terrible," Billy says, staring at the strange sight.

Gus nods and, pointing, hands him another note: *They're all dead. All except him.*

"Yes. Well, he must be very lonely."

Gus nods and, holding the small glass rectangle up, unhinges the opening at the top. He places the ant farm in the soft grass of the front lawn and the two of them watch the lone red ant as it quickly makes its escape.

The boy detective returns to Shady Glens to find Nurse Eloise in the kitchen, baking a cake and crying. She smiles sadly at Billy, a touch of flour on her nose, and asks if perhaps he would like to stir. Billy nods silently and the two stand beside one another—Billy holding the wooden spoon, Nurse Eloise still sobbing, staring down at the creamy batter—until finally she whispers, "I have received some terrible news."

"What might that be?" Billy asks.

"My boyfriend, the magician, has been in a terrible accident. He has accidentally been sawed in half."

"Is he . . . Did he survive the accident?"

"The doctors said the top part arrived at the hospital dead, but the bottom part was completely fine."

"I see."

"What will I do now, Billy? He was the only one for me, I see that now. I feel as if I too have been cut in two."

Billy stares down at the batter which, at this point, has been mixed quite well. He hands the bowl back to Nurse Eloise and awkwardly touches her hand. Nurse Eloise smiles and goes back to crying.

In an hour, Billy, following the sweet smell of frosting, wanders down to the television room and finds the cake finished: It is a great white skull whose gumdrop mouth is set into a frown. He places one finger on the cake, expecting a sweet sugary confection, but instead it is bitter and unappetizing. He backs away and returns to his room, then he stops and turns, and hurries down the hallway. He finds Nurse Eloise standing in the medication room, eyes soft with tears and runny mascara, staring down at her hands full of blue and white pills. Billy smiles sadly at the young woman, who nods and smiles back.

Nurse Eloise slowly places the pills in Billy's hands and resumes crying. "I am so embarrassed, Billy," she says. "I am so embarrassed."

Billy holds the young woman's hands and then carefully shows her his scarred wrists.

"Oh, Billy. Billy, I didn't really want to die. I just didn't think I could get through this."

"Neither did I," he says. "Neither did I."

Sitting in the television room, accompanied by Mr. Pluto, the trio plays Hearts until finally it seems the darkness has passed and the tears have run out. Nurse Eloise kisses each of them on the cheek and says, "Thank you both. Tomorrow night, how about a nice Angel food cake for the two of you?"

Billy lays in his bed then and smiles, watching the silvery snow fall across his eyes. He goes to sleep, and instead of caves, he dreams of dove wings, of clouds, of everything nice. What he dreams looks this:

cloud   cloud   cloud
cloud   cloud
cloud   cloud   cloud

cloud   cloud   cloud
cloud   cloud
cloud   cloud   cloud

cloud   cloud   cloud
cloud   cloud
cloud   cloud   cloud

girl with a singing harp

cloud   cloud   cloud
cloud   cloud
cloud   cloud   cloud

TWENTY-FOUR

The Mumford children wander the dark woods along the murky river:
There, the sounds of lost secrets echo in their ears and disappear. Effie Mumford, in her purple and white winter jacket, black headphones
covering her ears, holds the tape recorder close to the brambly ground,
doing her best to capture long forgotten whispers. Gus Mumford, who
walks quietly behind her, watches the needle of the compass as it ticks
back and forth. Marching over fallen trees, past sinkholes, and under
the fading canopy of the night as it comes into view, the children pause
suddenly. Effie Mumford catches sight of something odd, simply left
there in the solace of the wet leaves and dirt: a small black shoe.

The Mumford children stare at it for a moment, Effie going so
far as to hold the microphone of her recording device close to it, and
then, slowly, she begins to inspect it, kicking it with the tip of her
own foot.

"Look how out of place it seems lying here in the woods," she
whispers.

Gus Mumford nods, holding the small compass beside it. The
needle barely moves.

"It looks new," Effie Mumford whispers. "There's no scuff marks
anywhere on it."

Gus Mumford nods again. He hands his sister a note: *It is a girl's.*

"Yes it is. A girl with very tiny feet," Effie replies, holding the small
shoe in the palm of her hand. Setting it back down in the dirt, the two
Mumford children glance around. Gus Mumford hurries off, finding
a second shoe, just a few yards away resting silently beside a log. He
hands his sister another note that reads: *It is the same.*

Effie Mumford stares down at the shoe and then looks up, catching sight of something else glinting in the near darkness.

"Look!" she shouts and the two children hurry off.

Up ahead, near the very sharp declination of the woods, right where the greenish rush of the river meets the sturdy whitened trees, they see something red. It is a ribbon, caught there in the thorny fingers of a fallen branch. Grasping it in her hand, Effie Mumford discovers something else: Down at the tangle of weeds and cattails, along the gray stones and dark pebbles of the riverbed, there is a soft white blur—a girl's nearly naked body. There are the bare white legs and soft arms and a flash of a navel, all of which is covered in dirt. The compass in Gus Mumford's hand begins to tick in all directions, and the two run as fast as they can while Effie Mumford shouts for help.

At school the next day, everyone stares at Effie Mumford. In the cafeteria, in study hall, walking alone down the hall, her heavy textbooks held like a shield against her spindly chest, it seems the entire world is glancing at her—not glaring, no, only looking at her and wondering what it is she has seen.

When she finds her seat in history class, Lauren Marks, a popular blond girl, leans over the aisle and says, "Was she all gross and everything?"

Effie Mumford frowns and then nods her head, enjoying this little attention.

"Did she say anything?" the other girl asks.

Effie shakes her head, and looking the pretty girl in the eyes, replies, "I gave her my coat and then she asked if she was dead. I told her no, because she wasn't, I guess."

* * *

After school, that very same day, there is an unexpected phone call from a mysterious stranger.

"Hello?" Effie Mumford says quietly.

"Hello," the voice comes. It is unfamiliar and weak, the breath sharp and spindly against the telephone receiver.

"Hello?" Effie says again. There is the sound of machines on the other end, of small pumps rising and falling, of the slow, continuous rattle of some steady beat. After a moment or two, Effie Mumford realizes it is the sound of Parker Lane's empty hospital room. The girl, barely alive, is trying to speak.

"Thank you," comes the voice. "Thank you, thank you, thank you."

TWENTY-FIVE

At school, Gus Mumford is again the only child in class. He has no one to whom he can brag to, even if he did want to speak. He sits in his chair, nervous because Miss Gale's wooden desk is also empty. He lowers his head against his arms and stares up at the clock. He watches as the small black hand chases the larger one around its blank white face. An hour goes by. Nothing happens. He lifts his head and looks around. He stares at the blank white room. He imagines this is what being dead must be like. He blinks. He blinks again. He blinks once more, very fast, hearing the sound his blinking makes—it is like a soft fluttering. He places both feet against the tile floor. He taps his foot once. It makes a loud snap, the sound vibrating and echoing in the large, vacant space. He taps his foot again, then the other. He pounds both on the floor, proud of the clomping rhythm they make. He bangs on the wood panel of his desk with his right hand then the left. He begins to hum. It is the first time he has heard his own voice in some time. It is unusual and spectacular, like the sound of a narrow buzz saw. He continues throttling the desk, humming along, making up a song about a dinosaur who eats tanks:

Tanks, tanks
I eat tanks
Every kind of tank, tank, tank
Tanks, tanks
I eat tanks
I don't even say thanks

Gus Mumford does not even realize he is singing. He is saying words out loud—many of them. He hollers and shouts, clapping his hands and singing until finally, many hours later, the classroom door opens and Miss Van Winkle, the school's fourth grade teacher, a young lady with puffy brown hair, big brown eyes, and glittery blue eye shadow, steps inside.

"Gus Mumford?"

Gus Mumford nods.

"Have you been in here all alone, honey?"

Gus Mumford nods again.

"We've made a terrible mistake. Miss Gale believed all of her students were absent today."

Gus shakes his head.

"Would you like to visit with my class today? We're doing a science project with clay. We're discussing dinosaurs."

So excited is the boy that he opens his mouth and whispers, "Yes," before he knows what he is doing. It is the first word he has spoken to anybody in nearly three months. Without regret, he hurtles from his chair and Miss Van Winkle takes his hand, the two of them hurrying down the hallway.

It is as he steps into the colorful, unfamiliar world of the fourth grade, and it is as Miss Van Winkle asks question after question about dinosaurs, that Gus Mumford most happily answers, that the small boy then realizes this: The most important things in your life are almost always impossible to predict.

Walking home that afternoon, smiling, Gus stops and watches a single red ant cross his path. He pauses and stares as it hurries into line, marching merrily away, joining a tiny red parade.

TWENTY-SIX

The boy detective sits beside the Mumford children, staring at the front page of that day's late-edition newspaper. In a blurry photo, beneath a headline that reads *MISSING GIRL FOUND*, Effie and Gus Mumford stand pointing at some indefinite spot in the woods, both children in the photograph appearing serious, bright, and charming.

Billy looks at the picture, then up and into their smiling faces.

"But now, of course, like all detectives, you must reveal how you did it," he says, smiling back at them.

"We did something very simple," Effie says.

"Yes, and what was that?"

Effie Mumford stares off the porch into the night sky. The first stars of the evening are quietly arriving, and Billy, following her gaze, listens as the small girl speaks.

"We allowed ourselves, for one brief moment, to believe in something we could not see."

The boy detective, on the bus again, stares out at the dull lights of the evening. Dreading having to go to work, he quietly begins to remember the Daisy Hollis case.

Of course, it was Billy's wondrous sleuthing that led them to the mansion on the hill. Daisy Hollis was heir to the Hollis Dry Cleaning fortune and lived in a very large estate beside many other large mansions in the hills just outside of town. At first the police were sure the girl's disappearance was the work of the Pawn Shop Kidnapper, who had abducted as many as five girls already. Taking their prized jewelry and possessions, he turned the children free without waiting for a ransom. It seemed Daisy Hollis had been a victim of the same treachery, as she was famous for wearing a mammoth ruby heirloom pin, worth several thousand dollars. However, unlike the other children, Daisy was not soon returned and the police chief began to get worried.

When Daisy had been missing for a fifth day, the police once again performed a search of the Hollis estate but, sadly, no clues were discovered. Billy, insistent that there was always a clue to be found, undertook a serious investigation.

With Caroline and Fenton, Billy gave a very close search of the grounds near Daisy Hollis's immense house which, to the Argo children and their companion, looked like a museum: There was an enormous aquarium with many colorful fish, there was a conservatory with real-life coconut trees, there was a musical hall with a piano that played by itself and a swimming pool as large as any of the children had ever seen. But there wasn't evidence of mischief. With magnifying glass in hand, Billy investigated the topiary garden, its giant trees cut in the shapes of dancing elephants and giraffes. With the fingerprint set, Caroline searched the stables. His stomach rumbling, Fenton questioned the kitchen staff. Before long it was growing dark. With their flashlights, the children crept through the large maze Daisy's parents had erected for her, then past the petting zoo, where small deer and antelope were going to sleep.

As the silent moon began to rise, marking the end of the fifth day poor Daisy Hollis had been missing, Billy made an important discovery: The mansion on the hill, a spooky old house at the very edge of the highest cliff overlooking town, was mysteriously glowing. A small colored light was glimmering in one of its many windows, and reflected there in the mist of the night, the mansion seemed to burn with a very strange red haze.

Without delay, the boy detective and his assistants headed up the steep cliff, past the enormous, wrecked wrought-iron gate, to the heavy wood doors which served as the mansion's entrance. Sneaking inside, the children walked silently through the dark, following the strange flashing of the mysterious light. Up the creaking stairs missing their banisters and down a cobwebbed hallway, at last the children found the reason for the strange red glow: There, at the foot of an enormous dressing mirror, was a very large ruby. The colossal jewel, reflected by the moonlight through the mirror, was causing the whole room to sparkle red.

"Look!" Billy exclaimed. "A ruby. Just like the one in Daisy Hollis's pin." He knelt beside the clue and glanced around the empty room. "I believe someone left it here as a hint."

Billy stood and placed the evidence in the pocket of his sweater. He took a few steps, then began to inspect the enormous dressing mirror, which ran from the ceiling to the floor. Billy gave the shiny surface a push and it quickly opened, revealing a narrow passageway.

"Look!" Caroline exclaimed. "A hidden door."

"It sure is dark!" Fenton chimed in.

"It certainly is," Billy agreed.

The children switched on their flashlights and followed Billy into the narrow passageway. It seemed to turn this way and that. The children realized they were heading into a series of caves somewhere within the heart of the cliffs. Along the way were a number of other jewels—a diamond ring, a pearl necklace, a set of antique amethyst earrings. Finally, the passage led to a very large cave. At the end of the cave was an opening which led out to the river. A small motorboat was tied there, as were a number of other interesting clues: several suitcases which seemed packed and ready to leave, a chair and rope, and a black blindfold.

"Look! Evidence!" Billy exclaimed.

Caroline immediately began to test the items for fingerprints.

"Look there," Fenton whispered, opening the first suitcase. "There's jewelry."

"It seems the Pawn Shop Kidnapper has been quite busy," Billy replied.

Opening one of the other suitcases, Billy found a variety of children's clothes and shoes. Beside the second suitcase was a third which, when the clasps had been opened, the children discovered was filled with wigs of all kinds; short, long, blond, red, and brown.

"So this is how he manages to nab his victims!" Caroline gasped.

"Of course," Billy said, nodding. "The poor children are forced to change clothes and wear these wigs so he can escape with them and later sell their belongings."

"Perhaps we should contact the police," Caroline remarked. "I'd hate to run into the Pawn Shop Kidnapper out here alone."

"Yes, of course, I'll go," Fenton agreed. In a dash, their chubby friend hurried back through the passageway, his flashlight marking his path.

"Perhaps there is another clue that can lead us to Daisy Hollis," Caroline said. "We ought to look more carefully while we wait."

"A very thorough idea," Billy replied.

However, searching through both suitcases once more, the Argo children did not find anything new. When they had finished their search, the young detectives replaced everything as it had been and stood in the dark, wondering what to do next. That's when a light began to shine from the secret passage once more.

"Look," Billy whispered. "Someone's coming."

"Could it be Fenton already?" Caroline asked.

"I don't think so," Billy answered. Quietly, Billy and Caroline did their best to hide behind a stack of crates, holding their breath so as not to give themselves away. Just then, a man dressed as a ghost entered, and began to place the suitcases within the motorboat.

"Hold it right there!" Billy shouted, flashing his light in the villain's eyes.

"Who's there?" the ghost responded angrily.

"Hurry, let's make a run for it," Caroline whispered, frightened. Billy nodded, flashing the light in the ghost's eyes once more. The villain cursed as the children darted past him into the secret passageway and back into the dark. The ghoul quick on their trail, they began, as loud as they could, calling for help. Pushing the doorway behind the mirror open, they ran through the spooky old house, along the cobwebbed hallway, and then back down the old steps. Pulling on the enormous front door, the Argo children found it locked, and looking back over their shoulders, they heard the villain laughing at their misfortune.

"Now you'll see what happens to meddlers," the ghostly scoundrel said.

"We're not afraid," Billy replied. "We know what you've done."

"Well, for such smart brats you *ought* to be afraid."

Hidden by the dark, Caroline quietly took Billy's hand, now quite frightened. The ghost slowly crept down the stairs, step by step, until he was standing before them, laughing.

"Now you'll have a chance to solve your greatest mystery, boy detective: What happens when meddling children poke where they don't belong?"

The ghoul raised his hairy hands toward them and Caroline screamed.

It was then that the police, with Fenton in tow, crashed through the mansion door. Very quickly, the ghostly villain was surrounded and, just as quickly, was put in handcuffs. Captured now, the Pawn Shop Kidnapper lowered his head and Billy removed his ghostly mask. It was none other than Killer Kowalzavich, a hoodlum Billy had come across once or twice before on his adventures.

"Now that you're under arrest, Killer Kowalzavich, why not confess?" Billy asked. "Tell us where Daisy Hollis is and perhaps the police might go easier on you."

"Daisy Hollis? I never had the chance to nab her. Sure, I had planned on it, but someone beat me to her first. All the others, sure, I admit, I kidnapped and took their expensive jewelry and toys to sell. But I never had the chance to nab Daisy Hollis. Honest, I don't know where she is."

"What about the ruby?" Billy asked.

"What ruby?"

"This one," Billy said, holding the jewel out in his hand.

"That one belongs to Hazel Maryweather, the daughter of the mining company magnate. It's from her prized necklace."

"Very interesting story," Billy replied, shaking his head. "Maybe you'll have a different ending when you meet the chief of police," the boy said, watching the nogoodnik being led away.

The three children walked out of the mansion and stood beside a rusty wishing well, staring down at their own reflections.

"Do you believe he's telling the truth, Billy?" Fenton finally asked.

"Of course I don't," Billy said. "We only need to look at the evidence. Within an hour, Killer Kowalzavich will tell what he knows and Daisy Hollis will be found quite safe."

Caroline, however, was unconvinced. "Billy, I believe Daisy Hollis may still be in danger," she said. She opened her small satchel, and finding a shiny penny, tossed the coin into the wishing well.

"Now what was that for?" Billy asked.

"I made a wish that Daisy Hollis would be back home safe and sound quite soon."

"A wish will not bring her back," Billy said, scoffing. "We have discovered the truth."

"But what if we are wrong?" Caroline asked. "What then, Billy?"

Billy did not reply. He just stood there and watched as the shiny penny sank, drifting down into the cold black water, disappearing.

"We are not wrong," Billy whispered. "Simply consider the evidence."

"Billy is right," Fenton said, staring up at his friend. "Anyway, it's past midnight and our parents will all be worried."

"But what if we're wrong?" Caroline asked. "What then, Billy?"

Again Billy did not answer. He only stood there and wondered, not saying a word.

On the bus, Billy looks up and sees he has gone many miles past his stop. The boy detective thinks, *I was so very wrong*. He thinks, *I was so very wrong and afraid to ever admit it*. He stands suddenly and signals the bus driver, who pulls over at the next stop. Billy climbs off the bus and stares at the shadowy cliffs rising along the edge of town, the cliffs which have somehow moved much closer than Billy has ever dared to remember. He begins running along the street, the sun falling from the sky, the dark shadows of the hills now as heavy as a handprint upon his back.

TWENTY-SEVEN

At work, his head laying on the desk, the boy detective does not rest easy. He dreams of the cave once again. It is quicker, this dream: As he moves through the dark, he hears the familiar screaming, and finally begins to follow it. At the end of the cave, there is his sister Caroline and Daisy Hollis, sitting on the ground, sorting out a puzzle, arranging its small red pieces. Daisy looks ghastly, slightly decomposed, definitely dead. Billy sees Caroline playing with the dead girl, and grabs his sister's arm.

"Hurry, we have to go. You can't play with her."

Caroline resists, pulling her hand back. She folds her arms across her chest. She won't budge.

"What? What is it? Say something! Tell me what I should do, please tell me."

Caroline shakes her head, then points to Daisy. Daisy nods and opens her mouth. Hundreds of quarters, nickels, and dimes pour out. Billy begins screaming.

He lifts his head from the desk, and then dashes toward the elevators.

Past midnight now, back at Shady Glens, the boy detective knocks on Mr. Pluto's door very gently. In a moment, the giant stumbles to answer, still wearing his enormous blue hospital gown.

"Please, I need your help," he tells the much larger man.

Mr. Pluto blinks once, then again, and then nods, smiling.

Arriving at his childhood home in the quiet suburbs of Gotham by taxicab, the boy detective and Mr. Pluto stand staring at the house which sits sad and silent in the dark, wondering what it is they are exactly doing. In a hurry, the boy detective climbs beneath the worn white porch and immediately begins searching, digging his hands through the dirt, finding a corner, then another, then the third and fourth, scraping with his fingertips, then his thumbs, until he has uncovered the tiny gray strongbox which houses the remains of the dead dove, Margaret Thatcher.

"Abracadabra," Billy whispers, and holds it up to the light cast down by a happy-faced moon. He crawls quickly back out from under the porch and gently hands the small metal box to the giant man beside him.

"I need you to open this, please," he says.

Mr. Pluto nods, stares at the tiny silver lock, which reads *unbreakable* in small lettering, and with one hand crushes the device into flaky silver dust. He hands the metal box back to Billy and grins.

"Thank you, sir," Billy says, opening the strongbox as quickly as he can.

Strangely, Margaret Thatcher's small withered body is missing. Instead, there is only a note—the missing page, torn from Caroline's detective notebook. Holding his breath, Billy begins to read:

maybe i have made a mistake;
maybe someone with more smarts can figure it out
if they try and follow the clues which lead to the saddest thing
i've ever seen
left lying like that in a wishing well
their eyes looking up into the
light, all i can do is stare at myself in the bathroom mirror and
wonder why, why did this happen? to them? to me?

evil is all around i know, but still: who could have done this?
what clue, what motive, what reason can explain this
riddle? none, none, none.
maybe only someone as daring as Billy might
search and discover the answer, but
i do not have the brains to do it and, worse, now my
courage is gone and
i feel so sad, as if i have failed him and everything
as if i am at the end of this wonderful adventure and now,
and now i don't know what else to do—do i just hope in
vain that there will be some way out of this awfulness?
i'm afraid i already know the answer: that
everything, in the end, will always be a mystery to me

The boy detective stares down at the torn diary page, quickly discovering the secret message his darling sister has left behind. The cursive letters unstitch themselves from their perfectly-straight lines. Their tiny loops begin to uncurl, the sweep of each curve revealing the secret kept hidden now for more than ten years. He sees all but a few letters simply fall from the page. It is now very clear: *MILLER'S CAVE.* Reading the missing entry, starting with the first letter of each sentence and then every other on down, he smiles at Caroline's charming inscrutability. He folds the small paper in half, slips it in the pocket of his blue cardigan, and, grabbing Mr. Pluto's hand, dashes back toward the waiting taxicab.

TWENTY-EIGHT

In his room once again, the boy detective lifts off the newspaper clipping that reads, *THE HORROR OF THE HAUNTED MINE: WHAT LURKS INSIDE MILLER'S CAVE?* He puts on a new blue sweater, opens the dresser, and takes out the detective kit.

He lays the kit on the bed and stares at it for a moment. Then he leans over and, very slowly, very carefully, he opens it. All of the items are coated in a ghostly sheen of dust. The magnifying glass has been terribly cracked. The pencil has been altogether broken. The lock picks are missing. The pair of binoculars have been separated at the joint. The mustache and beard are wilted and fall apart in Billy's hand. The only item that remains is the flashlight, narrow and silver, which somehow, miraculously, still works. Billy switches it on and nods, then stands.

The boy detective glances at himself in the mirror, and frowns suddenly, his heart beginning to rebel, to retreat. The boy detective thinks, *I was wrong before many times.* He thinks, *What if I am wrong once again?* He stumbles around the darkness of his room, searching for an antidepressant and frowns as he remembers that no, there are none. He can hear himself whimpering now. He can feel his knees wobbling.

The boy detective thinks, *The only thing all men have in common with one another is their inherent capacity to make mistakes.* He reasons, *But there is wonder in the attempt, knowing we are all destined to fall short, but forgoing reason and fear time and time again so deliberately.* He takes a deep breath, grasps the trusty flashlight, and hurries back into the night.

TWENTY-NINE

The boy detective is riding in the backseat of the taxi, staring as the dark woods flicker by. Shadows like the limbs of the dead fall across his face. The cabbie, red-bearded and bright-eyed, speaks to Billy, mumbling over his own shoulder.

"Awful suspicious, if you ask me, driving to the woods in the middle of the night. Awful suspicious, I'd say."

The boy detective does not reply.

It is raining as the boy detective exits the taxi. Without another word, the cab pulls away, its taillights disappearing into the dark. Billy, looking terrified, his glasses foggy, his flashlight held tensely at his side, creeps past the wooden barricade and signs which read, *Miller's Cave* and *No Trespassing* and into the entrance of the cave.

Strange noises, water dripping, animal sounds, moans reverberate in the dark. He lets out a small whimper and makes his way beneath the soft wood barring the entrance. A scream rises, coming closer. Billy begins to back away as the scream gets louder. He turns to run but falls in the wet mud and just then sees an owl fly past, screeching as it goes. He laughs softly, admonishing himself, shaking his head. *OK, Billy*, he thinks. *You're OK.* He stands, brushes the water and mud off, and continues on. Further along, he walks, holding himself up against the cave roof, which is slick. Water rushes around his feet. Billy stops, rubbing his fingers, and looks up, glimpsing hundreds of small bats. He shouts as the bats take flight, fluttering around him. Further still, he discovers a number of blind baby rats, nearly drowning in the rushing water, scurrying about, squeaking and hissing. He looks around, finds a small hunk of rotten wood, and places each baby rat, one by one, on the plank, sending it along. Further still, he comes to the end of the cave. He touches it with his hand, feeling the cave wall, disbelieving. It is the end. There is nowhere else to go. Only blackness. Only nothing.

"Nothing. There's nothing here. No answer."

Billy sadly turns and begins to walk away, when he notices the water around his feet. He shines his light at the cave floor and sees all the water rushing deeper still. He follows the water with his flashlight, finding a very small opening in one of the cave walls beneath dozens and dozens of stacked rocks. Frantic, Billy begins removing the stones. A strange silvery-blue light emanates from the opening and Billy kicks the rocks aside, faster, more desperate. Finally, there is room for him to crawl through and he does, getting covered in water and mud.

Billy stumbles around in the dimness, following the bluish light, casting his own flashlight along the cave walls. Then he stops, frozen, looking up. Upon a flat expanse of smooth rock is a small handprint. He looks very closely at it. Beside the handprint is a single word, written with dirt: *Abracadabra*.

Billy shines the light around more and sees hundred and hundreds of handprints everywhere. Looking for an answer, Billy calls out.

"Caroline?"

He runs his hand along the message.

"Caroline?"

Billy presses on, taking off his jacket, then his sweater. He wipes his face and notices dozens of articles of clothing along the path: high heels, purses, stockings, ribbons, dresses, undergarments, sweaters. Billy stops, investigating, opening a purse. It is filled with money. He continues on, following the trail of clothing. Up ahead, he sees a shiny white sweater, with the monogram, *DH*. He stops, picks it up, and nods. It is soft and light and turns to dust in his hands. Beside it, lying on the ground there, is the silver-jeweled, monogrammed pin. The ruby pulses red like a heartbeat, Billy's flashlight making it glimmer and move. He detaches the pin and turns it over. An inscription on the back of it reads, *To Daisy, from Daddy*.

"Daisy Hollis . . . It was not Killer Kowalzavich after all." He holds up the silver pin. "Surely, he would have pawned this."

Billy sets the pin down and moves on. The bluish light becomes brighter and brighter until finally, following the water and trail of floating clothing, Billy finds the end. It is a large pool of water, with a rush of small waterfalls among shiny silver and brown rocks. Pointing the flashlight into the water, Billy discovers a naked body, a girl's body, her long hair rippling like seaweed. Her eyes are each covered by a silver dime. Covering her body, and piled beside it, are hundreds of other dimes, nickels, quarters, and pennies. Billy lets out a cry, covering his mouth.

"Oh no . . . no."

Billy flashes the light away and notices a second body in the pool, another girl, also naked. Again, there are more silver coins, flashing brightly. Billy leans closer to the water, trembling, terrified, holding his hand over his face, and sees the full horror of his discovery: The secret pool is filled with dozens of bodies, all young girls, all naked, like mermaids, their hair gently drifting in the current, their eyes open and glassy, sunken among thousands of quarters, pennies, dimes, and nickels.

Billy shines the light up and sees a small opening, about a hundred feet up. He stares, squinting through the dark.

Through the opening and into the night—which has cleared and reveals small pricks of white stars in the sky—Billy hears someone laughing. Someone else giggles, and in a moment, two small dimes drop from the opening, down into the water.

Billy holds his breath, whispering his realization.

"A wishing well . . ."

The bodies, eyes full of silvery dimes, look up at Billy.

Billy, in horror, begins to crawl away, then stops. He turns back and stares at the water.

"Who? Who did this? Why? Why would *anyone* do this?"

For a brief moment, Billy stares into the water and sees Caroline lying there, the sight of her in her casket drifting beneath the water, looking back up at him. The flashlight cuts out for a moment and when it clicks back on, she is gone. Billy stares down into the pool and understands what happened to his sister, finally.

He smiles, staring into the water, whispering.

"You found your way down here, didn't you? You *were* smart enough."

Billy leans in closer to the water.

"You found your way down here, and then . . . saw all of this. You saw all of this and you couldn't find the answer. You couldn't find the answer because there *was* no answer for all this, was there?"

Billy places his hand out, touching the water, just for a brief moment. He apologizes both to his sister and the poor girls he could not save.

"I'm sorry . . . I'm so sorry."

Billy nods, turns, climbing out, and stops, seeing Caroline's message. He touches it and frowns. He stares and then smiles, his eyes filling with tears, turning away. Billy climbs out of the cave and sits down exhausted, beside the opening, too tired to stop himself from crying.

THIRTY

Imagine, if you can, a time-lapse photograph of several police officers arriving at the entrance of the cave, backlit by the flashing lights of an ambulance. The police officers are very serious and ask the boy detective many, many questions. He nods and points. He holds his head up and frowns, exhausted. It rains and it rains and it rains. The chief of police, with his pointy white beard, pats the boy detective on the back, excited, congratulating him. But Billy only stands, soaked by the rain, staring back at the cave.

Our evening newspapers report that every
light in our town has switched on suddenly.
Unplugging the plug or switching off the
switch is useless. The lamps, nightlights,
streetlights, flashlights, and headlights
of our town all refuse to stop beaming.
It is a lovely surprise: the soft song of
one million light bulbs humming along in
harmony. We stare at the beautiful glow of
our small world and wonder *why,* content
with the silent response gleaming there
as an answer before our wide-open eyes.

CHAPTER THIRTY-FIVE
THE CASE OF THE SECRET TREASURE

We have devised a theme song for the
boy detective. It goes like this:
It is a spooky night / but don't anyone be afraid
Because the boy detective / is close on his way
No case too big / no case too small
With his trusty kit / he will solve them all
Boy detective / detects every clue
Boy detective / solves every crime for you
Boy detective / he's our favorite
Boy detective / ba-da-bum-ba

ONE

The boy detective stands outside Penny's, covered in mud and water. He looks terrible. We mean *terrible*. He gazes up at Penny's window and sees the light is on. He stands for a moment, just watching. What might he say? He does not know. He walks over to the buzzer and presses the appropriate button. Penny answers, nervously, her voice sad and resigned.

"Yes . . . who is it?"

"It's me, Billy. May I please come in?"

"Of course, Billy."

Penny buzzes the door open. Billy rushes in, his wet shoes squeaking like an alarm on the steps. He kicks them off and runs up the stairs barefoot and stares as Penny opens the door and lunges forward, attacking Billy with a flurry of kisses. She pulls him inside. Penny continues to kiss Billy, who smiles, holding her, exhausted.

"Look at you. What happened? What happened to you?" she asks.

"Please, I . . . I don't want to be alone. Not tonight."

Penny stops kissing him and holds him. She wipes the dirt from his face and begins undressing him. They resume kissing, falling onto the couch, knocking over a stack of stolen shoe boxes. From there the boxes fall, spilling over to the window, where Penny's hand slowly draws the blinds. A lightbulb is suddenly made dark. Outside, two doves huddle in the rain, cooing.

TWO

The boy detective lies on the couch, asleep, with his head in Penny's lap. Penny sits, staring down at him. He awakes and smiles.

"I thought it was a dream."

Penny places her finger over his lips, hushing him.

"Shhhh, it's OK now."

"No, I should, I really ought to be going."

Penny kisses him. She places her hand on his chest, then feels something underneath. Billy sits up, smiling. He pats down the small lump on his chest, feels inside his shirt pocket, and finds his notepad, opened to Mr. Lunt's riddle. He reads it and smiles, handing it to Penny.

"How would you like to solve a mystery with me?"

"A mystery? What kind of mystery?"

"The best kind: one with treasure at the end of it."

"How do you know there's treasure?"

"I don't know for sure, that's the mystery of it, I guess. Would you like to help me?"

"If you don't laugh. I get clumsy."

Billy smiles, staring into her brown eyes.

"We can hold hands if it helps," he says.

THREE

The boy detective and Penny walk along the street, staring down at the riddle on the paper.

At the beginning of a silver line, and the end of another made of twine, if you have old lungs, the treasure you will find.

Penny is excited, clapping her hands. Billy stares at her and grins.

"Yes, so, where do we begin to look?" she asks.

"A silver line, perhaps? That sounds like jewelry."

"Or a machine of some kind."

"Or a geographical place, like a mineral deposit. *The beginning of the silver line*. Perhaps in the mountains? Hmmmm," he says.

Penny looks up and stares at the bus stop sign on the street corner.

"Or . . . the bus line."

"The bus line?" Billy says with a smile.

"The silver line."

There on the corner is a sign that reads, *SILVER LINE: Weekdays, Weekends, Late Hours.*

Billy stares at the sign while Penny nods victoriously.

"The beginning of the silver line," he says, impressed.

Billy and Penny hop on the next bus, excitedly. Trying to solve the next part of the riddle, sitting together, looking at the piece of paper, Billy realizes he cannot concentrate. He is counting the number of freckles on Penny's nose. He blinks and counts again and realizes there are fourteen beautiful amber dots sitting there.

"*The end of another made of twine,*" Penny whispers. "That sounds like a rope, doesn't it? The end of a length of rope. Well, we'll have to wait and see about that."

"Yes," he says, sighing as he stares at her.

The city flies past the windows of the bus. Billy notices he is holding hands with Penny and his face becomes flush, watching as the town hurries by.

"What do you think we'll find?" Penny asks.

"I don't know. Maybe we won't find anything," he says seriously.

"Oh, we'll find something. And inside, there will be a giant precious diamond. Or hundreds of rubies. Or a locket, with a photo of a lovely woman from long ago, maybe."

The bus driver calls out, from over his shoulder: "OK, it's the beginning and end of the line, folks. Everybody off."

At the bus station, which is old and silver and dilapidated, Penny and Billy get off the bus and look around. There are some woods, train tracks, a field. Their hearts are pounding. They look around happily.

"Now what? The end of a length of rope. Where would that be?" Penny asks, peering about. She spots something, then grabs Billy's hand and begins running.

There is a small, rusty gray sewer grate at the end of the train tracks which has caught Penny's attention. There are several rail ties and rusty lengths of track surrounding it, and she quickly moves them to one side.

Penny and Billy stare past the metal grate, down into the murky sewer. It is dark and dank. Billy shakes his head, still unconvinced.

"It's down there, I'm sure of it," Penny says.

"Do you think so?" he asks.

"Yes. That's exactly where I'd hide something—if I had to, I mean. It's very close to the bus. You could hide something and hurry back without anyone noticing."

"Well, I don't think it's such a good idea to go down there," Billy says.

Penny takes off her glasses and hands them to Billy. With one forceful tug on the sewer grate, she lifts the metal covering aside and places it near Billy's feet.

"Look," she says. "They left the rope." Just as Penny claims, there is a worn-looking yellow rope knotted to a sturdy black pipe, which is caked in rust and grease. Without another word, Penny grins widely and begins to lower herself down the well.

Billy shouts: "Just a minute! Just a minute!"

But Penny is at the bottom of the well, already, shouting back up.

"It's not very deep at all, just dusty!"

"Be careful!"

"What's the next part of the riddle?"

"It says, '*If you have old lungs . . .*'"

"Maybe they mean the dust? It makes you cough like you have old lungs!"

"What else do you see down there?"

"Well, there's some change. And an engineer's cap. And there's also an old accordion down here. It looks very old. And broken."

"That's it!" he shouts, clapping his hands.

"OK!"

"I'll pull you up!"

Billy pulls Penny up in a hurry. She hands him the broken accordion, which is red and gold and withered. He fiddles with it, pressing the dusty white keys. It doesn't make any noise at all.

"Well, it seems to be broken, all right," he says.

Penny gently lifts the accordion, hits a key, then shakes the accordion and smiles.

"There's something inside of it, I think."

Billy and Penny carefully find a way to open the bellows, detaching a series of small springs, and there they find a note, which has been blocking the air valves inside. They stare at the note and read it together, silently:

> *To the boy or girl that finds this:*
> *Mr. Howard Lunt, aged 9, hid this April 24, 1902. Congratula-*
> *tions! Put back in spot so others might find.*
> *Signed,*
> *Mr. Howard Lunt, President, League of Amateur*
> *Whodunit Enthusiasts.*

Billy and Penny look at each other and smile. He nods, quite pleased. The boy detective slips the note back into the bellows, seals it up, and lowers the accordion back into the drainpipe. They walk back toward the bus station. The sun begins shining over their shoulders.

FOUR

We would really like to think that you were holding hands with some-body while you read that last part. If not, you might read it again and ask someone to hold your hand right now. You might then write that person's name somewhere here on this page with a heart glowing around it. Why not? It might be fun.

FIVE

Billy and Penny sit on the bus, smiling, side by side. Billy looks across the aisle and sees a young boy with glasses in a red cardigan sweater doing a crossword puzzle, sitting beside his mother. Billy eyes him, smiling, and, digging into his pocket, pulls out his pad and pencil, and begins scribbling something down.

It is this: a treasure map with a big X marking the spot.

Billy finishes and tears the drawing from the pad of paper. He hands it to Penny, who smiles at it. Billy nods toward the child across the aisle. Penny looks from Billy to the boy and nods, understanding. She stands and very carefully slides the treasure map into the kid's sweater pocket without anyone noticing. She sits back down and winks at Billy.

Billy and Penny sit side by side, slightly dirty but smiling, staring straight ahead. In a moment, Billy frowns and Penny notices.

"What is it, Billy?"

"It's all over now. I'm not young anymore. No more adventures, no more mysteries, no more secrets."

Penny hugs him. Billy smiles at Penny, holding her hand.

"We'll make our own secrets now, maybe."

THE END

NURSE ELOISE'S ANGEL FOOD CAKE!

You will need

4 c. egg whites

4 tsp. cream of tartar

3 1/2 c. sugar divided into 1 1/2 c and 2c.

2 c. cake flour

1/2 tsp. salt

1 scraped vanilla bean

Put egg whites and cream of tartar into mixing bowl. Using your mixer's whip attachment, whip until soft peak. Gradually add 2 c. sugar and scraped vanilla bean and beat until stiff peak. When beater is pulled out and held upside down, a curl should hold its shape.

Sift flour, 1 1/2 c. sugar, and salt.
When whites are ready, slowly and gently fold in dry ingredients—*don't over mix!*

Dollop into two angel food cake pans—*ungreased*!
Run a knife around the pan edges to get rid of any large air pockets.
Sprinkle top with sugar.

Bake at 350° F approximately 35-40 minutes, until cracks in top no longer look moist.

Eat and enjoy—*yum!*

BOY DETECTIVE PUZZLE!

The boy detective needs your help! Assist him with escaping the mystery of the haunted maze.

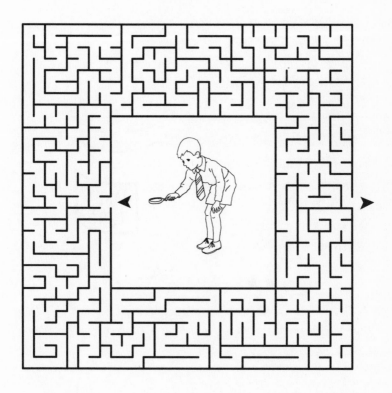

BOY DETECTIVE CONNECT THE DOTS!

Help the boy detective face his darkest fears!
Connect the dots to reveal what is hidden.

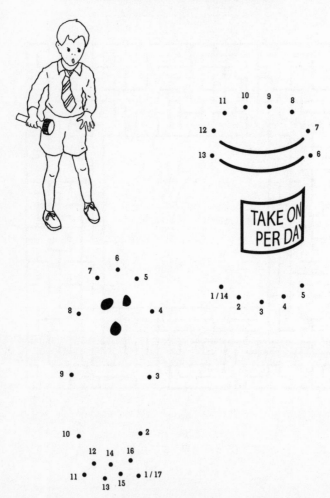

HIDDEN MESSAGE WORD SEARCH!

Search for the missing words to reveal Billy's secret message.

C	A	R	O	L	I	N	E	D	E
E	L	Z	Z	U	P	B	Y	E	I
B	L	O	O	D	Y	L	E	T	F
L	I	E	E	T	L	V	E	N	F
I	N	M	M	I	S	Y	S	U	E
T	E	R	B	I	C	O	Y	A	H
P	E	N	N	Y	R	L	H	H	I
N	O	T	N	E	F	C	U	G	N
L	I	A	F	S	U	G	E	E	V
U	G	F	T	L	I	A	I	A	Y

Billy	Effie	Gus
Bloody	Fail	Haunted
Caroline	Fenton	Penny
Clue	Ghost	Puzzle
Crime		

Starting at the top left, the letters not used in the words you've found spell out Billy's secret message to you:

_ _ _ _ _ _ _ _ _ _ _ _ _ _ _ _

ACKNOWLEDGMENTS

With many thanks to: Koren, Dan, Johnny, Anne, Johanna, Todd and Ashley, Jon Resh, James, Mark Zambo, my folks and family, Jenny Bent, Michelle Kroes, Jay Ryan, Todd Dills, Mickey Hess, Sean Carswell, Jonathan Messinger, Quimby's, the House Theatre, and the Columbia College Chicago Fiction Writing Department.

What I listened to while writing this book: Belle and Sebastian, the Coctails, Wilco, and the Beatles.